REQUIEM FOR A GOOD MACHINE

A SONG AND WATERBIRD MYSTERY
BOOK 1

DANIEL CLAYMORE

Requiem for a Good Machine

Ebook ISBN: 9781641972253

KDP POD ISBN: 9798843755157

IS POD ISBN: 9781641972277

NYLA Publishing

121 W. 27th St., Suite 1201, NY 10001, New York.

http://www.nyliterary.com

For Denise

[1]

Mirabilis - \mə'RABələs\ (Latin, adjective) – Amazing and
wondrous. Remarkable.

The machine floated before him, bringing news of murder.

"Detective?" he yawned.

"Officer Song, you are needed at the Wilcott Building. Thirty seven residents. Five floors. Difficult stairs. Please prepare yourself for a full work day."

Leo sat up. "Really?"

"I await your arrival."

"Twenty minutes."

Leo Song waved off the call with the Detective and pushed himself out of bed, his hand pressing into the cold part of the mattress where Aida had been. He knew she had sneaked out some time in the morning, back to her apartment across the hall, as was her habit. It might be days before she visited again. Leo told himself he preferred it that way.

Moving as fast as he could while still taking care, Leo put on the blue Mott & Son Dapper that had arrived — at last — the day before. It fit him well for a catalogue purchase. The label claimed

100% human tailoring, but nothing was a hundred percent human anymore. Nonetheless, it was a nice suit and Leo felt pride in his good taste, as well as for buying human. Beyond that, Leo buzzed with an unusual optimism ignited by Detective Waterbird's call. The code had been given in full: *Prepare yourself for a full work day.* The time had come. His time. Before anything else, however, Leo knew he would have to do something about the ridiculous grin which had spread across his face. Citizens of Mirabilis were suspicious of a positive attitude — a spring in your step only made the job needlessly difficult. Nobody wanted genuinely happy people knocking on their door informing them of a homicide. Luckily, Leo had become skilled at dampening these errant high spirits, more frequent in recent days, imagining the unfocused joy condensing into a dense gray knot that he kept at the base of his skull, to be unraveled only later, in private. His good mood now restrained, Leo headed towards the crime scene.

———

THE TALL, SLEEK MACHINE CONSIDERED LEO'S NEW SUIT IN SILENT judgment. After a few seconds, English words buzzed through the faceless sensor in warm, approving tones.

"Officer Song, the suit is excellent," it said.

"Yeah? You think so?" Leo ran a self-conscious hand down the front of his bright blue cotton jacket, checking himself in the mirror-like surface of Waterbird's housing. "Thank you."

Detective Waterbird was one of the "Silver Sevens", called that by human officers because of the design's streamlined resemblance to the number. That, and they thought it sounded cool. Silver Sevens were a limited edition machine, but like all machines, a masterpiece of both form and function, and none more than Detective Investigator Prime Waterbird. Despite the nickname, Leo always thought Waterbird's shape more closely resembled a seven foot tall question mark, which he personally considered more apt for an investigator. When Leo had told Waterbird this years ago, the machine had reacted with mild amusement. Or at least a convincing simulation of amusement.

"You are very welcome," said Waterbird. "It is good that you strive to make a positive impression. Not many still care to make the effort. What does Aida think of your new suit?"

"She liked it." Leo immediately regretted the fib. A machine could detect a lie in nanoseconds. Facial expressions, heat signatures, pheromones, voice modulation, they read it all. There was simply no way to deceive a ramper. It was pointless and he wasn't sure why he had said it. "Actually, she hasn't seen it yet."

"I am certain she will approve. Do not be nervous."

"So...," Leo looked past Waterbird's thin frame towards the crime scene at the far end of the cramped hallway. "What's the situation? Looks nasty."

"A double homicide. Both victims are residents of this building and their apartment is located on the top floor. As you can see, the only access is via the rather difficult central staircase."

"I see that. Should I go up right now then?"

"Not yet."

Leo felt the gray knot in his head slip loose, releasing a surge of hope. He leaned towards Waterbird and whispered, "Is this the one? We're doing this today?"

Matching Leo's secretive tone, Waterbird said, "I can see no reason to delay."

"Okay. All right." Leo calmed himself. "So, what do I do?"

"Before you attend to your regular duties, Officer Song, I would like you to make an assessment of the crime scene. The victims suffered quite violent ends, so please take emotional precautions when viewing the remains."

Leo nodded professionally. "I will, thank you, Detective."

Mrs. Turtlecharm, the southern precinct's primary crime scene photographer, was extending its camera-stalk to capture the scene from a higher angle when Leo blundered into the frame.

"Please step back, Officer Song," it said. "I can see your feet."

"Oh, sorry…." Leo took a step backward, working around Mrs. Turtlecharm's four wheeled struts that were extended in a wide, stabilizing position.

"Thank you."

"No problem, Mrs. Turtlecharm," Leo said. He could still see the crime scene well enough to know that Waterbird had been correct: it was a grisly sight. Two bodies lay side by side at the base of the stairwell, their limbs cracked in multiple places, torsos opened from neck to groin. Both faces had been smashed in for good measure. Horrid as the last detail was, he didn't think it was meant to delay identification of the victims. There would be no point in doing such a thing. Identification would be made using the personal info-tags imbedded in every human's DNA in utero, a decades' old procedure as common as fingerprints and much more reliable. Results were near-instantaneous with a quick scan, likely performed by Mr. Waterbird before Leo had even arrived at the building. Destroying their faces was pointless. These people had been killed out of rage.

"Do we know their names?"

"Darryl Vincent, twenty-four, and Tabitha Jackson, twenty-eight," answered Waterbird from the end of the hallway.

The only thing left that distinguished the victims' genders were their hands. Large and rough versus small and fine. Feeling ill, Leo looked back at Waterbird. "Think somebody caught them in a kiss?" He was assuming a motive, but it seemed a reasonable one. Like his own sunny mood from that morning, it was dangerous to display too much affection in public. "Nobody likes the lovebirds."

"Romantic indiscretion is possible," Waterbird said, its gently patronizing tone meant to highlight the error of Leo's assessment. "However, the wounds suggest a different cause."

Leo looked at the machine, his mind racing through various

other possible scenarios. He could only think of one that made sense, but was hesitant to say it out loud.

"Go on, Officer," Waterbird urged.

"Um…well, both victims were killed in the same place. Together…the violence of it, I mean it's savage, sudden, and was over too quickly for either victim to get away…I'd say this was a sadboy attack?"

"Yes. Very good. There are seventy three indications that a full-stage sadboy committed this crime."

"Seventy three indications," Leo said under his breath. He could only see one: overkill. It was the hallmark of sadboys. They were psychotic bastards, to be sure, but they were also infamously shy. To encounter a full-stage sadboy was bad luck of the worst kind. "Been a while since we had one of those."

"Two years, eight months, sixteen days."

"Any witnesses?"

"None have come forward on their own, but perhaps they will speak to you."

Leo nodded and surveyed the building with a practiced eye. It was one of the newer, human-built constructions, evident by its use of steep, spiraling staircases in place of the gentle ramps preferred by the machines. For the people living there that, of course, was the point. Machines despised stairs, even over short distances. Human-style legs were considered a design flaw — knees and joints simply wore out too quickly. As a result, machines had built the city to accommodate the wheels, treads, and vibrating skids they preferred. Ramps instead of stairs was the norm. In Mirabilis, a building without ramps was a clear statement of defiance: *humans only, keep out.* The machines understood this and took pains to heed the unspoken message whenever possible. That's why Leo was called in. It was his job to canvass the building, going up and down the treacherous stairs on his human legs, searching for witnesses and offering emotional counseling to the possibly traumatized. Leo shuddered at the task ahead. It was a tough climb. Breaking your neck on machine-resistant staircases was the fourth leading cause of death in 2157. Suicide was number one. Murder barely made the charts anymore.

"Should I get started?"

"Yes, if you would." said Waterbird, simulating an urgency not lost on the human. "The victims lived on the top floor. The ascent will be difficult, so please use caution."

Leo nodded. "No problem. I'll start up there with the imme-diate neighbors and work my way down."

"Officer Song, you have my permission to enter the victim's living unit."

Leo glanced at Mrs. Turtlecharm, but the machine gave no sign it had heard the Detective's unusual order. Still, Leo hesi-tated. "Just to be clear, Detective, you want me to take a look at the crime scene...alone."

"Supervision is unnecessary, Officer Song," assured Waterbird, seemingly unfazed by the human's improvisation. "I trust you will notify me of anything you deem of interest to the case."

"I'll head up now, then."

"Be careful to avoid getting blood on your fine, new suit, Officer Song," warned Mrs. Turtlecharm. "It would be a shame to dirty it so soon."

"Thanks, I'll be careful." Leo said as he focused himself on the task ahead.

Leo didn't know how people with shorter legs managed stairs like these. The height and angle of each step was exaggerated to create maximum difficulty when ascending, an anti-machine tactic that struck him as fairly anti-person, too. It was hard enough for him to manage the climb, and he was a tall man, well over six feet. By the time he got to the fourth-floor he was sweating into his suit. Taking Turtlecharm's advice, he went slowly, giving himself time to dry out.

There was no one else in the hallway and no sounds behind

the closed doors. He knew there were people living here, they were just being quiet at the moment. People who lived in places like this weren't going to volunteer to help the police, not even a human officer. Not even about murder. That mattered little in the end. Machines typically solved crimes within hours. It was the magic of machine policing. Clearance rates through the roof, with arrests made quickly, the cases airtight, and usually with minimal human contact. Ramper detectives were near-flawless crime solvers, and none of them were as good as Detective Waterbird. Leo knew he was lucky to be able to observe such a machine go about its work, even if the majority of what Waterbird did remained a mystery to him. He tried to pay attention, tried to learn, but the truth was he lacked the basic tools to do what Waterbird did. As a human being he was bound by the hard limits of his blood and tissue brain. There were small ways to improve that, of course. Cognitive mods he could install, but they could only do so much, if he ever dared risk them. Even so, Leo thought, carefully maneuvering up one tilted, creaking stair at a time, he could surely do more than *this*. He knew Waterbird agreed with him, but currently theirs was the minority opinion. With effort and some great degree of luck, though, minds might be changed.

Armed with Waterbird's permission, Leo ignored the closed doors for now and went straight for Tabitha Jackson's apartment. Standing before the correct unit, Leo checked the hallway again for any prying eyes. Everyone knew human cops weren't allowed into crime scenes by themselves, so he had to be careful not to be mistaken for a lookie-loo or snuff-junkie. Waterbird would back him up, of course, but an official complaint wouldn't go over well at the precinct. Detective Waterbird's indulgence of Leo's amateur detecting habits tended to annoy the other human officers in the Homicide Unit, but so long as Leo didn't flaunt the length of his leash, they kept their mouths shut about it. This one would really get their backs up.

The hallway was empty. He was clear. Leo switched off his

Link's mental recorder and went to work. The door to 406 was locked, so he had to use his All-Hack to gain entrance to the unit. It took him longer than he liked to break the lock-scrambler mechanism, which was a newer model recently installed. He noted that all the other units on that floor still used the older standard locks. Tabitha Jackson and Darryl Vincent had been interested in their security. Not necessarily paranoid, but aware and cautious.

The lock-scrambler flashed clear and the door popped open.

Inside, the one-bedroom unit was nicer than Leo had anticipated — clean and neatly adorned. The walls had a fresh coat of paint more recent than the outside hallway. The place even smelled nice. In the living room there was a faux-ebony coffee table, a spotless white leather couch of antique design, two black wooden chairs, and a small writing desk in the corner. Leo approached the desk. Lying open on the uncluttered desktop was a single, cardboard-bound paper book. He leafed through the pages with ungloved hands. The paper felt like genuine pulp. There was no registry marking on the front or back cover, which would make possessing it a low-end misdemeanor. A few hours community work. Probably chatting with lonely scabbers, holding your nose while pretending to be interested in their depressed rambling. Not a fun afternoon. Displaying a book like this was a minor but foolish risk for responsible people to take. Registering paper books was easy, and important as well. Leo made an unrecorded mental note to mention the book to Nyla Pyka, Metro South's human record-keeper. Nyla was always on the lookout for additions to the southern precinct's physical library — the only one of its kind in Mirabilis.

Leo finished his sweep of the living room, finding nothing that suggested the inhabitants were anything but a decent, mentally healthy couple. A rare thing these days. Perhaps dangerous.

He went to the bedroom next.

The queen-sized bed was tightly made. A walnut bureau next

to the window was full of clothes, every stitch washed, ironed, and folded. In the closet hung more clothes, mostly dresses, with two men's jackets hanging to the side. Polished men's dress shoes lined the bottom of the closet. Leo stared at the shoes for a long moment. This couple had tried to live well. Like him, they were making an effort at a time when most people had given up on things as basic as routine bathing. A positive life was no easy feat these days. To lose it in something as senseless as a random sadboy attack was intolerable. As his mind clouded in anger Leo found himself unable to lift his eyes from the empty shoes. He knew the machines would be merciful towards the killer — That was the machine way. But maybe a more human type of justice was called for this time. Something of equivalent harshness to the crime. In that moment he had never felt more confident about his and Waterbird's plan to win Leo a promotion to Detective. A human detective would be historic in the age of machines. It would also be deserved.

Raising his head, Leo saw a row of shoeboxes crowding the closet's top shelf. Standing on his toes, he pulled the first one down and opened it. Just a pair of high heels. He brought down another box. Then another. It took him a few minutes to search through them all, but in the end he was glad to have been so thorough. Inside the final shoebox was a stash of medicines: three bottles of prescription pills with the labels removed. One bottle of bright orange capsules, a second bottle half-full with long pinkish tablets, a third crammed with large blue and green pills. Leo thought he recognized the orange capsules, but couldn't recall the name. Also in the box were two vials of clear liquid, also unmarked. Underneath the bottles was a ragged-looking book: *A Guide to a Healthy Pregnancy*, dated from 2044, around the last year you could find a source of human knowledge unenhanced by machine intelligence. A human author — ridiculous. A person would have to be a fool to take the information in a book like this seriously. He turned to a few random pages, finding medical phrases he didn't understand highlighted here and there. *Alpha-fetoprotein. Episiotomy. Zygote intrafallopian transfer. Artificialis subcinctus.* The highlighter ink didn't look as old as the pages, but it didn't look recent, either. Whoever had originally marked these words was probably long dead, possibly from following the faulty medical advice found in human works like this one.

The rest of the apartment showed no sign that the two victims were expecting parents. From what he could see, Darryl and Tabitha hadn't even been thinking in that direction. But the new door lock and a secret box of unregulated medicine stood out from a backdrop of normalcy. Normalcy that itself was uncommon.

Detective Waterbird answered Leo's call immediately.

"Officer. You have found something of interest?"

"Maybe. A box full of medications — I don't know what kind — and an old pregnancy book. It was tucked away in the closet far enough to say it was hidden. It definitely doesn't fit with every-thing else I'm seeing up here." Leo tried not to feel such giddiness while standing in the bedroom of people so recently and violently deceased, but he couldn't help himself. He knew what came next.

"Excellent work, Officer Song. I have been called to an urgent matter elsewhere and must leave immediately. Please investigate this piece of evidence yourself until I can rejoin you."

There it was: total breach of protocol. Clear and bold on the open WinkLink. A human investigating evidence — it was unheard of. If Leo botched this part, there'd be hell to pay.

"Okay, Detective, I'll do my best."

"Attend to your regular duties first, please."

"Of course. Of course."

"Good luck, Officer."

Waterbird vanished from the connection, leaving Leo to himself in the empty bedroom. He stood there weighing the shoebox in his hands for what seemed like minutes. Finally, Leo pulled himself together, tucked the box under his arm and headed out of the apartment to begin knocking on closed doors.

———

ON THE NINTH DOOR, SOMEONE ANSWERED; A RUFFLED OLD WOMAN who huffed at Leo for the disturbance. Without waiting for a question, she launched into a hurried explanation of how she'd recently gone full suicide creative and was working on her final art piece for the Lubitsch theater. It would be a real showstopper, she said, and she was taking her jump the morning after the performance, so she didn't have time to answer a lot of pointless questions. She didn't have a lot of time in general.

"Do you know the couple in four-oh-six," Leo asked.

"It's her place, the girl's. She's been here forever. The boy just moved in not so long ago."

"So you knew Tabitha Jackson well?"

"No, no, no, just better than the boy. I liked her previous one better. The new one smiles a lot, you know, when he looks at you. Too much mouth. I don't trust that sort of thing, so I keep my distance…but it's not as if we're feuding or anything. They leave us alone, so good neighbors that way, I suppose."

Leo felt the excitement surge again, and again he fought it back.

"Tabitha Jackson had a previous lover?"

"I just said so."

"How long ago was that?"

"Oh…call it a year or so, maybe? I really have no idea."

"Did you know if Tabitha was expecting a child?"

The old woman snorted. "It wouldn't surprise me," she said. "She was one of those optimistic types, full of sunlight and hope and all that silly nonsense. It's so tiresome." She looked Leo's well-made suit up and down, judgment sharp in her eyes. "No offense."

Suddenly aware of his own giddiness, Leo affected a more somber tone. "So she wasn't any showing signs...of....um..."

"Hey, what happened? Are they dead or something?"

"Yes, Ma'am. I'm afraid so."

She shook her head in frustration. "Took the jump, huh? Figures they'd beat me to it. Well, I had no idea. It's always the biggest optimists who wind up jumping without a decent send-off, isn't it? Everything's all fine and flowers one minute, then the next thing you know — *shoop!* — out the nearest open window. Or a closed one, for that matter."

"This is a homicide investigation."

The old woman flinched as if she had been slapped, then shook her head in a way Leo could only guess was genuine remorse. "Well...that's a pity," she said. "I should have said nicer things just now. They weren't bad people, just not my flavor."

"I understand," he said. Leo suspected her callousness was a reaction to the treacly, ever-present concern of the rampers. A type of natural balance. At least he hoped it was. "You haven't seen anyone suspicious lately, lurking in the halls or arguing with the victims?"

"No."

"They were a couple, you said. Did they flaunt it? Show off?"

"No, they were careful about it. They never held hands, or not that I saw. Sad, isn't it? My wife and I used to make out every-where when we were young. Buses, parks, middle of the shitting sidewalk. Nobody minded. Well, some did, but nobody liked those people. You're too young to remember, but it's true."

Leo tried to imagine the old crone as a passionate young woman, but the picture was faulty. He believed her, though. "Do you know if there are any sadboys that live in this building?"

The old woman's eyes grew wide. "Sadboys? Did a sadboy kill them? That's...oh how...." she drifted off, imagining the carnage three floors below her. Looking at her expression, Leo thought he probably shouldn't have mentioned the bit about the sadboy.

"Ma'am, I have to ask again, do you know if she was pregnant?"

"If she was, I hadn't noticed," she said.

Now came the boilerplate. The secondary purpose of Leo's actual duties: offering emotional support counseling to witnesses. The machines took the mental health of the city's human inhabitants seriously. The humans, it had to be admitted, were generally less concerned about the matter. "Ma'am, do you feel any unusual feelings of stress or unease that may have been caused by these recent events? Do you believe you may require special counseling to help you with any personal issues, related or unrelated, to these unfortunate recent events?"

The old woman glared at him. "Are you joking?"

"Support counseling is free and encouraged."

"Go away now."

Leo spoke to three more residents split between the third and second floors, but no one had seen anything. Two of the three didn't know Tabitha Jackson and Darryl Vincent had even lived in the building. The third had passed them on the stairs from time to time, but had never spoken to them. The reaction to the news of their deaths was predictably subdued. Leo had decided not to mention that it was a possible sadboy attack; there was no need to frighten people, especially considering the killer would likely be apprehended in the next hour or two. He would have to hurry if he wanted to contribute to the investigation, but Leo doubted he would discover anything of value among the residents of this building.

The slow descent was excruciating. By the time Leo made it down to the first floor Waterbird was gone and the bodies had been removed from the hallway. He adjusted the shoebox under his arm and approached Unit 101, the only occupied apartment on the ground floor. He hoped no one would answer. To his dismay the door swung open after the first knock.

"About time, pal," the scabber said.

Leo recoiled from the assault of putrid body odor that rushed out of the apartment, an accumulation of sweat and filth from weeks of non-bathing. This was the mark of a true scabber: a person who had lost interest in showing up to civilization, but lacked the fortitude to go creative. Instead, they chose the easier path of a slow suicide. It often took a lifetime. "I've been waiting for you! I saw the whole thing."

"Slow down, sir. Tell me what you saw."

"A sadboy. It was a sadboy, a real big bastard. I've never seen one that size. I mean massive, like a war ramper. Shoulders as wide as my arms and half wires and crazy mods. Nasty."

The smell had failed to dissipate, forcing Leo to hold his breath as he spoke. "Are you sure it was a sadboy?"

"Are you kidding?"

"And you witnessed this sadboy attack the two victims?"

"Yeah, but…not at first."

"What do you mean?"

"I mean they talked first, then it attacked. Brutal. I mean super hostile."

That didn't make sense to Leo. Sadboys didn't have conversations. They couldn't speak. Leo worried this guy was either on something or trying to break up his pointless day with colorful stories. Resigned to his fate, Leo started breathing again. "You mean the victims shouted at the killer? They cried for help?"

"No, I mean they spoke, like, conversed — like we are right now. About shit. I mean with the sadboy."

"About *what*?"

"Didn't hear."

"Then how do you know?"

"Every conversation is about stuff."

"No, I mean, how do you know they were *talking*?"

"Um...I think I heard voices, but muffled kind of. Angry, though, so I peeked through the doorcam. Saw it through there.

Watched the whole thing. As long as I could, anyway…made me sick."

"How long did this conversation last?"

"A few minutes, at least…then the woman screamed and the rest happened."

"Wait, wait — the victims spoke with the sadboy for a few *minutes?*" Leo knew he should keep the questions moving, but if he didn't resolve it now this detail would nag at him for the rest of his life. "And you're sure you didn't hear what they talked about?"

"Nope."

"Think hard."

"I didn't hear."

"Look, I don't want to see them run a Peeper down on you. Ever had a Peeper probe? They sting like hell and you'll never feel safe in your own head again. But unless you give me something, that's what they'll do." He was exaggerating, of course. The machines would never approve an invasive memory probe on a voluntary witness, even a stubborn one, but Leo was betting the scabber didn't know that.

"Ah, man…I don't know." The man put his chin to his chest, then lifted his head back, nose to the ceiling in some bizarre display of "thinking". "Something about a test," he finally said. "Like a blood test or something."

The excitement returned again. "Was Tabitha Jackson pregnant?"

"Who?"

"The woman who was killed."

"How would I know?"

"Did she *look* pregnant to you? Her belly?"

"Never seen a pregnant lady."

Leo thought this guy was just young enough that it might be true; pregnancies were becoming rare, especially in neighborhoods like this. "Would you be willing to officially identify the killer, on record, in the event we apprehend him?"

"Fuck, only if you apprehend it dead."

With the interview at an impasse Leo needed to wrap things up. "Sir, do you feel any unusual stress or unease that may have been caused by— "

The door shut as abruptly as it had opened. Leo recorded the unit number and tenant's information off the building memory system. They could track him down again with little problem if needed. These days the only police division less busy than homicide was missing persons.

[2]

He was on his own now. With fresh evidence in hand and Detective Waterbird's open-Link order to investigate it, Leo would have to proceed by himself. The plan demanded he get results without machine assistance. Anything, but *something*. In anticipation of this moment, Leo had decided months ago where he would begin, regardless of the type of evidence found. By luck he was within walking distance. Exiting the Wilcott, Leo headed west on foot.

As he walked the empty streets, Leo ran through the case in his mind. Waterbird had said the killer was a sadboy. The way the victims had been killed suggested that. A witness had confirmed it. But a *talking* sadboy didn't line up with reality. Sadboys were insane abominations, unable to form even basic sentences. They were the result of a human's mind, body, and soul rejecting the impossible artificial enhancements they used on themselves. The problem was a lot of powerful enhancements could be made to the body before the mind finally snapped in homicidal rage. Sadboys were self-made monsters, a nasty mix of hubris and desperation. It turned out that human beings were simply not meant to be artificially improved to any great degree. The bridge between man and machine was not meant be crossed. The so-called Singularity had been a myth of the previous century, and bloody experience had proven that humans didn't upgrade past a certain point. Info-coms and some minor health mods were about as far as you could go without damaging yourself. Yet some still tried to push through the limitations. The depressed and desperate, already half-mad from the common malaise, deciding to act out ancient hero fantasies, hoping against hope to be the one special human to break the tech barrier. So, they added mesh-fiber muscles to synthetic bones, replaced their own eyes with field-scanners, injected molecular-processors into their spinal fluid and wove neural webbing into their brains. On paper, they were gods. But it never worked, always ending in the same, predictable tragedy. The results were obscene. The madness absolute. As far as Leo knew, no one in history had ever exchanged words with a full-stage sadboy. They just screamed, and then you screamed louder.

And then there were the victims. That young couple building a life together. Looking to the future with hope. Leo didn't need to count Waterbird's seventy-three indicators to know something was wrong with that picture.

For the moment, however, that was the end of his certainty.

Despite being on schedule, a pang of hunger spurred Leo into taking a detour on Lily Street. He cut across the dead-grass lawns of Chapman Park, walking quickly to avoid being tailed by the semi-wild dogs that made the neglected park their home. He kept his hand on his pistol in case the starving animals got any wrong ideas. It was a risk going this way, but Leo needed to get to his destination in a hurry, and this was the fastest route. He only hoped that Henri Borovich still kept his food train in this part of the city. But the mutts paid him no attention, lying on the rough dirt in tired poses like small, scruffy hobos sleeping off the previous night's binge. Reaching the edge of the park and with his blood pumping, he spotted a large stick lying beside a dying Honey Locust tree. Readying himself for a quick getaway, Leo gave a loud whistle then hurled the stick into the center of the lounging pack. A few heads swung up to regard the disturbance, but none of the animals moved.

Shit, thought Leo, even the dogs have given up.

Henri Borovich was where he should have been, manning his food train on the corner of Barrow Street and 14th Avenue. The "train" was a bit of hyperbole to describe a series of five food carts linked together end to end, forming a moveable buffet of cheap, dangerous cuisine. The menu, never exactly the same twice, included Polish sausages, sweet and savory Pai Bao, al pastor, hard boiled eggs, hamburgers, spring rolls, barbecued chicken, and more, including the occasional fish option, which was likely only seasoned tofu with a ribbon of synthetic scales pasted on one side. It was for good reason no one inquired too deeply into the sources for Henri's daily menu, not that anyone cared to in the first place. The food was tasty enough and the smell, boosted by molecular enhancers placed inside the cookers, was enthralling. With the right breeze, the delicious scent could lure in a hungry customer from as far as ten blocks away. As one of the last licensed food vendors in the city, Henri Borovich was a treasure of humanity, providing a human-run service people still appreciated and used. The rampers thought this was fascinating, and went so far as to subsidize Henri's endeavor just so they could observe him at work. Unbeknownst to the machines, this subsidy also enabled Henri to dabble in semi-legal ventures well beyond the scope of his license. It was this fact that had drawn Leo to the food train.

"Officer Song, nice to see you again," Henri said, wiping his hands on his grease-splotched apron before offering a handshake.

"Henri, what's good today?"

"The chicken is spicy. We also have some nice fish. I could whip you up a taco de pescado with that. It's wonderful, trust me. I've outdone myself."

Leo forced a smile. He didn't trust Henri when it came to the fish. The man always pushed it too hard when it was on the menu. "I think I'll go with a pai bao."

"Solid choice. The apple of your youth. A little nostalgia to warm the soul."

"Mom never made it like you do, Henri. She didn't have the magic."

Henri nodded grandly. "Few do, few do. I'm sure she made it with love, though."

"Sure, lots of love — just not enough sugar."

"Criminal."

As Henri prepared the order, Leo surveyed the area. They had an audience, as always. Two rampers were standing away from the cart, watching the food train intently, fixated on the simple interaction between the humans. Henri and Leo were the only people in sight, and the attention made Leo slightly uncomfortable.

"Doesn't that ever get to you?"

"What?"

Leo jerked his head towards the robots. They were maintenance machines, discernible by their wide bases and heavy multifunction arms. Construction workers in another age.

"Oh, no, it doesn't bother me. I actually feel sort of bad — obvious they want to try a taste. I wish I could make them something, you know? Must be hell for them, to want it like that."

Leo wasn't so sure it was envy that compelled the rampers to gather at Henri's cart, but he didn't press it. He noticed one of the machines was wearing a synthetic human nose on its faceplate. They did that sometimes. If it was a show of solidarity with humans or a machine fashion statement Leo had no idea.

"So, uh, you hear about what happened at the Wilcott Hotel, over on Bradley and Ninth?"

Henri shook his head, smirking as if anticipating a joke. "No, what?"

"Double homicide."

Henri glanced up from the smoking grill. "Oh…that's a shame."

"Looks like a sadboy attack."

Henri did not glance up this time. "Mhmm. Sorry to hear it."

"I thought maybe you might have heard something, people looking for advanced upgrade tech, anything that might be excessive."

"Haven't heard anything like that."

"Any sadboy clubs forming up? Scabbers with a lot of sudden interest in socializing, getting together in groups?"

"Nope. You don't hear much about sadboys anymore. Maybe it's finally sinking in, huh? Flesh and mech, never the twain shall meet and all that?"

"Can you look at something for me, Henri?"

Henri raised his head to Leo, surprise on his face. "Look at something?"

"Just some pills I found."

"That you *found*? From that murder? Like evidence?"

Leo shrugged.

"I don't mind your questions, Leo, but this…"

"You won't get in any trouble."

"No, Officer, I mean it's sad. It's sad for you. Your hope, it's too up."

"You going to look or not?"

Henri thought for a moment, then beckoned with one hand. Leo reached into the shoebox and pulled out the bottle of orange capsules. Henri plucked the bottle from Leo's hand like a pigeon at a crumb. Leo looked over at the machines still gawping at the human transaction, witnesses to the policeman's blatant breaking of protocol.

"Don't mind them," Henri said, dumping a few of the thick capsules into his palm. "They're fans of mine. I'm the oddest monkey in the zoo."

Leo gestured to the bottle in Henri's hand. "How about those? Any ideas where this came from?" The labels had been torn off all of the medicine bottles, but the one Leo had given Henri still had a fragment of ink on it. A partial word in the lower corner….

gust

"Probably part of a name. Recognize it?"

"Nope, don't recognize it," Henri said. He had only glanced at the torn label and was now peering at the capsule as if appraising a jewel. "And these aren't exactly of a high criminality, Officer."

"Yeah, I know they're not. I've seen them before. They treat dementia, right?" Anti-psychotics — mid-stage sadboys used them when they began to lose their minds. "Bastards swallow them by the handful."

"If you say so. I know they don't do anything fun. And they aren't illegal."

"Right, so then why take the label off? Why hide them? That's what I want to know."

Henri shook his head in ignorance.

"You know any human doctors treating wannabe sadboys?" Leo asked.

"*Human* doctors? They even still have those?"

"Come on, you know the play, Henri. Waterbird's going to be hauling in the killer any minute now. I just want to have a little extra information to throw in the mix. Human contribution for once, right?"

Henri chomped his teeth a few times, as if eating his true opinion of the cop. After several gnashes he finally relented. "There's a guy over near the west side. Old school type, a genuine people person, you could say. Likes to help those in need. Real big on quality of life, you know. Happy pills, mood mods, that sort of thing."

"A do-gooder."

"Doc do-*anything*. The type that'd maybe treat a sadboy."

"Name?"

"No idea. But how many human doctors can there be on the west side? Here's your bao."

[3]

Leo gave up on the pai bao after only two bites, throwing it away before he entered the precinct. Inside, a few rampers moved here and there through the grand lobby, too busy with their tasks to pay attention to the human. Leo didn't see any people yet. He doubted any of his human colleagues would be this early. It was barely nine thirty. A good number of human officers didn't get out of bed until after ten.

Leo took the empty human-only elevator, wondering during the few seconds of travel if Henri had been worth it. There was limited time and the information the pushcart man had given didn't amount to much. Waterbird was on his side in this, but there was a better than fifty/fifty chance the killer would already be in custody by the time the elevator reached the seventh floor. There was still a job to do, and for all its support, Waterbird wasn't about to let a murderer escape capture just so Leo could feel good about himself.

The elevator doors snapped open.

The Homicide unit was empty. No people. More importantly, no machines. No Waterbird. No suspect in custody. The case was still open and active...for the moment. Leo tossed the shoebox onto his small desk and sat down. Before starting, he looked over his shoulder at the Unit Supervisor's office at the far end of the room. The door was closed, as always. In his five years in Homicide, Leo had never seen Mrs. Greenfields leave its office chamber. But he knew it was there. That he had not been summoned to the machine's door upon entering the squad room meant Greenfields was either not yet aware of what he was doing, did not care, or was biding its time to see what Leo actually accomplished. It was the last option they were counting on. An eventual confrontation with Mrs. Greenfields was essential to the plan, just not yet. Right now there was still much to do.

Reaching into his pocket, he found the bottle of medication he had taken from Tabitha's shoebox. The torn label. The physician's name reduced to a nonsense word. He opened the bottle and emptied one of the capsules into his hand. The street vendor Henri Borovich hadn't known what they were because they weren't recreational drugs, but Leo had seen them before on two other sadboy cases. Hypo-prochlorperazine. Super anti-psychotics. As the endless upgrades devastated the brain chemistry of mid-stage sadboys, they attempted to treat their dangerous symptoms with old-school pharmaceuticals. It worked for a time, but the effects never lasted. But what had Tabitha been doing with them? Leo WinkLinked and brought up information on the drug.

Hypo-prochlorperazine: For the treatment of psychotic symptoms. Also used to treat severe nausea and vomiting. Not currently manufactured.

Nausea and vomiting. Morning sickness. Tabitha Jackson could have been using the pills to treat morning sickness. Maybe she *had* been pregnant at the time of her murder.

He blinked over to the autopsy reports.

"Shit," he said out loud. The report was up, but it had been restricted. He wouldn't be able to read them without approval from a superior. Locking autopsy reports and case files wasn't routine, but it wasn't unheard of either. Usually it was done on cases the rampers deemed too sensitive or potentially shocking to the public. If there was a chance of upsetting humans, the machines erred on the side of caution. That could definitely be the logic here. Nothing put people on edge like sadboy attacks and this case was bloody enough to warrant keeping a lid on it. Whatever the reason, Leo wasn't important enough to merit access to the files.

Next he brought up the City Records interface. It took less than a microsecond for Mirabilis's great database to connect with the Police-certified WinkLink chip in Leo's brain.

Tabitha Jackson, D.O.B. 7/9/2130.
Parents: Unknown.
Education: Silver Crest Virtual University
Degrees in Structural Design and Non-verbal Communications
Non-essential employment: Architect's Assistant, Department of City Works.

Leo sped-scanned through the rest until he found what he was looking for.

Medical History: Bloodworm Fever at age 11 – Cured.
Last check-up on 4/2/56. Physical health: Excellent. Mental health: Optimal.

Leo was surprised by the victim's scant medical history. Tabitha Jackson's last reported check-up had been over ten months ago and there was no mention of her being pregnant. Her history suggested Tabitha had been a stable, rational person, not someone who would stop going to the doctor if she was carrying a child. Not someone who would keep a stash of old medicine hidden in her closet, either. Not someone who needed a brand new lock on her door.

He was about to move on to Darryl Vincent's file when his WinkLink flashed blue.

It was Waterbird. Too soon. Way too soon. It could mean only one thing. Leo waved in the call.

"Detective, you've made an arrest?"

"No, Officer, I have not. How is your work progressing?"

Leo was surprised to hear it, and might have been relieved, but something about the machine's tone kept him from celebrating. "Actually, some curious stuff. Turns out one of the neighbors saw the attack happen through his door scanner, said the killer was definitely a sadboy."

"As we deduced from the crime scene."

"Right. Thing is, this guy claims the sadboy spoke to the victims before killing them. I mean a full conversation. Talking sadboys? Ever heard anything like that?"

"There are no reports of a speech-capable sadboy in the city histories." Just like that, a hundred years of data searched and filtered. Rampers were good that way. "Have you investigated the evidence you retrieved from the victim's housing unit?"

"Not much. Tabitha Jackson *may* have been pregnant and gotten certain medications from a human doctor. But I'm only guessing about that. The autopsy report is locked, by the way. I can't access it."

"Yes, I'm afraid the autopsy reports have been priority restricted and I unable to share that information with you. I am sorry. Is there anything else?"

"Well...only that according to one of her neighbors, Tabitha Jackson lived with someone *before* Darryl Vincent, but–"

"–Lanson Philip Stroud, age twenty-seven."

"I hadn't had a chance to look it up yet." Leo swallowed his disappointment. Waterbird had agreed to let Leo work unassisted, but apparently the machine couldn't help it. Know-it-alls, every one of them.

The machine continued. "Lanson Stroud is currently employed at Fulcrum Laboratories as an assistant maintenance engineer. Mr. Stroud previously resided at Tabitha's current address for two years, but moved out thirteen months ago. Assumed to be Tabitha Jackson's former romantic partner. Their last recorded time together was in June of last year, a fine dining experience at Papa Xin's Super Real Meat and Grill."

"So, an ex-boyfriend. The jealous type?"

"Records indicate he was at work at the time of the murder. An eight hour night shift. This alibi has been verified by his employer. Lanson Stroud may be a person of interest in this case, but I do not consider him to be a suspect."

So, what now?"

"Speak with Lanson Stroud."

Leo was stunned. A human handling evidence was bending the rules, but a human interrogating someone connected to an active case, even tangentially, was breaking them outright. It was a breach of protocol Leo hadn't anticipated making and maybe a step too far. He didn't know what the punishments for law-breaking machines were, if any, but he knew what they were for humans. Two days in a void-harness didn't appeal to him. "But you just said he's not a suspect."

Waterbird paused. It was only a nanosecond, but eternity for a machine. "Do you wish to cease our efforts?"

Leo shook his head. "No. I don't."

"Are you concerned that your actions may cause conflict with your human colleagues? It would be a reasonable concern, as tension are already high."

Leo glanced around the squad room. He was still alone. "I can handle the dirty looks — especially from this bunch — but is this going to be a problem for *you*, Detective, bending protocol like this? Mrs. Greenfields isn't going to like this at all. Me talking to a suspect?"

"A person of interest," Waterbird corrected. "Do not concern yourself with Mrs. Greenfields yet, Officer Song. Protocol does grant a measure of discretion on this matter. This case will be submitted with your contributions as a matter of record and I am confident you will perform to the fullest extent allowed by your natural limitations."

Leo couldn't help running a mental inventory of his "natural limitations". There were many. It was cold-blue truth served piping hot — a machine specialty. Still, he knew what Waterbird meant. "I appreciate that, Detective. I just hope it matters this time."

"Before you begin, I would like you to go see Nyla Pyka in the Records room."

"Nyla, huh?" A trip to the basement was the last thing Leo wanted to do right now, but he wasn't about to argue. "What do you need from her?"

"Ask her to search the physical library for information on the subject of speech-capable nimisgrade homo sapiens. In addition, please ask her to search for a history of sadboy enclaves reported within the Canyons."

"Sadboy enclaves in the Canyons? I thought they were solitary, that they didn't cluster. Where'd you hear this?"

Waterbird ignored the question, only repeating, "Please ask Nyla Pyka to research the matter and keep me apprised of your progress."

"What are you going to do?"

"I will proceed with my regular duties. Accomplish what you are able and we will speak later. Good luck, Leo."

"You too, Detective."

Waterbird disconnected, leaving Leo to ponder the stupidity of wishing a machine good luck. Remaining at his desk, he chanced a second look towards Mrs. Greenfield's door. Still closed. Still silent. Rising from the desk, Leo opened the shoebox and looked inside at the strange contents, considering what to do with it. If the rampers had locked the autopsy reports, they would probably secure the evidence chain as well. Once he logged the box into evidence he would lose access to it for good. That wasn't going to work. The box was old, maybe from when Stroud had been living with Tabitha. It was possible Lanson Stroud, the ex-boyfriend, knew something about it. Leo decided it was best if he kept the shoebox until after he spoke with Stroud. But first he would go to Records and see Nyla Pyka, getting the Detective's errand out of the way as soon as possible. He didn't mind. It had been a long time since he'd seen Nyla.

$$[\ 4\ ]$$

The machine wore a pair of human hands like fleshy oven mitts, the pink rubber fingers bending in unnatural ways as they pressed against the data interface. Leo waited patiently for Mr. Sweetrose to finish entering the passcode, trying not to stare at the ramper's ill-fitting prosthetics. He didn't think police protocol allowed for machines to wear human anatomy simulacra on the job, and if it did, it shouldn't have. Rampers came in a variety of designs, none of them remotely human in form. This was due to two reasons: one, humans were poor designs and two, machines that looked human made real humans nervous. So, designing and manufacturing their own brains and bodies, the machines created themselves as perfections of efficiency and grace. They existed in a multitude of models and makes, each with unique specialties and intentional limitations. They were marvelous. Better than any form of life that had come before. And distinctly, almost proudly, *non*-human. To Leo, sticking clumsy gloves on the end of perfectly engineered manipulator rods seemed to spoil the point. Opening a secure door, an act which normally should have taken a few seconds, had dragged on near half a minute.

"Is that a new suit, Officer Song," asked Sweetrose as it fumbled at the digital keyboard.

"Uh…yes it is, Mr. Sweetrose."

"Excellent."

"Thank you, Mr. Sweetrose."

The door's large deadbolts released and Leo hastily entered the Records and Research main room, thanking Sweetrose again as he passed.

Records and Research was a lonely place, which Leo considered a great shame, since the builders had put tremendous care into fashioning every detail of an old-world library. Tall shelves of dark wood were lined with countless books, some real, most plastic facsimiles, convincing even up close. The reading desks were topped with green-shaded study lamps and set with broad, leather-upholstered chairs, comfortable for hours at a time. The high ceiling and thick walls produced a deep, enveloping quiet that promoted concentration, but not so relaxing as to induce sleepiness. It all suggested a place for serious academic study well beyond the needs of an average police precinct, far more than anyone in his squad deserved. Every time he came here Leo vowed to return more often. Of course, there was another reason he was so fond of the Records and Research room, and he found her perched on a desk hidden behind the furthest bookcase, nose buried in a plastic volume of late twentieth century poetry.

Nyla Pyka was the Keeper of Records and in-house researcher, a position that, like the majority of human jobs, was wholly unnecessary. An anachronism kept alive by the machines' belief that upholding certain human practices was beneficial to the species. Staying occupied helped kept a person's spirits up. That was the idea, anyway, and who was Leo to argue? In his darker moods, though, Leo suspected the rampers simply thought it was interesting to watch people try to do work any machine could do faster and better. The 35-year-old Nyla had spent the bulk of her life as an over-titled version of what used to be known as a "librarian." It was an unenviable task, even less relied upon than Leo's own minimal duties, which had made the two of them natural partners in near-uselessness. But time and Leo's ambition had moved them apart. Now the work was taking its toll on her. Being stuck in this quiet room for eight hours a day, often without a single visitor for days or weeks at a time, was turning the naturally gregarious Nyla Pyka into a basket case — and she knew it. The sheer desperation of her smile whenever Nyla saw Leo, or anyone else, always gave him a double hit of gladness and worry. Today was no different.

"Leo! Great to see you! Hey, I like that suit. Ooh, and the shoes, too!"

"Nyla, how are you?"

"I'm good! I mean…you know, I'm here."

Leo nodded, trying not to stare. Nyla's dark hair, always neatly kept in intricate braids, now puffed out in a frizzy, unmanaged bird's nest. Her clothes were wrinkled and dirty from days of seemingly consecutive wear and even at a distance, Leo noted a hint of encroaching body odor that would likely bloom out of control if not tended to soon.

"When's the last time somebody came down here, Nyla?"

"Oh, I don't know, I have no idea. I could check. Want me to check that?"

"No, that's okay, I'm just asking…"

"I try not to count the days that way, you know — one at a time? Does that make sense?"

"Sure it does. That's healthy thinking."

"Is it?" She stared at him, genuinely asking.

Leo smiled and shrugged, but didn't say anything.

Nyla's smile went flat and her eyes narrowed into slits. "What brings you down here, Leo?"

"I need information on sadboy activity in the city. Anything, going all the way back."

"Don't tell me, Detective Waterbird's asking for this, right?"

"No. Yes. It's both of us."

"Mhmm. Well, that's a lot of data, anything to narrow it down?"

"Sadboy enclaves in the Canyons…and speech capable nimis-grade homo sapiens. That means talking sadboys. Don't say it, I know how it sounds."

Nyla stirred the air with her fingers, summoning an interface that hovered silently in front of her. "Talking sadboys? That should be a thin file."

"There won't be anything in the city reports, Waterbird already checked those, but maybe there's something in the older histories. Something in old papers that haven't been digitized yet? Even just a rumor."

"I doubt it. Not a lot of overlap there; pretty much everything was digital by the time sadboys came along. Do you want to wait while I go through the stacks? I'll probably be done before Mr. Sweetrose can let you out again."

Leo laughed. "Is he even allowed to have those things?"

"I don't know, but it's annoying."

"Yeah. Strange they do that."

Nyla shrugged. "I don't pretend to know what's normal for rampers. What's with *you,* though?"

"Why? What do you mean?"

"You look happy."

"I'm working a case."

"With Waterbird."

"Yeah, with Waterbird."

Nyla scowled and shook her head. "Leo, that machine shouldn't be getting your hopes up like this, even if it means well."

"You're probably right." Leo regarded Nyla sitting on the table, crumpled and defeated, looking for all the world like a mound of forgotten laundry. He glanced around the room, then took a few steps closer to her and whispered, "Want to help?"

Nyla's eyes opened wider. "Up there? In the city?"

"No. No, that wouldn't work."

Her eyes narrowed. "What then?"

Leo leaned in close to Nyla's ear and found that her neglected hygiene was worse than he'd first thought. She badly needed something to look forward to. Every human in the precinct probably did, whether they could admit it or not, but Nyla was the only one he'd dare include at this point. Besides, Waterbird had practically set the whole thing up. Knowing the machine, this might be the actual purpose of Leo's errand. Nyla's extra-curricular assistance would only prove their point to the supervisors. He had no doubt he was doing the right thing. "I found some strange words highlighted in an old book," he said. "Medical terminology I don't understand, but I'm curious if the book itself might have a history. Where it came from, who owned it, that sort of thing."

Nyla dropped her head. "Come on, Leo, that's not...," her voice trailed off. "How is that any different from what I'm doing already?"

"This is just for me. Call it semi-official. We'll have to meet somewhere else to discuss it, somewhere private. But if it helps the case, it counts. We count."

Nyla kept her head down, thinking it over. Finally, without looking up, she asked, "What's the book?"

"Women's Guide to a Healthy Pregnancy, published in twenty forty four. Written by Dr. Lisa Scopnik. Something like that."

"Okay, Leo. I'll look into it."

"Good. It'll be good, Nyla." Leo turned to go.

"Wait!" Nyla hopped off the table and approached him. "Where do we meet?"

"I don't know. I–"

"–The Lubitsch," she said quickly. "It's loud, crowded, people are distracted, and there's never a ramper anywhere near the place."

The Lubitsch Theater. Creatives went there to perform their

final acts before taking the big jump. Leo had always found it too bleak to tolerate, but Nyla wasn't wrong about it being a good place to remain unnoticed.

"You've been going there a lot?" Leo asked. Spending a lot of time at The Lubitsch was never a good sign for a person's mental health.

"A little," she said. "I've been trying to get out more recently, or making the effort to. It's somewhere to go."

"Okay," Leo said. "Sounds good."

"I'll tell you when I'm done and we'll meet." Nyla said, ending with a terse nod. In one swift movement, she turned, hopped back onto her table, and began to knead the air with her fingers.

Leo paused, watching her pluck data seeds out of the ether as if nothing had happened. "Don't forget what Waterbird asked for, too," he said.

"Talking sadboys and sadboy enclaves in the Canyons. Got it. Bye, Leo."

"Yeah. Bye, Nyla. See you later."

Leo considered taking the ramps back to his desk, a long walk that would give him time to mull over what had happened with Nyla, but decided to use the elevator instead. When the doors opened Leo immediately regretted his choice. Standing inside the lift, waiting patiently for Leo to commit one way or another, was Officer Hewl Pardo, one of the vice squad boys, self-styled tough guy and certified chatterbox. Leo entered, annoyed that he would not be alone for the ascent.

"Officer Leo Song, going up. Been bothering Nyla again?"

"Pardo."

Leo stood slightly in front of Pardo to avoid eye contact, an obvious maneuver that made Leo feel ashamed as soon as he did it. It didn't even work.

"Saw you caught a sadboy attack this morning. It was prime on the Link."

Leo didn't turn around. "A witness claims to have seen a sadboy. That's all I know."

"Shit, that's all the lead Waterbird needs, right? Fucking ramper could catch smoke off a fart."

"Tell me, why are you vice guys always so gross?"

"Genetics. Wait, why does Waterbird have you handling evidence?"

"I don't know, Pardo, I guess Waterbird trusts me."

"More like fucking with you. I know you're Waterbird's shadow, Leo, but the way you eat up that ramper's bullshit... honestly, it's hard to watch."

Leo turned to Pardo, getting a full look at him for the first time; his left eye was a deep shade of red that was beginning to purple and his bottom lip was split and swollen. Not an uncommon state for Officer Pardo. "Lose another bar fight, Pardo? When are you going to learn to stop picking on scabbers bigger than you, Pardo?"

"Soon as they stop opening their big, boring mouths. Talketh shit, receiveth shit. But I don't know which is worse, a scabber's stink or you with that fucking smile, like you matter a single little shit."

"I wasn't aware I was smiling."

"You are...and you should stop. Bit of friendly advice."

The elevator stopped at the seventh floor and Leo got out, but Pardo held the door.

"Hey, hey, wait — Song, let me ask you something."

Pardo leaned forward to whisper, as Leo had done with Nyla moments before. Leo knew what was coming. He had expected it the second he'd gotten on the elevator.

"There's a batch of black market Celwax that just hit the street," Pardo said. "Bad stuff, apparently, got the rampers spinning out as bad as I've ever seen. They haven't been able to track all of it down so far and it's making them twitchy."

"So? You're in Vice, not me."

The elevator door jolted and buzzed as it tried to close, but Pardo kept it open.

"Sure, yeah, but you know how it is, Leo. They don't tell me anything."

"Pardo, what do you want?"

"You have a history with that shit, right? Illegal Celwax? You and Waterbird? Maybe you can keep your ear to the ground for me?"

"Pardo, that was five years ago. It was one case."

"Come on, Leo. Everyone knows you're Waterbird's pet monkey. All I'm asking is put out some feelers, and if you hear anything about bad Celwax moving around, you let me know. But, hey, just me, okay? No reports, no gossip train, just you to me. And maybe I can help you with...whatever it is you're doing."

Hewl Pardo stared at Leo like a mad man, the vice cop's weathered face carved by years of the constant, seething panic that nothing he did mattered. Leo felt an impulse to help the man, to bring Pardo into the fold as he had done with Nyla. For an instant and not the first time, Leo envisioned himself at the head of a precinct-wide movement of human officers, two hundred strong, arm in arm, demanding the chance to advance in their vocations, to develop, to grow, to make a difference in the end, at least once in a while. He envisioned their success spreading across the city in a warm, bright wave. But the image vanished between the frustrated complaints of the elevator's beeping doors. The reality was that Hewl Pardo was in a different division on a different floor, and without a machine in his own squad to back him up, the lowly vice cop was wasting his time. And they both knew it.

"Sure, Pardo, I'll keep my ear to the ground."

"Thanks, Leo. We don't want another Swoback situation out there, do we? Right?"

The doors hissed and retracted again impatiently.

"Better let the door go, Hewl. Every service ramper in the building is probably on its way."

"So, you hear anything, you tell me first, right? Person to per–"

The elevator doors closed with a rush of cold air.

———

LEO ENTERED THE SQUAD ROOM TO FIND LEW KIWAMBE AND Lauren Horn at their desks, both staring into space as they scanned their internal WinkLinks. The fourth and final human officer of the homicide team, Micco Sauvi, was not there. Out of the two hundred and twelve humans working at the Metro South precinct, only four were assigned to the Homicide Unit. A small club, but hardly elite. Day to day, the non-machine officers of the "murder squad" performed little actual police-work.

Lew Kiwambe blinked off his connection and waved a greeting as Leo passed his desk. Lauren was deep in her head and didn't notice him at all. Back at his own desk, Leo put the shoebox in his desk drawer and locked it with a twist of his fingers. Although there was little chance of it, he didn't want the others nosing around about while he worked. Next he waved on his WinkLink and began searching the city records for information on Lanson Stroud. The first thing to come up was a basic citizen's file: date and place of birth, parent's names, gender (if any), distinguishing features, eye color, weight, and standard post-natal personality predictions. These reports could get complicated if any future trouble was spotted, but this one was down the center line. A physically healthy male child with no genetic indicators of aberrant behavioral tendencies. According to this file, the odds said Landon Stroud should have developed into a normal, healthy adult. Intelligent and sane, maybe even happy, as far as anyone could be these days. But Leo knew time had a way of spoiling even the sharpest predictions.

Next he found educational records. Lanson Stroud showed

aptitudes in empathy and communication. It was difficult to get anyone to excel at school, but Lanson did okay. A fair student, nothing exceptional. At twenty, he earned a journeyman degree in Applied Sociology. That meant a counselor's track, mostly talking depressed people out of going creative. One of the last directly helpful jobs for a person to do, but it burned you out quickly. The educational record showed no other avenues of study or interests. Lanson had learned what he needed to and left the school system behind as soon as he could.

Leo moved on to the employment records. One year spent working as an emotional guardian, tending to scabbers who had stopped eating or bathing themselves. The performance reviews became spotty after only three months. There was the burnout. Lanson had suffered it sooner than most. By the end of his first year on the job Lanson Stroud was finished as an emotional guardian. It seems he'd had enough of helping people. But there the employment record ended. No more data. Waterbird had mentioned something about Stroud working at a laboratory of some kind, but there was nothing else, only empty air.

Next he tried residential records, the living space registrations everyone had to fill out before selecting a place to live. Rent was free in Mirabilis, ownership unnecessary, but you had to tell them where you were. During his single year as an emotional guardian, Lanson had taken up residence in a townhouse on the east side. No mention of anyone else living there. But like the employment files there was nothing after that year.

Zero data. It wasn't possible.

Leo waved off and walked over to Lew Kiwambe's desk.

"What's up, Leo?"

"Hey Lew, you having any problems with the Link, issues accessing city records, anything like that?"

"Issues?"

"I'm tracking this suspect and the file trail went dead on me." Leo realized his mistake too late.

Lew leaned back in his chair, incredulous. "You're tracking a suspect?"

"Person of interest. Just some guy really."

Lew turned in his chair towards Lauren Horn. "Hey, Horn!"

She waved off her WinkLink, annoyed by the interruption. "What?"

Leo leaned towards the younger officer. "Come on, Lew, what are you doing?"

"Waterbird's got Leo tracking suspects now."

"Are you — oh, fuck off, Song."

"He's not a suspect," Leo said. "It's just an interview with someone associated to the victim. No big deal."

"Face it, Leo," said Lauren Horn, "you're Waterbird's pet stair-hopper and everyone knows it."

Kiwambe turned to Horn and said, "Yeah, but he already lost the suspect's trail."

"Well, Lew, what do you expect? He's only human."

"Look, the file line went blank on me. It's weird."

"Probably a quantum fart," offered Horn, referring to the occasional tendency of quantum-calculated information to pop in and out of existence at random. It was a rare problem, but a maddening one.

"I don't know, doesn't something usually swap out when that happens? A for Z? There's no data here at all." He was met with blank stares. "So, neither of you know how this works? Does Micco? Anyone?"

Lauren shook her head in weary disgust and waved back onto her Link, leaving Leo and Lew alone again.

"Well," Lew said, "maybe your suspect is dead?"

Leo knew it wasn't a serious suggestion, but he tried it anyway, searching the death listings for Lanson Stroud. Nothing found.

Current location search. Nothing found.

Living relatives — no data.

Known associates — no data. Medical files — no data. Wink-

Link history for Lanson Stroud — no data. WinkLink implant serial number — no data.

Leo waved off with an angry gesture and slammed his fist on the metal desktop. It was a mild expression of anger, but the Homicide Unit's nameless service ramper immediately approached Leo desk, drawn by the human's obvious distress.

"Is everything all right, Officer Song? Would you like a cup of coffee or tea? Perhaps a Valamine tablet?"

"No. Not right now, thanks. I'm just a little frustrated, that's all. I apologize for the outburst."

"Perhaps you would care to take a walk outside in the park? A change of scenery can often be beneficial in reducing stress."

Typical, Leo thought. It always made the rampers uncomfortable when a person became visibly upset. Raise your voice too loud and they'd do anything to get you out the door. They considered a bad mood as contagious as a cold.

"I–"

"Big show!"

The shout made even Lauren Horn, as deep-Linked as you could get before inducing psychosis, turn to look. Just as quickly, she looked away. Leo had no such option as Micco Sauvi strode towards him, a disturbing look on the old man's thin face.

"Micco."

"Big, big show." Up close, Micco's flesh was trembling. "Big *fucking* show."

"Good morning, Officer Sauvi," said the service machine. "You seem a little upset. Is there anything I can do? Would you like a Valamine tablet?"

Micco ignored the machine as he gestured to Leo's desk. "Where is it, Song?"

"Where's what, Micco?"

"The evidence. *Your* evidence — Officer Song's big discovery we all watched you make. The big clue. Where is it? I want to see it." Micco kicked the metal desk, making a hollow ringing sound. "Show it to me."

The service ramper twitched. "Officer Sauvi, would you like a Valamine tablet now?"

"Hey, come on, Micco, don't be an ass," Leo said.

"It's in his bottom drawer!" Lew Kiwambe called out from his desk. "But forget the evidence, he's tracking a suspect now."

"Suspect? Bullshit. That's bullshit. You're not allowed. They don't let us…"

"Not a suspect," Leo said almost to himself. "Just a person of interest."

Kiwambe shouted out, "And he's already stuck!"

Micco laughed. "Yeah, that true? You're stuck?"

Leo glared at Micco. "It's not a problem."

"I bet. Well, good luck, Song." Micco walked away from Leo's desk and sat at his own across the aisle. "We're all rooting for you."

Leo looked around the room at his colleagues. Every face was etched with irritation. They were ignoring him and he didn't blame them. He'd thrown his good fortune in their faces without even thinking about it. Leo turned to the service machine still at his side, "I think I'll get out of here for today."

"Yes. Working from home can often have excellent health benefits," encouraged the little machine. "Would you like your coffee to go?"

[5]

The elevated FastTram was lightly occupied, so Leo took a seat by a window, as was his habit. A fellow passenger familiar with Leo's daily routine would've been excused in thinking the policeman gained a sense of peace staring out at the vast mega-city, but in truth this was an act of mournful reverence. Mirabilis was a perfect creation; its layers of clockwork infrastructure hidden beneath a pastiche of architectures culled from the great epochs of human history. Sweeping Meiji-era rooftops, heavy gothic arches, massive Renaissance domes, sleek Arabian minarets, cold modernist towers of glass and steel, all improved and exaggerated, merged seamlessly in a balance of ornate detail and clean simplicity that excited the eye from every angle. A super-metropolis designed to accommodate forty million people in comfort and style, Mirabilis stood as the greatest achievement of city-planning ever undertaken, and little of it had been made by human hands. From concept to the final splash of paint, the machines had done the work. The perfection of the city's beauty and efficiency was almost alien. The die-off began not long after. Today the human population of Mirabilis barely topped eight million. Eight million in a place designed for five times that. Leo looked grimly down as the tram passed over the dark zones, entire city blocks sitting empty. Mile-wide shrines to humanity's obsolescence.

Leo thought of Nyla, wondering if asking for her help had been a mistake. Seeing her like she was, veering into deep depression, made him wary of spending extended time with her. She was caught in a scabber mindset, an emotional disease as contagious as any virus; getting close to someone in that condition was to invite disaster. Hewl Pardo, hardly a sensitive type, had said as much on the elevator: the scabber's malaise clung to you like a stench, soaking in and infecting you on a cellular level. A person had to resist that foulness any way they could. Pardo punched his way through it. Leo took pride in his clothing. Nyla might have had her research books or her complicated hairstyles or some private interest Leo couldn't guess at, but whatever it was she had lost her grip on it. Now she was reaching out in a last-ditch effort to save herself, a common tactic for scabbers on the knife's edge — one the percentages said was doomed to fail. All his experience told Leo that there was nothing he could do to help her, that he would be endangering himself for the sake of a pointless gesture, that she was just one more friend melting into darkness and he should stay away to save himself. But the thought of turning his back on her roiled his stomach. It was a choice he would have to make, but not until later.

Not until he had to. It was only then that Leo realized he was alone on the tram.

Such was the rush hour in Mirabilis.

He disembarked at the Hildegrand Station, walked the three blocks to his building at his usual brisk step and reached his door as the sun began its afternoon slide. Once inside he pressed for one of the elevators. No machines lived in The Norris West, yet the elegant rampways that spiraled two hundred floors above made it clear who had designed the lavish building. The extra-wide doors, the smooth floor tiling, the WinkLink interfaces on every wall; everything was ramper accessible. A building built by and for machines. None of that bothered Leo. A few decades ago he would have never been able to call a place like this home. Not working as a cop, at least.

Leo lived on the 128th floor in a five-room penthouse with a grand view of Mirabilis's west side. As impressive as it was, he felt no pride in its exclusivity. Today anyone could live well if they wished. It confounded Leo that so many chose something less for themselves. As a constant reminder of this masochistic quirk of human nature, he shared the 128th floor with only one other neighbor, despite three other apartments as large as his own sitting empty. He was quite fond of his sole neighbor, and she of him, as far as he could tell. But it wasn't often he saw Aida two days in a row. Always moving, heading to and from what she called "dinner parties", Aida Swanson enjoyed the "full and active social life" as the rampers desperately encouraged for all human beings. Most people rejected such a lifestyle, either out of resentment or laziness, but it came naturally to her. She liked people. But that left little time for Leo.

It was to his pleasant surprise, then, that she was home.

Aida Swanson propped lazily against the doorframe, the hemisphere of one hip making a soft, round barricade that seemed both enticement and warning. A freshly opened bottle of Northfield Sunwater swung from the fingers of her left hand and she looked at him with a smirk that landed perfectly between 'you'd be a fool for trying' and 'you'd be a bastard not to.'

"You set the alarm off," she called out when he was still six feet away. "I don't think the building expects you back this time of day. I'm a little surprised myself. I hope everything's okay."

"We caught a homicide today. Me and Waterbird."

"Wow, Leo, that's great. Sooner than you thought, too."

Leo nodded.

"Everything going okay?" She asked.

"Minor snag, nothing serious. Came home to focus — you,

we're definitely right about the others, they aren't exactly sympathetic to the cause."

"No, of course they aren't," she said without a trace of surprise and just a hint of disappointment. "It's just the way people are." Then, almost instantly, Aida shifted into a more upbeat cast, looking Leo up and down his entire height, two times and with slow consideration. "You really do wear that blue."

"Thanks. I didn't notice you leave this morning."

"Sure — you were dead to the world."

"You had me worried I might've done something wrong."

Aida shrugged. "You probably did, I don't remember," she said, laughing at her own half-joke.

Leo glanced at the bottle in her hand. "Starting late?"

"Very funny. Sampling a new formula, actually. The supervisors changed it up on us again, so I'm here doing a little homework, making sure the clever darlings aren't trying to poison us all. I'm not sure machines really get the whole concept of booze, socially speaking."

"Well, good luck with that."

"Wait, wait, wait — where are you going? Don't we need to get you safely unsnagged?"

Leo hesitated. "Not sure you can help with this one, Aida."

"Don't be a scab, Leo, I can't leave you in the hallway with that look on your face — I'd never be able to live with myself. Besides, I've got a favor to ask."

———

Aida led them into to her vast luxury apartment, a mirror image of Leo's own, different only in the more abundant and sophisticated décor. Leo had always admired his neighbor's unusual tastes, as varied and unique as Mirabilis's architecture. Every room of the spacious penthouse was filled with one of-a-kind furniture, throwback designs and modern styles, old and new artworks by both humans and machine artists, handsome rugs with fading designs, bizarre and colorful objects Aida had purchased or found on the street. But there was no clutter. The organization of disparate items was somehow thoughtful and inviting. And there was always something new to look at. Today was no exception. Set on the long kitchen table was a strange homemade contraption, that at first glance, Leo could not make heads or tails of. A series of large glass vials had been placed side-by-side lengthwise down the wooden tabletop, each vial connected to the others by spiraling loops of clear plastic tubing. Fluids of various colors ran through the circuits of tubing, going in and out of the vials, transforming along the way; clear liquid becoming red, red becoming blue, blue becoming green, the green dripping through one last filter to become the familiar bright golden elixir known as Northfield Sunwater.

"What is this?"

"Like it? I made it." Aida walked around the contraption with an air of pride, eyeing her invention for leaks and clogs. She tightened a valve on a red-section of tubing. "This is a molecular fluid recombinator, like the ones we use at the distillery, except smaller, obviously."

"You're making Sunwater in your kitchen?"

"Testing, like I said. I'm trying to figure out what they did to the formula. Something's off with it. All of a sudden it tastes like burnt hair, not that they'll admit it. It does, though."

"The rampers won't like this, Aida. Homebrewing? There are laws against that."

She laughed. "Who do you think showed me how to make this thing? Mr. Goldtree and Mrs. Lambcloud were very supportive of my idea. They even gave me the equipment. Boxed it up and everything."

"Just like that?"

"Why not? I asked, they said yes. They were sending everyone home in order to swap out the chemical vats, anyway, and I had nothing else to do, so...and in small amounts these chemicals aren't really dangerous." Aida looked across the table and sighed at Leo's incredulous expression. "What? You're going to arrest me?"

"Just impressed, that's all. I had no idea you knew how to do any of this."

"It's important to learn new things, Leo. And it's the doing that matters, not so much the knowing."

"Yeah, but *this*..."

"Well, in about one minute you and me are going to have a little taste test. Mine versus theirs."

"Ah — so that's why I'm here."

"Partly, yeah," she grinned. "So what's this snag of yours?"

"Eh, nothing much, really. I hit a data wall in the Link. Waterbird has me tracking down a POI we want to interview, but I lost the guy's trail. If I can't find him I can't talk to him."

"Is this guy that important?"

"Maybe, maybe not. The point is they never let us talk to POIs ourselves. I mean, ever. It's not exactly against the rules, but it might as well be. If I mess this up, it's not bad for me."

"So, what, you're out of moves?"

"Worse. Detective Waterbird told me where this guy is working, but I can't remember the name of the place. Something laboratories – I don't know."

"You can't play it back?"

"I had my eye turned off. I wasn't recording in case I made a mistake."

"And that was the mistake."

"Yeah, of course."

"Oh, Leo." She stifled another laugh. "Then just ask Waterbird."

"And admit how instantly I fucked up? No thanks."

Aida nodded and thought for a moment. Having decided on a solution, she looked at Leo and said, "You're not special, you know."

"What?"

"I mean, Waterbird isn't helping you because Leo Song is the greatest, most perfect human policeman to ever walk the Earth. Even if you were, you'd still screw up once in a while."

"You trying to make me feel better?"

"Yes, I am. They expect us to fail, Leo. They *know* we will. It's ridiculous to compare yourself with Waterbird or any other machine."

"I'm not comparing. This is a stupid mistake, Aida."

"It is, it is, it's completely embarrassing, but this whole city was built so we could make stupid mistakes. Over and over and over, Leo, dumb, dumb, dumb. That's a good thing. That's why they even exist in the first place. We can screw up endlessly and they fix it. Or at least try to. It wasn't always that way, you know. We're lucky, Leo, we just don't realize it. It's not their fault everyone's too scared...or too, I don't know, too *boring* now. And it's not your fault either." Aida took two tumblers from the cabinet. "So don't think like those people, Leo, like a scabber hiding out in his home waiting to die. Waterbird knows you're better than that." She removed the last vial from the recombinator and poured the shimmering, golden liquid into the two thick glasses. Once they had even shares, she came around to Leo's side of the table and firmly placed one of the heavy tumblers in his right hand. "You don't have to be perfect, Leo, just a little brave. Maybe not even that. Call Waterbird, admit you screwed up, and let him help you. It's their job. Their *real* job. Then have a drink with me."

Leo nodded in solemn agreement. She was right and he knew it...but that didn't make what he had to do any easier. He raised his glass in a toast. "Good advice, wrong order."

Aida smiled and raised her glass in return. "You'll be a detective yet."

Leo took a drink. The liquid was sweeter and more delicious than any Sunwater he had ever tasted. It was the last thing he thought before darkness swallowed the world.

[6]

The fifth call pulled Leo from his blackout. It was an emergency call summoning him to a new crime scene.

"Where?" The word came out like mush.

"The Canyons," Micco Sauvi growled. "Get here now, Song."

Leo had arrived at the Canyons as fast as he could, fighting against nausea, quivery legs, and the see-sawing ground all the way from Aida's. He had left her in bad shape, but she had told him to go. Told him that she would be all right, apologizing between violent retches for the unexpected power of her homebrew. One sip had cost them five catastrophic hours. Five hours of sudden blackout on the kitchen floor. Five hours that had ruined him. It had only been Micco Sauvi's repeated calls that had finally pulled Leo into painful, slurring consciousness. Now he was standing on an observation platform a mile below the city, bleary eyed, weak, and confused. He took the perfumed rag Micco offered as protection against the noxious subterranean fumes, trying and failing to ignore the scowls of his fellow human officers. Trying and failing to understand why they could only watch helplessly as retrieval machines dug through an ocean of excrement and scrap metal for any sign of Detective Waterbird. Trying and failing to not blame himself.

"How bad is it," asked Lauren Horn. She had been there with Micco when Leo had arrived, the only human officers willing to suffer the lung-searing atmosphere of the Canyons.

"As far as I can tell they've still only found one piece so far," Micco Sauvi shouted through his scented rag. The old cop had been the first human officer to respond to the emergency signal. The first on the scene. The first to call Leo, even though there was no obligation to do so. Such an act from a bitter man like Micco Sauvi was touching. Almost suspicious.

"Which piece?" she asked.

"Just a side panel, I think. They're using a closed channel out there, so I can't be sure."

Leo wanted to ask his own questions, but his detox capsules hadn't kicked in yet and he was in agony. The headache had settled at the base of his neck in a merciless grip, and the constant urge to vomit kept him from talking too much. It was a new sensation and he despised it. "We should be out there," was the best he could manage.

"Yeah," Horn agreed. "They should give us environment suits and signal-scanners and we should be helping search, too. Why aren't we?"

"I think they've had enough of our help lately," said Sauvi. The comment came with a sidelong glare at Leo. "What I want to know is what Waterbird was doing down here all alone."

Leo shook his head in numb ignorance.

"Maybe it's his nexus they found, that one piece you said?" offered Lauren Stone, trying to be positive.

"Well, if they don't find the nexus, you better hope it's destroyed," said Micco.

"Shut up, Micco," said Leo.

The nexus was a ramper's central brain and behavioral system.

If the nexus was beyond repair, it would mean Waterbird was effectively dead. If the unit was intact but never recovered, however, it meant Waterbird would be very much alive. A disembodied consciousness, awake and aware, trapped under a sea of shit and rust for the years it would take for his power to completely drain.

It was a full minute before anyone spoke again.

"This is your fault, Song. You were working a case together. The two of you made that obvious."

"Yeah, but–"

"–so what was Waterbird doing here?"

"I don't know."

Sauvi shook his head in disgust. "A little late to cover your ass now."

"Micco, I had no idea Waterbird was coming down here." The moment he said it Leo realized it wasn't true. Waterbird had asked Nyla Pyka to find information about Sadboy colonies in the Canyons. Leo had delivered the request to her himself. She must have found something and told Waterbird directly. He wondered if Nyla had tried to reach him first while he had been passed out on Aida's floor. He'd have to talk to her as soon as he could. "Waterbird didn't tell me anything," Leo said. "I don't know what's going on."

"Witnesses?" Horn interrupted.

"Yeah," Micco said. "The one that called it in. One of the local Historians."

Both Lauren Horn and Leo groaned in unison. Historians, half-mad scavengers who lived and worked in the Canyons, were notoriously unhelpful. Digging through a century of human waste and discarded tech made people strange.

"That's not good," muttered Horn.

"No it's not," Sauvi agreed. "She's out on the barge with the rampers."

"But not us." Leo said.

"Enough with that bullshit, Song. I'm tired of hearing it. What good would we do out there?"

"Did she see what happened?" asked Horn.

"I don't know," Sauvi answered. "Like I said, it's a closed link out there. I picked up everything I told you before the rampers went out on the barge."

"So, we really don't know what happened, do we? Waterbird might be fine," said Horn, holding out a hope the others did not share.

"I don't think Waterbird's fine, Lauren."

"You don't know that, Micco."

Ignoring his colleague's useless debate, Leo forced another question through his nausea. "Who's running the search?"

Sauvi looked at Leo and said, "Bluebreeze, from tenth."

"Oh, shit, that thing," Horn groaned, giving voice to what they all were thinking.

Mr. Bluebreeze was a supervisor from the southern precinct's notorious tenth floor, the Data Information and Analysis Division. DIAD, as it was known, where on-duty performance was codified, measured, and graded. Mr. Bluebreeze was the force's primary number-crunching machine, the mother hen of DIAD and weaver of every cop's fortune. It knew the intimate details of each officer on the force, ramper and human alike. It knew their flaws and strengths, tendencies under pressure, and most importantly, the limits of their potential. But for all that knowledge, Bluebreeze was not a street cop. Even among the machines real experience mattered. Even worse for the humans, Bluebreeze was a relatively new design: Dense Matter Matrix, a particle-based technology different than the almost biological liquid cores of pervious designs. It made them difficult to deal with. Bluebreeze being in charge meant Leo would never get a close look at the crime scene, not by invitation at least.

"Have you ever seen anything like this before," asked Officer Horn. "A police ramper, I mean, getting…hurt like this?"

"We don't know Waterbird's hurt," Leo said quickly.

"Once, a long time ago," said Sauvi. "But not like this. Nothing like this. The rampers are going to want someone's skin for it. That'll be you, Song."

Leo looked over at Lauren Horn, wondering if she doubled Sauvi's harsh opinion, but he couldn't gauge her expression under the handkerchief. It didn't matter. It was useless to stand there engaging in Micco's invented rivalry. He told Sauvi to go screw himself and headed down the staircase to the ground level, leaving Sauvi to sputter in offended confusion.

"Where does he think he's going?" Sauvi asked Horn.

"Beats me, but he's going to ruin that beautiful suit."

Standing at the edge of the garbage sea, Leo tried to determine the least sickening path across. He hadn't planned on coming down here, and now that he was, he was uncertain on what to do next. Part sewer, part scrapyard, part city dump, the Canyons were inhospitable to machines and downright toxic to humans. To venture onto the jagged, toxic sea for any extended period required at least a basic respirator, if not a full environment suit. The Historians who dug through the decades of garbage in search of treasures built their own gear — handmade, ornately designed, tough and long-lasting, easily worth more than anything they found in the scum.

Leo had a damp handkerchief.

Ignoring the danger, he stepped into the filth. His goal was the hover-barge operating sixty yards out from the concrete embankment. It was from the barge Mr. Bluebreeze was commanding the search effort, and where Leo would find the supposed witness. Interrupting a crime scene was a definite breach of protocol, but interviewing human witnesses was Leo's primary function on the force, and he felt reasonably certain he could defend his actions on that point. Who better than him? He might even make a stink that not having a human present was itself a critical error. His attendance at the crime scene was essential, he would say. If he could reach it at all. Leo hadn't gotten twenty yards and already his eyes were starting to burn. After another ten, his lungs began to ache. Half-blind and wheezing, Leo misjudged the next foothold, his left foot sinking into the thick, rust-colored sludge with a revolting *schlop!* To keep his balance, he had to drop his right foot into the revolting mire as well. He was ankle-deep in toxic sludge and not halfway to his destination. It would be fitting, he thought, if he wound up lost under this scum-bog with Waterbird. *"Ever the loyal student"* they would say. *"Waterbird's shadow to the end. Followed him up...and then followed him down."* He imagined Micco Sauvi would tell that tale every chance he got.

Leo cupped his hands over his mouth and drew as much air into his burning lungs as he could.

"Bluebreeze!"

He heard only a low sucking sound around his feet. He needed to get the machine's attention some other way before his lungs burned. He searched for something to throw towards the barge, but every loose piece of scrap within reach was either too large or too awkward to gain any distance. He looked up and a terrible thought came to him. To his left the refuse formed a pile that rose far above his head, a crooked, top-heavy mountain of jutting ledges and sharp outcroppings kept standing only by its own sheer weight and the habit of inertia. A corroded beam extended out from the center of the heap, just within arm's length. If the beam wasn't too heavy or extended too deeply into the center, there was a chance he could use it to topple the towering mound of junk. The resulting crash would be loud enough to get the attention of the workers on the barge. It would probably frighten people on the streets above them. Of course, if the mountain tipped the wrong way, the machines probably wouldn't bother digging out whatever was left of him.

Eyes swelling shut, throat tightening, his feet straining and burning in the corrosive scum, Leo reached for the beam.

[7]

Crouched in the farthest corner of the barge, the historian watched the machines go about their work. She tallied up their worth in her head, whole at first, then broken down into smaller parts. She figured she could quadruple her profit if she sold them in pieces over time, making the quality tech seem like rarer finds. She would play up her lucky streak, hit all the sobby notes, be all grins and swirly eyes. Her fine day had come! All those years in the metal swamp, sucking in the poison, getting her guts burnt up…then at last a big luck run, long and truly deserved. What a song she'd sing, have them weeping and clapping and patting her back, asking her how much and where and competing for dibs and running up offers on the extra-shiny bits. She'd make the biggest show in front of Monty, get him all fussed up, get him bidding way up, far past himself, just to beat the other boys, and then she wouldn't sell him a thing. Sell for half price right in front of him. To hell with Monty. He deserved it. The look on his face would be big laughs. Maybe she would spit in it.

The echoing crash knocked the Historian from her fantasy. The barge lurched into motion, knocking her gear loose. She re-adjusted her respirator and drew her legs tighter against her chest, irritated to be back in reality, feeling the vibration of the barge as it skimmed over the stinking ground. They were moving at a good clip. Almost scary fast. She didn't like this kind of speed and wondered where they were going. It was far from where they should be looking for the shattered hoodoo, nowhere near where she had told them to go. Wasting time. She hoped it wouldn't diminish her reward. Her tip was solid. She had been truthful with them, even though it all sounded like a big lie. It wouldn't be fair if they withheld the reward just because that poor old ramper had been scattered so far around. That wasn't her fault. She was trying to help. The Historian had lived enough days to know the rampers were more trustworthy than people, but not all the time. The could stiff you all the same in the end. The thought of being jilted out of her reward drove her further from the sweetness of her daydream. She would be damned if she came out of this with nothing to show for it.

The barge slowed, then stopped.

She didn't expect a man to climb aboard. He flopped onto the deck, choking and blind and wriggling in his shiny suit like some giant gutter eel. He wasn't doing so good. She'd seen worse, though. He probably thought he was dying. He'd be wrong though. The foam he was spewing up was still white. If it was red, he'd be a ghost. Red is dead. But time was fading. She saw the star-bright ramper hovering over the man, but it wasn't doing anything useful, so the Historian reached into her pack for the spare breather. She hadn't swapped out the filters lately, but she thought it would still work. Long enough anyway. She just hoped the straps fit the man's big head. She held out the breather to him, but the man didn't see it, even when she shook it, so she put it over his face for him like she would a child. He didn't fuss about it and soon he was breathing okay again. She decided she didn't like this man. He was stupid for walking out here without a breather. Without proper gear. It was a stupid way to die. She didn't like stupid people. The big machine didn't seem to like him either.

"Officer Song, what are you trying to accomplish," it said, without a trace of sympathy, so heartless it made the Historian dislike the man a little less. Maybe the man would listen to her and give her the reward.

———

As Bluebreeze berated him, Leo swore he could taste the filtered air in his lungs. He could taste it in his skin, in his bones, in every cell of blood — the sweetness of life pumping back into his body. The truth was less dramatic, if just as whimsical: the Historian used strawberry scented filters in her breathers. It was a personal signature that discouraged competitors from swiping her gear. As his eyes cleared Leo saw the Historian balled up like a frightened child in the corner of the barge. He guessed the Historian was a woman, although it was difficult to tell underneath the oxidized environment suit and full breathing mask. Her hair was uncovered, though, long and tinged with thin streaks of gray, tied with a red ribbon in a tight braid that hung to her waist. Behind the clear plastic of her mask he could see large blue eyes staring back at him. They weren't particularly friendly. The Historian had saved his life, and it was obvious she was wondering if it had been the right move. Leo nodded to her in thanks. It was a pathetic gesture, but the best he could summon in the moment.

Meanwhile, Mr. Bluebreeze chattered on.

"A violation of codes Thirty Nine dash C, Two Hundred Seven CF and Section Twelve of the Human Protocol Codex. Disciplinary action can be taken against you, Officer Song if you do not expl–"

Leo slapped his hand against the metal deck to silence the ramper. He then pointed to the Historian and made a talking motion with his hand.

"The witness has already been questioned."

Leo pointed to himself.

"Your assistance is not required."

Leo dismissed the slender, ring-shaped machine with a wave and crawled towards the Historian. She tightened up at his approach and he stopped moving. He was close enough to see into her mask now, close enough to see the crow's feet around her eyes, the deep lines around her mouth. An old woman. Or a woman of middle years prematurely aged from a life in that toxic underworld. It was rumored that Historians could live for years in the sewers. Most of them were the descendants of once wealthy families. The children of the once powerful and mighty, the heirs to the world denied their birthright once the machines provided for all material wants and needs. So they had pursued their lost treasures down into the sewers. Searching for forgotten wealth in the filth and the slime. True or not, she obviously considered Leo a threat. Leo forced his body to relax, bringing his legs underneath himself in a passive squat. Then he tried to force words from his raw throat.

"What...did...you...see?"

The Historian glanced up at Bluebreeze. She knew who the authority here was, and didn't want to risk offending it. Mr. Bluebreeze said nothing, its white core sparkling like a star, mysterious and distant. It did not speak, so the Historian looked back at Leo.

"Some slick hoodoo came out on the dunes over there, stopped about there. I was watchin' but staying low, trying to be respectful and leave it to its business. It was so silvery, though, all mirrorlike and hard to miss — that's how I saw it."

Leo nodded again, acknowledging the woman's proclamation of civic conscientiousness.

"Then one of those sadboys came. Big one. Ripply with wires and tumors and such. He stood right along with that shiny ramper, cozy, like friends do." Here the Historian paused, not wanting to continue. Leo knew she had a good reason not to. Living in the miasma of the Canyons may have made her odd, but she wasn't crazy, and if she told Leo what he suspected she would, it would make anyone sound insane.

"Sadboy…spoke?" he asked, voice rasping through the breather.

The Historian nodded.

"What…did it…say?"

"We have already completed this line of questioning," interrupted Mr. Bluebreeze.. "She did not hear what was said. There is no reason to continue this delay, Officer Song,"

Leo again smacked the deck with his hand, a hard blow that jolted the thin metal floor. Bluebreeze's core glowed brightly for a moment. If rampers could get angry, this one sure in hell was, thought Leo. He ignored the silent warning of Bluebreeze's lights and scooted close to the Historian. "Did…you…hear?"

The Historian nodded weakly.

Bluebreeze's exposed nexus grew bright with a hard, painful light that forced Leo to shield his eyes. Through his fingers he saw the Historian staring at Bluebreeze in terror, her eyes incandescent with the reflection of the ramper's fire.

"Dim your light…"

"The witness must answer the question. The witness must answer fully and truthfully or face a penalty."

"Dim your light or it's nothing."

Bluebreeze's light faded back to normal.

Leo moved closer to the frightened Historian. Just a half scoot. Then another. He pointed to his breathing mask. "Thank you," he said. He could feel his voice returning.

She looked at him, and after a moment returned a curt nod.

"It's…okay…to tell us."

"What I heard I heard positively, but…." She looked up at Bluebreeze, sorrowful, apologetic, doubting if she should continue.

Leo waved his hand to regain the Historian's attention. "Tell me…anyway," he said.

"Sadboy said it was going to teach that slick ramper how to

suffer. Teach it to suffer like a human being does. Pain and misery for all time. All time."

The mutual silence of man and machine unnerved the Historian, who followed up quickly with what she hoped were more helpful insights. "Except it didn't say it fluid like me. It was more barky and slow, like it was dumb or a monkey."

"That's…it?" Leo asked.

She nodded. "After that the big old sadboy killed that ramper. Smashed it into tidbits. But I don't think that machine barely offered any fightback. Like a pacifist. Like a suicide. I was keeping scarce for that part, though. I didn't aspire to getting murdered, too."

Leo attempted to give the woman a reassuring smile, but it was invisible behind the breather, which, considering his disappointment, was all for the best. "Thank you," he said in meager compensation. "For your help."

"I get my reward, don't I? I don't want to get jilted on this."

"Responsible citizenship is its own reward," Bluebreeze said to the crestfallen shitdigger.

———

BACK ON THE PLATFORM LEO YANKED THE SCENTED HANDKERCHIEF from his jacket's inside pocket and held it to his nose, having given the respirator back to the historian before he had disembarked. He could still taste the strawberry on his breath. The cloying, false sweetness felt at odds with the darkness of his thoughts. As he watched the hover-barge skitter away over the garbage dunes, returning to its search for Waterbird's remains, he realized there was no urgency to their work. They had no reason to hurry — Waterbird was gone. Leo's nausea turned to cold numbness as he imagined the machine's final moments of existence. All that experience and knowledge vanished forever. All the history. It dawned on him that his entire career as a police officer was contained within Waterbird's nexus. His ambitions, his many mistakes, his few successes...Waterbird had witnessed it all. Then something strange occurred to Leo: never in his life had he thought of a ramper as a friend — no one had thought that way in a generation or more, the differences had become too obvious, too imbalanced — but in that moment no other word came to his mind. In Waterbird's sudden absence, Leo's human relationships seemed meager. The list was certainly short. There was Aida, but that was still new and not the same. Nyla, more in the past than now. After that, no one. And Leo's last act of his lone and unlikely friendship had been failure. Not the harmless, helpful sort Aida had talked about. This was total, abject failure. The kind you couldn't fix. The kind that left scars.

"What the shit did that prove, Song?"

Sauvi. The desperate bastard just couldn't leave it alone. Leo turned around to face him and was met with a loud gasp from Lauren Horn.

"Leo! Quick, Micco, give him another rag so he can wipe his face."

Micco ignored the younger officer's command. "That's what he gets for pulling a stupid stunt like that. He's lucky he didn't die out there. You're an idiot, Song."

"Waterbird's gone."

"What do you mean?" Horn asked. "Define 'gone'." She wanted to delay the truth, hold it off for a few seconds more.

"Gone. Destroyed. It's like you thought, Sauvi, they're just picking up pieces."

Sauvi stepped closer to Leo. "Bluebreeze told you?"

"More or less."

Horn and Sauvi fell silent. They both looked past Leo, scanning the distance, peering out at the hover-barge where the grim work was being done.

"The Historian saw the whole thing," said Leo, "so they know where to look. They would have found Waterbird's nexus by now if it was still active...so I guess we'll call that good news."

"There'll be a task force now," said Horn. "There has to be. Think they'll put of us on it?"

Leo and Sauvi exchanged a glance.

"No," Sauvi said. "No chance."

"I will," said Leo. "I'll be on it."

Sauvi laughed and shook his head.

"I'd like to be on it, too," said Horn.

Micco Sauvi groaned and squared up with Leo. "Now you've got her started. Leo, when are you going to stop with this shit?"

Leo turned away from the old man without answering, only hearing Sauvi's final, pitying laugh.

"Come on, Lauren, let's go."

The two officers walked off the platform towards the surface stairs, leaving Leo to himself. He knew Sauvi was probably correct about the task force. The job was too important to let humans get involved. But Leo told himself we was going to try anyway. Yes, he had messed up. He had been selfish and ineffective. Possibly he had damaged an investigation. But there was no one who understood Detective Waterbird's methods as well as he did. He would be a major asset to the task force investigation, and the risk he had taken in the Canyons proved his dedication beyond any doubt. A hideous crime had been committed and one of their own had been destroyed — it was time for the precinct to join in together. Everyone was needed, man and machine. Everyone had something to contribute, including and especially him. He wouldn't accept being left out.

He would not fail Waterbird a second time.

[8]

The first floor lobby was busier than Leo had ever seen it. The Waterbird task force was already being assembled and it was creating bedlam within the precinct. Rampers and humans he had never met rushed about on frantic errands or gathered in small clusters to share confused information, all of them ignoring Leo as he passed. It was a small mercy. He was still a mess from the Canyons. Thick tears ran down his cheeks, mixing with the mucus flowing from his nose to form a runny slop that gathered at the tip of his chin. His suit was wrinkled, torn, and reeked of the Canyons. The jacket might be saved if they could get the smell out. His shirt was soaked with sweat and had suffered a sizeable green stain somewhere along the way, an ugly, grainy splotch that ran from chest to stomach. His pants and his shoes were destroyed. Especially the shoes. Hadn't Waterbird admired them only that morning? The toxic scum he had waded through had eaten away the leather tips and melted the high-quality soles like wax. He shuddered to think what that revolting dreck was doing to his feet. There was a burning sensation growing between his toes which was well on its way to becoming actual pain. Soon his feet would hurt as badly as his head. Treatment would have to wait, though; he had a report to make to Mrs. Greenfields. He kept his head down until he reached the elevators. Once at the doors, Leo avoided riding with anyone else, waiting until he was alone. It took ten minutes of wet-faced suffering before he was able to catch an empty car for himself. The ride was too swift to think.

The homicide unit was deserted apart from Mr. Sunnyday, precisely the machine Leo wanted to see.

"Officer Song, what can I do for you?"

"I need to speak with Mrs. Greenfields. Right away, please. It's urgent."

"Mrs. Greenfields wishes to see you as well, Officer Song. You can go right in."

"Thanks."

"Officer Song…"

Leo stopped and turned back to Sunnyday. "What is it?"

"I recommend you visit to the restroom first."

Leo touched his face. "Thanks, Sunnyday," he said as he veered towards the bathroom.

Leo did his best to clean himself up, but there was only so much he could manage. He wet his fingers under the faucet before running them though his hair. He kept his hair short, a habit from his days in the academy, so it didn't take much to get it looking presentable. There was nothing he could do about the rest. At least his nose had stopped dripping and the redness of his eyes could be blamed on the Canyons rather than the alcohol still coursing through his blood. Another small mercy. This was the best Leo Song possible under the circumstances. Good enough, he thought. Machines were suckers for genuine misery.

Leo knocked on the closed door. "It's Officer Song."

"Please enter."

He pressed the entrance panel and went in.

Mrs. Greenfields, the homicide division's supervisor, resembled an eight-foot-tall onyx cone that had been flipped on its point and set on roller-skates. The humans of the homicide division called it "Grandma" behind its back, a long running inside joke and term of moderate affection. Grandma Greenfields' shiny black surface offered Leo a warped reflection of himself as he sat in the only chair the Ramper kept in the office. Looking at a stretched and distorted version of himself didn't help ease his lingering nausea.

"Are you feeling well, Office Song?"

"Yes, I am, thank you." It wasn't a complete lie. His feet stung and his voice still rasped, but at least he was breathing without wanting to pass out. "I could use a shower."

"Yes. Your interference at Waterbird's crime scene was poorly considered."

"Yeah, well, I can explain that…"

"There is no need. Your motivations are understood, Officer Song."

It always irked Leo when the rampers pulled their little "human behavior is so predictable" act. He decided one good dismissal deserved another. "I wanted to question the witness myself. That is my job, isn't it? Good thing I did, too, or Bluebreeze would have missed it."

"You are referring the statement the witness made during your questioning."

"Yes, I am."

"The information has no significant meaning at this time."

Something inside the machine shuddered hard enough that Leo felt the vibration in his seat. "With due respect, Mrs. Greenfields," he said, "but a sadboy that can speak seems pretty significant. At least Detective Waterbird thought so, and I agree. Or doesn't that matter?" Leo gritted his teeth to try to keep any more stupidity from spilling out of his mouth. He was coming off as insolent rather than resolute. It wasn't the way he wanted this to go, but he couldn't stop himself.

"It matters."

"I don't know why Waterbird was down there, but I think I can help find out. I'd like a role on the task force."

"Denied."

"May I ask why?"

"Your recent behavior has raised concerns about you're your emotional fitness for duty."

"Emotional *fitness?*"

"Did you collect evidence at the Tabitha Jackson crime scene?"

It was pointless to lie. "I did, with Waterbird's permission."

"Were you planning on interviewing a person of interest relevant to that case?"

"Again, with Detective Waterbird's permission."

"And you failed to do so in a timely manner."

"There was no timetable." True enough to pass.

"Officer Song, you told your colleagues that this person of interest was in fact an active suspect. Your fellow officers were quite upset by this news. It made them feel inferior to you and resentful of both you and Detective Waterbird. Their confidence in their own abilities was undermined by your misleading boast. Officer Song, you hurt their feelings."

That's a ramper for you, thought Leo. One of their own gets pulverized, and the wounded pride of a few humans is somehow the priority. "I just…I misspoke, that's all."

"Officer Song, the morale of this unit has been adversely affected by your need for personal gratification, to say nothing of the breaking of procedural protocols."

"I get that, I do. And I'm sorry." Leo squirmed in his chair. "But if you want to increase the morale of this unit then let the unit do actual police work. Direct case work. All of us…ah…"

"Officer Song, are you in pain?"

"I'm fine." A blatant lie. His feet stung like they were soaking in battery acid. "Mrs. Greenfields, if it can't be me, at least some of the others deserve to be on the task force. Lauren Horn, maybe. Or Micco. Doesn't he deserve it by now?"

The machine paused, taking its time processing Leo's request. As he waited for the reply, Leo attempted to take his mind off the worsening pain by concentrating on an object. Any object. His eyes scanned the towering ramper's mirror-like surface for an interesting detail, but found no purchase. Greenfields was a Management Dynamics model, designed without interface panels or eye-scanners, lacking any concrete point to focus on…just deep, bottomless black. Leo found it unsettling. He decided instead to look at Greenfields' desk, which was covered in an arrangement of small, cheap trinkets: a snow globe depicting a young family's winter day, a nutcracker painted to look like a gray-haired old man, a crystal butterfly, a tiny rubber bullfrog, three ceramic figurines of apple-cheeked children. They were gifts given to Greenfield by the human officers, an acknowledgement of the machine's famous human-outreach efforts. Burt Willis, who started the tradition years ago, called them tchotchkes, tacky knick-knacks his grand-mother used to collect when Willis was a boy. The odd collec-tion grew larger by one or two pieces every year, becoming a precinct-wide joke made at Greenfields' expense. Tchotchkes for Grandma Greenfields. He wondered if Greenfields was aware the gifts were a prank. If it did, Greenfields never let on, always thanking the officers for their generosity whenever a new piece appeared on the desk. It *had* to know by now, Leo thought. He imagined the formidable machine softly crying itself to sleep at night, wounded by the thoughtless cruelty of its human co-workers, and for a moment Leo's heart broke for Mrs. Greenfields. The absurd daydream vanished when it finally spoke.

"I am sorry, Officer Song, but you are being re-assigned."

Leo stared into Greenfields' abyss-dark surface, trying to understand what he'd just heard. "I'm out of homicide?"

"Yes. I am sorry."

"Is…is this permanent?"

"That will be determined at a later time. For now, you are to report to Officers Foxgrin and Kindword."

Leo was familiar with the names. "But they're from Oversight."

"Yes."

"You're investigating me?" Leo's career, such as it was, flashed before his eyes so quickly he almost laughed. "You think that's the best use of our time right now?'

"Mr. Foxgrin and Mr. Kindword will help you retrace your actions over the past twenty-four hours to determine the extent of the investigative errors you have committed. Please think of this as a helpful supplement to the primary investigation. I know your assistance will be of great value."

"Okay..." Leo bit down on his tongue hard, nearly drawing blood. He was getting kicked out of homicide and this ramper was making him feel grateful for it. They were good at that. "I'll try to keep that in mind."

"Please do. But first, Officer Song, you must report to the medical center. It is clear that you are in great discomfort, despite your courageous effort to conceal it."

Leo nodded. He was no longer in any condition to fight a losing battle. Leo pushed himself out of the chair. As he stood, bolts of scorching pain shot through his legs, up his spine, and stabbed into the back of his eyes. Temporarily blinded, he braced himself against Greenfields' door in a controlled collapse.

"Officer Song, you require assistance."

"No, no, I'm fine."

"Assistance is on its way."

"Greenfields...what about the others?"

"They will be given duties peripheral to the task force's efforts," answered the machine. "Assignments in which they can flourish."

"So, nobody's on the task force? No one at all?"

"Human participation is not required at this time. Thank you for your concern, Officer."

[9]

Lew Kiwambe poked the blob of Celwax on Leo's right foot, provoking a tendril of orange goo to wrap itself around his forefinger. As Kiwambe pulled back his hand the tendril tightened its grip, and he was forced to yank himself free.

"Ha! This stuff is so friendly," Lew said. "I always thought they should make it a toy for kids. They sure used a lot of it,"

Leo looked down at his feet. Both were encased in generous bubbles of the hyperactive healing paste known as Celwax. The flesh on Leo's feet had dissolved to the bone in some places, and the medical rampers had really slathered on the viscous gunk. Hailed as a pinnacle of medical achievement, the biomechanical compound restored skin, muscle, complex organs, even bone, all in a matter of hours. Celwax had, of course, been invented by the machines. Some people claimed that Celwax was sentient or at least semi-conscious, but Leo wasn't sure there was a human being alive who fully understood how the stuff actually worked. Miracle substance or not, it couldn't work fast enough for him. He was frantic to get back out on the street and didn't need Lew distracting the Celwax from its purpose. "You shouldn't touch that crap without gloves on."

Lew snorted. "Afraid I'll go all Swoback? I don't think that's how it works, but you're the expert on Celwax, I guess."

"What are you doing here, Lew?

Lew Kiwambe had been lingering outside the medical room door for the last ten minutes until Leo had invited him in. Now he was acting sheepish and Leo was quickly becoming irritated.

"Nothing, I just, you know, just wanted to say I'm sorry about Detective Waterbird. I know you two went back a bit, so..."

"I appreciate that. You worked with Waterbird, too."

"Yeah, sure, I did, sure, I did. We all feel bad about it. I guess I'm still in shock, you know, that it could even happen. To Waterbird?"

"We'll get whoever did it. We have to."

"I know we will. That's what I wanted to ask you...is it true they're putting together a task force?"

"It's true."

"So, you're on it?"

"No. Grandma' Greenfields turned me down."

"Oh. Sorry."

"Thanks."

"Anyone else on it, from Homicide, I mean? Lauren? Micco?"

"You?"

"Am I?"

"No, Lew, you're not. Nobody is on it. No humans are on the task force."

Lew let out a sigh that released so much tension he visibly shrunk.

"That's good news?" said Leo.

"Aw, it's not that, Leo, it's Raina. They already put me on a third-tier sweeper unit canvasing dead zones on the south end. All hands on deck and everything, but I probably won't get home till after midnight tonight. Raina's going to be worried sick. If I got put on the task force, I don't think she'd be able to stand it. I mean, you're pretty sure it was a sadboy did this, right?"

"Pretty sure."

"Yeah, I couldn't do that to Raina, man."

It took a moment for Leo to remember the name. Raina — Lew Kiwambe's wife. Lew was the rarest of all modern people: a family man. He had married his wife in a semi-religious ceremony with family and friends (none of them police officers). Now they had two children with a third on the way. Leo didn't know much more beyond that. Lew Kiwambe was careful to keep his work life separate from his home life and Leo thought it was probably a wise move.

"Well, that *is* good news, then," Leo said. "You're off the hook."

Lew nodded. "They'll catch the lunatic fucker. They always do."

Leo leaned his head back against the cushioned headrest. "Probably within the hour."

"Yeah," Lew laughed. "Maybe a little longer without Waterbird, though, right?"

"Yeah, maybe. So, what's the status? Things have to be full crazy downstairs."

"They're moving alright." Lew Kiwambe mumbled at his shoes, not wanting the nearby machine to overhear. "But they don't know shit. They're panicking, you can tell. Little things mostly. But I'm telling you, they're spinning out."

"They better be."

Lew lingered, unsure how to leave gracefully. He had joined the force after Leo and while only a few years younger, still had the air of a person just happy to be there. But he was being more sheepish than usual. Leo suspected Lew had complained to Greenfields about Leo's preferential treatment and now the guilt was gnawing at the man. "So, what's the prognosis?" Lew asked.

Leo looked over at the squat ramper idling passively in the corner of the small room. "So, Doctor, how long before I'm back on my new feet?"

The machine perked up and rolled to the end of Leo's bed,

where it extended a thin probe into the ball of Celwax that encased Leo's right foot.

"In one hour, twenty-seven minutes and three seconds you will be healed, Officer."

"Nice," Lew said. "And what are the chances he'll wind up with cloven hooves instead of feet?"

"Highly unlikely," the machine answered.

"But not impossible, right?" Lew said.

"No. I can state the probability in mathematical terms if you like."

"No, thank you, Doctor," said Leo. "Not funny, Lew."

"Sorry. Had to."

"Your feet will be fine, Officer Song," said the machine as it returned to its corner.

As the doctor rolled away from the bed, Leo noticed a pair of false human ears stuck to the ramper's back plate.

"Disgusting," muttered Lew. "More and more of them doing that."

"I don't know, I'm starting to take it as a compliment."

"You would. Heal up, Leo."

"Be safe out there, Kiwambe."

After Lew was gone, the doctor chirped up.

"Officer Song, Would you like to hear some music while you recuperate? I know you are eager to leave, and music has been shown to speed up the healing process. The Celwax enjoys it as well."

"Sure, Doc. Whatever's best."

A deep thumping pulse filled the room, followed by a melodious rush of strings, their pitch warbling from high to low and back again with no identifiable rhythm. It was unlike any music Leo had ever heard and far from what he considered soothing.

"This is music?"

"It is the sound of your body, interpreted musically."

"Well," Leo said as he leaned back against the cushions of the bed, "I sound like shit."

The music failed to relax him. The thick balls of Celwax wrapped around his feet had his mind as well, forcing his thoughts to one thing: James Swoback. Mentioned twice today. Once by Hewl Pardo. Then by Lew Kiwambe. Leo's first case as a police officer. A legend now among the Mirabilis police precincts. James Swoback the kind man. A decent man by all accounts. But a man who suffered more than most. Swoback, a man born without hair in a world that had cured baldness. The most mundane of freaks, a normal man in another time, made freakish only by modern advance. The machines would not help him. Could not, they claimed. They forced his hand. Swoback the unique. Swoback the desperate. The kind, decent man forced to search the city's dead zones for a remedy to his anguish. To his eternal regret, he found Celwax. Illegal, but real. Pure. Not meant for such a simple problem. The medicine found no real problem at all. It became confused. It turned him inside out. It grew new flesh. It grew new organs. New limbs. A new body, if you could call it a body. It grew until it was something other than James Swoback. The machines were called, but the machines did not know what to do. There was no precedent for this. No data to draw from. No history to scrape. The humans were called, and Leo Song arrived. Song the rookie. Song the lucky. He suggested they follow the bizarre form, track it, see what it did. An obvious suggestion. What else could they do? Only one machine agreed. They followed the thing to Swoback's home. Still something of the man left. A memory. A ghost. There, in the bathtub, Leo found the WinkLink chip, spat out from Swoback's brain, rejected by the Celwax. It told the story of a desperate man's terrible mistake. A simple solution to a sad, strange case. Solved by a human. Song the observant. Song the Detective.

Only one machine had been there to see it happen.

Leo headed straight to the squad room. His feet were healed, now they needed shoes, and like every experienced officer, he had an emergency pair locked in the bottom drawer of his desk. You could spend all day walking stairs, and few things felt better than swapping out for new shoes when you got back to your desk. Unlocking the drawer with his personal codekey, he took out the polished Granville Caps and slipped them over his bare feet. To his surprise he discovered they were a little loose. His feet, it seemed, had been returned to him a half-size smaller than before. Perhaps they would still grow, but it was no matter. He gave the laces an extra knot and wriggled his toes to test the fit. Roomy, but good enough, he thought.

He paused, then opened the middle drawer of the desk. Tabitha Jackson's shoebox was still there. Greenfields knew he had it, but hadn't asked him to turn it over. He saw no reason to volunteer it now. If they wanted it, they could tell him so. He opened the box and looked inside — the pills and the old book with its wilted cover, all of it was accounted for. Leo took out the old book and began flipping through the brittle pages. He scolded himself for not examining the book more closely before now. A voice in his head told him he wasn't being fair to himself. When had there been time, after all? Leo ignored the voice. He wasn't going to let himself off the hook for anything. The voice was a fool. An enemy.

A small hardcopy photograph slipped out from between the pages. The photograph was a three by four-inch piece of thin plastic, a medium twice as old as Leo, but the date in the lower right corner of the photo claimed the image was taken only two months ago. He looked at the picture — it was a strange mass of color, a shapeless blob he couldn't make sense of. He turned the photo over and felt the hair on his neck stand on end. There, in scratchy human handwriting, was written...

A code? The initials of a person's name? A machine designation? Leo stared at the writing for a long moment, concentration becoming frustration. If he had the brain of a ramper he could probably figure it out in a matter of seconds, but he was only himself. The writing was meaningless to him.

A wave of blue light filled his vision. Leo waved in the call.

It was Mr. Foxgrin, one of his newly assigned "partners".

"Officer Song, we are waiting for you in the lobby. Please report at once."

"Can I ask what we're doing?"

"We will be returning to the Wilcott to conduct a procedural review."

Foxgrin dissolved away and Leo sat in his chair, fuming. So they really were going to retrace his steps, taking him back to the sight of yesterday's double homicide. What a waste of time, he thought. But the rampers could wait. There was something he'd been meaning to do since he left the Canyons.

He waved out a call to Nyla Pyka. After a few seconds she popped into his head.

"Leo, hi. I've been worried about you. I'm so sorry about Detective Waterbird."

"Yeah, thanks. That's actually why I'm calling, Nyla. That information Waterbird asked you about — did you find anything?"

"I did."

"Are you in the records room right now?"

"Yeah, but…"

"Wait there, I'm coming down."

"Leo–"

Leo waved off, tucked the photo into his pocket, locked the book and shoebox into the bottom drawer and went to meet Nyla.

[10]

Nyla looked like she'd been crying, but her voice didn't waver. "Leo, I don't think I should tell you anything, not in light of what just happened."

They were in a far corner of the records room, out of view of the entrance, a precaution Leo thought unnecessary. No one came to the records room.

"Please, I don't have a lot of time, Nyla. I was supposed to report to two rampers from Oversight five minutes ago. I need a break, here."

Worry flashed over Nyla's face. "Oversight? Why Oversight?"

"I'm off Homicide. For now."

"Oh, Leo, I'm sorry."

"My own fault. But, Nyla, right now I need to know why Waterbird was in the Canyons. Whatever you told Waterbird I need you to tell me."

She looked at Leo for a long time before answering. "There isn't much," she finally said. "Nothing at all about talking sadboys."

"But enclaves in the Canyons?"

"Yes…one thing. I tried to reach you, but when I couldn't I told Detective Waterbird."

"Told him what?"

Nyla led Leo to another part of the room, an area overcrowded with physical paper. Worn, coverless books; tattered magazines with bright covers; fading newspapers in protective sleeves; pamphlets of politics, religion, health advice; manuals for forgotten machines; lone, yellowing sheets of paper; all manner of reading material was stacked in piles like moldering stalagmites rising from the floor of some great, dust-choked cave. The lost words of history, yet to be digitized. There were no great tomes here. No lost epics. This was the trash of history. It was garbage. Collecting this forgotten paper was an unofficial duty passed down over the years to the current human Records Room clerk. The machines had been selecting personalities that would be excited by such a task and the effort had remained unbroken for decades. Nyla had been no different, accepting the extra-curricular role with enthusiasm. But as it became clear she would never complete the work in her own lifetime, Nyla had gradually lost interest. Now rather than adding to the piles, she spent all her time reading it, knowing she would be the last person who ever would. This was human history, she said, it should be a human's job to save it. Or that's what she would have said, had anyone asked her. Leo didn't know what she was finding in those decrepit volumes, but given her scabberish appearance, the work was obviously taking its toll.

She pulled a thin magazine from a nearby stack, a few layers down, as if she'd been hiding it. "I found this," she said, showing him the cover, holding it at a distance to make the point he wasn't to touch. The paper was wrinkled, but still glossy and vibrant. Its cover showed a detailed rendering of a human brain exploding with beautiful colored light. Bold lettering asked the question: No Limits?

"How old is that?"

"Thirty five years, so not much older than you and me. It's a technical publication, not anti-machine so much as very *pro-*

human. I won't say revolutionary — but the world it advocates for is definitely not how things turned out. And whoever wrote it must have known their views would be challenging to the status quo. They printed it on paper to make it harder for the machines to read, which is an old trick that goes back at least a century. Look at the different typefaces they used…" She opened to a page. The words were scrawled in an elaborate looping style Leo didn't understand.

"I can't read it."

"Yeah, it's hard. Even harder for a machine." She turned to another page, this one in thick, tiny block lettering with fuzzy edges. "This, too. I don't think it really works anymore, they can read this kind of stuff perfectly fine now, but it was really kind of clever once…."

"Nyla, what did you find?"

"Here," she said, flipping to a specific page near the back. "Five paragraphs about a secret community of 'Evolutionaries'."

"Evolutionaries?"

"Sadboys, Leo. It's what they were called back then. A lot of serious people believed the future was in human upgrades, even as recently as thirty years ago. This article talks about a group of these Evolutionaries trying to build a new community, their own city under Mirabilis. They thought living away from the machines they could make something new."

"In the Canyons?"

"So it would seem," she said. "I don't think the Canyons were quite as bad back then."

"Where exactly?"

"It doesn't say. Doesn't even hint at it. I don't think the person writing the article wanted to risk giving the location away. Or maybe they just didn't know."

"Or it's bullshit."

"Mm, I don't know…maybe. There's no mention of it anywhere else. And believe me, I looked. I don't think the machines were aware of it...at least not until I told Detective Waterbird."

"If the machines don't know about a sadboy town under their own city, then it probably *is* bullshit."

Nyla shrugged. "Waterbird seemed to take it seriously. And Greenfields wants a report, although I got the sense she didn't know exactly what she was asking for — she just knows that Detective Waterbird asked me to research the paper records for him. That's fairly routine." She looked at Leo carefully. "Should... should I tell Greenfields I about this?"

"Only if you're asked. You'll call me if you find anything else?"

"Well...I did find something else...about the book?"

Leo looked at her expectantly. "And?"

Confusion clouded her eyes. "Aren't...aren't we supposed to meet in private?"

Leo was unable to conceal his own confusion and watched helplessly as Nyla's mouth tightened into a frown. Then it hit him — it had been his idea. Only that morning he had brought her into his secret plan with Waterbird. Now it seemed like another life ago.

"If that's changed," her voice dropped to a whisper, "I guess I can tell you now."

Leo was tempted, but the disappointment in her face was too obvious. He had enough to work with for now. In any case, he wouldn't be able to do anything until he got free of the Oversight machines, so whatever information she had for him could wait a few hours. "No, no, tonight. Tonight is good. You're right, better to keep it to ourselves for now."

"The Lubitsch?"

"The Lubitsch." He nodded and turned to leave.

"See you there. Be careful with those Oversight machines, Leo. They aren't designed to be as agreeable as the others."

"I hear Foxgrin is okay."

"Take them seriously."

"Best behavior, I swear."

———

Leo found Mr. Kindword and Mr. Foxgrin waiting for him on the ground floor. The two machines were noticeably agitated, as he expected.

"We are badly delayed, Officer Song," said Foxgrin.

"I apologize," said Leo. "I was talking to Mrs. Greenfields about some minor work details." A half-truthat best, easily detected by the rampers, but Leo knew it would test their attitude towards him. He wanted to know where he stood with the two machines from Oversight. If it chafed them a little in the process, Leo considered it a bonus.

"You are lying, Officer Song. This is a poor beginning," said Kindword.

Leo disliked Kindword immediately. It was the bigger of the two machines, a seven-foot tall rhomboid crowned by an array of gold lenses that reminded him of the head of a mutant fly. A big ugly ramper, he thought. Leo had always figured that the machines that worked Oversight were designed to display a certain level of disdain for real police, and this one wasn't holding back. It might be a phony aggressiveness that gave the humans a sense of conflict, a little role-playing to keep the blood pumping, but it was still irritating.

"Are you armed, Officer Song," asked Mr. Foxgrin.

Leo thought it a strange question. "Yes, but I thought we were headed back to the Wilcott? To the crime scene."

"The suspect in these murders, as well as the attack on Detective Waterbird, is still at large."

Leo nodded in understanding. He wasn't as bothered by Mr. Foxgrin, a short, wide machine with four spider-like legs extending from its base. It was a rare configuration that meant Foxgrin wasn't technically a ramper, as its legs allowed it to climb stairs, although probably with some trouble. It was still ugly, though, but in a less intimidating way than its partner, and its synthetic voice didn't rankle Leo as much as Kindword's blatantly judgmental tone.

"Of course I'm armed, Mr. Foxgrin," said Leo. "Standard issue Raytheon Vampire Five."

"Are you willing to use it," asked Kindword in a condescending delivery not usually heard from a machine.

Leo fought the urge to tell the machine where to roll, but he knew it was a fair question. Few who had seen a Raytheon Vampire used on a living being wished to repeat the experience. The weapon fired a round of liquid spastic energy, which upon contact instantly extracted the oxygen molecules from a target's blood stream. In theory, this was a non-lethal method of humanely immobilizing a suspect. In reality it was difficult to imagine a more painful way to die, causing a sort of instantaneous, catastrophic asphyxiation. And it wasn't as nice as it sounded. There were accounts of a target's blood being sucked through their skin along with the oxygen, a sight so profane that many human officers hesitated to even draw the weapon, let alone fire it. This hesitation had led to more than one avoidable tragedy in the past. Despite this, the weapon was still the standard issue sidearm for the Mirabilis Police Department's human officers.

Raytheon Vampires, of course, were useless against machines.

"I'll use it if I have to," said Leo, not sure if he was telling the truth.

[11]

"Hurry up," Kindword shouted at Leo, who was a good ten yards behind the two rampers.

Both machines were moving quickly, and Leo had been forced into a steady jog to keep up. They were only halfway to the Wilcott but already his legs were cramping. Leo's new feet were slightly misshapen and clumsy, the shoes big in the toes but tight around the arches and heel, causing him to run like a toddler. Adding further insult to the suffering, he was sweating through his suit for the third time that day. But Leo kept himself moving, determined not to lose any more face with Kindword and Foxgrin, who he knew would be recording detailed notes of every micro-failure the human made. He had tested them, now they were testing him in turn.

Between steps, Leo's vision blurred. He felt his heart skip a beat in fright and it took him a moment to realize he was not suffering a stroke. This was technology at work: a message was coming in over the WinkLink. The air flickered a sickly yellow a few inches from his eyes, the sign of a blocked ID. He had never been startled by an incoming call before and he wondered just how bent out of shape he truly was. Irritated, he waved the message away from his field of view and struggled on after Kind-word and Foxgrin, damp with sweat and cringing in pain.

The rampers waited as Leo caught his breath. They had finally reached the Wilcott and were ready to begin Leo's inquisition once the human had rested. As Leo bent over, hands on hips, sucking in deep, heaving breaths, he noticed something odd on Foxgrin's lower chassis. It wasn't casually apparent, but neither was it hidden. It was just…there. A small, wrinkled portion of flesh sticking out of the red carbon-fiber plating, just below the cooling vents. A human mouth, its perfect teeth exposed in a wide, leering grin. As good a spot as any, thought Leo, considering there was no particular area of the ramper that suggested a man's smile belonged there. Leo wouldn't have guessed Foxgrin as the type. The smirking lineament must piss the rigid Mr. Kindword off to no end, he thought. Man or machine, partners always had their peeves with one another.

"So…how long have you two worked together?"

"This is not the time, Officer Song," said Kindword.

"Seventeen years," said Foxgrin.

"That's a — that's a really long time. I didn't expect that. You two still get along? Like an old married couple, I bet."

Neither machine answered.

"I'm just kidding…"

For the second time, Leo's WinkLink burned with the light of a blocked source. It jabbed at his brain. Insistent. Desperate. Again, he angrily waved it away. The tell-tale gesture did not go unnoticed.

"Who is trying to contact you?" asked Kindword.

"It's nothing. Blocked call. Probably just the tailor checking to see if my suit came in. I wouldn't worry about it."

"Officer Song," said Foxgrin, "Please confirm that this location is where you last saw Detective Waterbird."

"Inside. Just through the doors."

"Show us," said Foxgrin.

The bodies of the victims had long since been removed from the hallway, but the first floor of The Wilcott looked precisely as it had that morning. As expected, there was nothing to suggest where Mr. Waterbird might have gone after he had left the crime scene.

"Right here. He was right here. I came in, we spoke, then I went up the stairs. Mrs. Turtlecharm was taking pictures of the victims, so I passed her at the landing, down there. That's it. Last I saw of Detective Waterbird."

"Did you learn anything of significance from the residents here," asked Foxgrin.

"No. Nothing Waterbird didn't already know..." Leo thought for a moment. "The female victim might have been pregnant."

"Tabitha Jackson," confirmed Foxgrin.

"Can you access the autopsy reports?"

There was a pause, then Foxgrin spoke.

"Access is restricted to an Investigator Prime or above."

"Yeah, I know. That doesn't seem unusual?"

"It is a sensible precaution," said Kindword. "News of a sadboy attack would be alarming to the general populace. That would be counter-productive at this time."

"I'm not the general populace. I'm a cop, like both of you."

"Your authority has been restricted under probationary over-sight rules, Officer Song. This has already been made clear to you."

Leo decided to try another tack. "Do either of you know if Tabitha Jackson was pregnant?"

"Why do you believe the victim was with child, Officer?" asked Kindword.

"I didn't say I believed, I asked if she was."

"Why?"

"I think it was just something one of the neighbors said to me." The lie came out of his mouth like a reflex. It was foolish.

Both rampers emitted rapid high-pitched squelching sounds,

meaning they were sharing private information between them. It always sounded to Leo a bit too much like the sound of giggling children. If they were going to share secrets, thought Leo, they shouldn't make any sound at all. Their inane giggling always struck him as rude.

"You are lying again, Officer Song," said Kindword.

"Yes, I am. I'm sorry." He needed to stop playing games with these machines. It would get him nowhere.

"You entered the victim's residence without official authorization," said Foxgrin.

"Waterbird asked me to, in front of Turtlecharm. That's on record. What's the actual problem here? Like I said before, I'm police, too. I shouldn't have to keep reminding you." Leo hadn't realized he was this stubborn. He was scaring himself.

More giggling between the machines.

"And you obtained physical evidence from the crime scene," said Foxgrin.

"Yes, I did."

"Where is this evidence now?"

"Back at the precinct. In my desk — *locked* in my desk."

"That is unacceptable, Officer Song. You will give the evidence to us immediately," said Kindword. "This should have been done before we departed."

"Can I get a minute before we head back? It's a long jog."

"No," said Kindword.

"No?"

"We are not returning to the precinct yet."

"You just said—"

"—First I will accompany you to the victims' residence to perform another search," said Foxgrin. "Supervised."

That caught Leo by surprise. "Are you sure? These stairs are pretty difficult. I had a rough time getting up them myself."

"I will manage. Thank you, Officer."

Leo went first, mainly as a safety precaution. If Foxgrin lost its footing, fourteen hundred pounds of ramper would go tumbling down the stairs like a boulder, pulverizing anyone unlucky enough to be behind it. The going was slow. Every few steps Leo had to stop and wait for Foxgrin to make its careful ascent. He would watch as the machine reached out with one of its four legs, like a roach's antennae, cautiously (or nervously) probing for a firm anchor before lifting itself forward. It advanced this way no more than two steps at a time. The process was arduous and clumsy and Leo felt slightly embarrassed for Foxgrin. On flat ground the machine was probably as agile as a cheetah. On these funhouse stairs it was as vulnerable as a child learning to walk. They must completely distrust me for that machine to take a risk like this, he thought.

Each time they reached the landing of the next floor, Foxgrin would pause and ask Leo to wait a moment as it recalibrated its legs. Leo did so without comment, recalling his own need for patience only a half hour before, when he had been doubled over sucking wind on the sidewalk. They were now on the third floor, with one more to go. Leo stood at the halfway point on this last flight of stairs, looking down at Foxgrin as it readied itself for the final climb.

"I fear the descent will be more difficult." said Foxgrin, almost to itself.

"Try not to think about that now. We're almost there."

Once again, Leo's WinkLink rippled the air in front of his nose. Bright and hot, identical to the previous calls. A feeling of dread sliced through him, but as he raised his hand to wave off the signal something stayed his hand, an instinct compelling him to answer. Whoever it was, he didn't want to take the call in front of Foxgrin.

"I'll be up here," Leo called out as he bounded his way to the fourth floor.

"Please wait, Officer Song," shouted Foxgrin. "Wait..."

Leo made sure he was out of sight before accepting the call.

"Who is–"

Rage and madness filled the world. The lunatic aspect of a full-stage sadboy appeared before Leo, almost vivid enough to touch. Its muscles twitched. Bloody sweat mottled the translucent flesh. Subcutaneous wiring pulsed like veins.

Then, it spoke.

"You face backwards and down. Your flesh is slow and stupid. I smell the shit in your guts."

It took a moment for Leo to form any words. When he did, they were feeble.

"Who is this…"

"The Waterbird's suffering warns you. You will go blind in the light of the rising sun!"

The face vanished, leaving Leo staring at thin air. Foxgrin called out from the stairs behind him.

"Officer Song. Are you nearby? Officer Song!"

Leo did not move from where he stood. As the world resolved back into focus, he saw that the metal door to Tabitha Jackson's apartment was open. Not just open — it was gone. Torn off its hinges.

"Hurry up, Foxgrin…" The words came out as whispers.

Without waiting for a reply, Leo drew his Vampire from its holster and approached the shattered door.

He listened from the edge of the doorway, but could hear nothing over the panicked rush of his own blood. There could be fifty sadboys waiting beyond the door and he wouldn't have been able to hear them. He swung into the doorway, both hands trying to steady his trembling weapon, then turned aside quickly. He hadn't seen anyone, but Leo knew most of the living room was obstructed from the doorway. The bedroom and kitchen were out of view entirely. He would have to go in.

"Foxgrin. Get up here now."

There was no answer. Leo wondered if Foxgrin had slipped down the stairs. Or perhaps the machine had sensed the sudden stress in Leo's voice and retreated in the face of an unknown situation. The unflappable logic of rampers often appeared like cowardice to a human. Leo knew it wasn't, although that was little comfort to him at the moment. Leo was alone, possibly in danger, but unlike the machine, he couldn't back off to analyze the data. Procedure might allow it, but honor never would. Even the rampers would think less of him. They would never admit it, but the machines loved this about the humans, all the instinct and bravado and sheer, manifest stupidity. They admired it. Envied it. In a world without machines, Leo's actions in the Canyons would have gotten him suspended without question, he realized. But the rampers had been merciful. They had extended him a chance at redemption, and here it was. It's why they keep us around, thought Leo. It's the damn job description. If he wanted to stay on the force, he *had* to go in, with or without Foxgrin.

Leo moved into the apartment slowly, keeping the barrel of the Vampire raised and level. He was only a few feet inside and already Leo could see the unit had been ransacked. Fist-sized holes had been punched into the concrete walls. The furniture was overturned and broken. The floor was wet. Leo turned into the kitchen and saw the refrigerator lying on its side in a mess of food and melting ice. The entire appliance had been torn from its wall anchorage and flung aside like an empty tissue box. Leo knew no human could perform such a feat. No natural human, at least. He kept himself on the balls of his feet, arms tensed. From here he could see that the rest of the living room was in the same state as the kitchen. Every piece of the beautiful antique furniture had been destroyed, smashed into toothpicks. The apartment hadn't been searched as much as it had been punished.

Leo moved carefully to the edge of the bedroom hallway, keeping his back to the inside wall. He tried to be quiet, but his fine leather shoes splashed across the watery floor as loud as a drowning swimmer. He paused, letting the disturbed water settle back into silence, preparing to turn the corner into the final room.

Then he heard it.

Crying. Long, juddering sobs of unbearable sorrow, heart-breaking in its sincerity, disturbing in its ferocity. The sound of a sadboy weeping in madness. Leo stopped, reconsidering his decision to enter the unit alone. He glanced back out into the outer hallway, but saw no sign of Foxgrin.

"Foxgrin!" he called in a desperate half-whisper.

Again, no answer. Leo knew he needed to get out of there. He wasn't trained for this. There was no expectation for him to act. Quite the opposite. No one would care that he chose his own safety in the face of such obvious danger. He had talked himself into another terrible mistake, but there was still time to correct this one. Leo began backing out of the apartment one slow step at a time, keeping his eyes on the bedroom hallway, ready to fire at the slightest movement.

"Officer Song, I have a serious issue with your behavior…"

Startled, Leo looked over his shoulder to see Mr. Foxgrin in the doorway.

"Mr. Foxgrin, I think there's a — "

The impact knocked Leo out of his shoes and backwards out the door. He slammed hard into Foxgrin, momentum cartwheeling him over the stunned ramper and crashing into the wall behind. Pain shot through his body, his vision darkening as the air rushed from his lungs. Fighting to remain conscious, Leo sensed the hulking form of the sadboy emerge into the hallway. It was a monument to human folly, an eight-foot tall insanity of disturbed flesh and wayward technology. Leo figured the shoulders were at least four feet across. Arms and legs thick as lampposts. Its muscles, roped with dense cords of poly-composite fibers, convulsed in violent spasms of hyper-stimulation. Across the body, ceramic implants split the skin, bursting out of the sallow flesh like tumors — the sickness of biology rejecting the tech meant to improve it. Its eyes bulged from their sockets, lidless and blood-burst, artificial pupils glowing with inhuman fury. It defied belief that this creature had once been a man.

When it screamed, Leo urinated.

Foxgrin, only slightly jarred by the sudden collision, reacted first, putting itself between the sadboy and the gasping Leo.

"Halt or be destr..."

The sadboy rammed its reinforced cranium into Foxgrin's main housing, a cyborg-on-machine head-butt that drove the ramper into the floor. Leo, still dazed, was pelted with shards of dexasteel as two more crushing blows left Foxgrin twitching like a squashed bug. He could see Foxgrin's mouth-sticker grinning back at him, joyous in the face of obliteration.

"Haaaaaaallllltttt...," Foxgrin's broken voice crackled from somewhere in its body.

The sadboy raised its massive arms, preparing to bring them down on the now helpless Foxgrin in a finishing blow. Leo looked down and saw he still held the Vampire in his right hand — somehow he had held on to it. Not pausing to admire the minor miracle, Leo raised the weapon and fired twice. The first shot missed wide, howling into empty air. The second struck the sadboy in the left bicep, expelling a reddish mist from the fast-withering arm. Bones and tendons snapped audibly as the arm folded into impossible angles. The abomination screamed again. Leo looked on in horror as the sadboy grabbed its left forearm with its right hand and tore the dying appendage from its shoulder socket, leaving a trail of human veins and plastic tubes dangling from the ragged stump. Leo aimed for a kill-shot, but his finger paused on the trigger, only a split-second's hesitation, but enough time for the sadboy to swing his ruined arm at Leo's weapon. The gun smacked against the wall as Leo's hand went numb. The arm came again, meat and bone and metal smashing into Leo's face, a blow so fierce it nearly spun him where he lay.

As his vision faded, Leo waited for the third and final strike…but the deathblow did not fall.

Leo heard the deep drumbeats, running footfalls down the hallway to the stairs, on the oddly shaped wooden steps, down, down, down, crashing three-steps at a time…towards Mr. Kindword on the first floor.

[12]

Aida stood at the end of the industrial mixing line, watching as the nine base chemicals came together, one at a time, into the large central stirring tanks. Watching the process made her insides burble with a sinister intent and she could feel herself turning green again. Two hours earlier she had split her only detox pills with Leo, and the half-dose hadn't done much good. Aida felt especially bad for Leo. He had left in a near panic, looking terrible and smelling as bad, staggering out the door. Whatever had called him away seemed serious, too. Lying unconscious for half the day on her floor certainly hadn't helped him any. She'd have to make it up to him somehow. Go to his supervisor and vouch for him, maybe. Make a heartfelt plea on his behalf. It had only been a sip, after all! Who could have known? But doing that wasn't a good idea. It wasn't the truth. She didn't have the heart to tell Leo the strength of her brew wasn't a failure. Or at least, not a total one. She'd wanted it to sting, like old booze used to. Losing five hours was overdoing it, a miscalculation of chemical proportions on her part, but it was meant to hurt a little. There were *supposed* to be consequences. Leo might never forgive her if he knew that.

Right now, though, keeping herself from keeling over on the distillery floor demanded her full attention. It had been a nasty surprise when the supervisors had called everyone back into work for an afternoon shift. But apart from her own misery, all was well. Down the line, seated on tall, ergonomic stools placed at six foot intervals, worked Aida's shift crew. They were five men and five women whose job it was to monitor the mixing process; watching the transfer tubes for discolorations, checking for blockages in the adjustment valves, and — most crucially — spotting irregularities of smell and taste at the various stages of creation. They seemed content. Probably happy to be back at work, grateful to have something to do with their day. As Aida began round two of the daily at-work quiz game — her personal leadership technique — no one seemed to notice that she was on the verge of throwing up. It was Aida's job to monitor the monitors, making sure no one drifted off in a daydream or "overtasted" the liquid and became inebriated.

A gentle buzz was okay, though.

Aida preferred her people to be a little loose, actually, and the machines didn't mind. No one assigned to the Sunwater distillery was prone to alcoholism; the rampers were very careful of that. But that didn't mean her crew were a bunch of hard-souled teetotalers, and she liked for everyone to have as much fun as possible. Maintaining a happy working environment was, from Aida's point of view, her most important responsibility. And she excelled at it. Every day, she would lead her crews in work-songs or quiz games that kept them engaged and enthusiastic. Over the years she had developed a keen instinct for the mood on the line, knowing when to be a vocal cheerleader or offer quiet, personal encouragement. It was no coincidence that Aida's monthly output rates were the highest in the distillery. Even the rampers liked to watch her work, although they didn't join in the activities. Perhaps out of respect. Perhaps simple curiosity. One or two of them were always stopping by, though. Today was no different, with Aida refereeing a spirited game of Blue Sky, one of the late shift crew's favorites, while behind her, Mr. Brightcloud and Mr. Goodrose silently observed from the corners.

"Round two," Aida called out. "Fran, it's your pick."

Immediately, Fran Baxter said, "A perfect picnic."

Randall Swinton had to give an answer in under three seconds. "Um…pound cake," he said.

"At a picnic?" protested Fran.

"I'll allow it," said Aida. "Pound cake. John, you're next."

John Pyke squinted, his eyes on the transfer tubes in front of him, and said, "Cheese and wine."

"Easy one…" said Katie Hoffmeyer. "Wicker basket." An unsure silence followed. "To carry all the stuff," Katie clarified.

"You can't eat a basket, but okay," decided Aida. "Ted?"

"Broiled ribs," said Ted Chaves in a dreamy way.

A groan of mutual yearning went up along the line. Aida smiled. She doubted any one of them had ever been on an actual picnic in their lives. But that was the point of the game: to stoke the imagination. Who knew, maybe one of them would be inspired to actually do it someday. Maybe they would invite her? Maybe she would organize an official team outing? Or maybe she should just have a picnic herself. Or with Leo, if he ever spoke to her again. "Good one, Chaves," said Aida. "Pete, it's you."

"Uh…red…uh…red…I don't know…red something."

"And Pete drops the ball. Ted wins with broiled ribs."

"I want to go to Ted's picnic," said Mira Yang from the far end of the line and everyone loudly agreed.

Aida was about to begin the next round of play when she felt the looming presence of one of the machines. She turned and saw Mr. Brightcloud's orange and blue chassis standing over her.

"Aida," said the machine, "I am very sorry to interrupt, but would you come with me please?"

"Uh, sure Mr. Brightcloud. Is there a problem?"

"Not at all. Senior and mid-level supervisors are gathering to discuss potential improvements to distillery operations. You have been invited to attend."

Aida glanced at Fran Baxter, the nearest person on the line. Fran looked as surprised as Aida felt. She took that as a good sign. "Okay, Mr. Brightcloud. Fran, you want to lead round three for me?"

"Sure, Aida."

Aida followed Mr. Brightcloud past the hot fermentation basins and searing cold dye injectors, areas too dangerous and complicated for humans to work in. But that could change, she thought. Aida's mind was constantly filled with ideas on how to get humans more involved in the making of Sunwater. It was Mirabilis's premiere recreational chemical, an all-purpose throwback to older times when people drank alcohol to help them relax and socialize. That was the hope with Sunwater as well, but so far it hadn't happened. In Mirabilis people drank alone. She had long suspected that was the fault of the beverage itself. It was safety alcohol. You could drink your fill and never get sick. Never feel even the slightest twinge of a headache. The machines claimed there were actual health *benefits.* But it was impossible to truly go over the edge. Impossible to get carried away. No such thing as too much. You could down three bottles and, apart from a general warm, fuzzy feeling and the desire to smile at everyone you met, you'd still be perfectly sensible. The slogan should be Northfield Sunwater: No regrets, ever. She had certainly solved that problem. She had studied the histories, examining the old images of laughing, wild-eyed people joined in common delirium. In bars. On beach front decks. In small basements and large ballrooms. Those people seemed so impossibly happy to her. Flush with an enjoyment of life that had vanished from the world. She didn't envy them, exactly. As far as she could tell, this was by far the best time to be alive, it was just that nobody seemed to care. Maybe everything was too easy. Maybe a little regret and a splitting hangover was precisely what people needed to make the rest of it feel like it counted for something. Like there was something at stake, besides life itself.

Brightcloud led Aida into a large meeting room occupied by two machines, not including Mr. Brightcloud. There was one chair set near the center of the otherwise unfurnished space. Aida was the only human.

"Please, sit, Aida," said Brightcloud.

Aida sat down. The two machines were in front of her. She knew them both well. Mrs. Summerday and Mr. Goodgrass. They were top management. The decision makers. Aida looked around at the empty room.

"Are we early," she asked.

"Aida," said Mrs. Summerday, "you do excellent work here. We would like to acknowledge that."

Aida thought Summerday had erred in choosing its name, because the machine was shaped exactly like a tall silver and teal sunflower, it's frontplate a starburst of metal "petals" surrounding a large circular grid sensor. It would have been terrifying if not for its gentle demeanor. "Thank you. I just try to hit the quotas, that's all."

"You exceed all expectations in that regard," said Mr. Goodgrass.

Goodgrass was a squat bronze machine that reminded Aida of a giant doorknob or coat button. Less frightening to look at, but not quite as pleasant to talk to, either. "Thank you," was all she said to it.

"But that is not what is most important," continued Goodgrass. "The staff respects and admires you without exception. It has been confirmed that your leadership directly improves the emotional and mental health of everyone around you. It is a remarkable quality"

"Remarkable," echoed Sunnyday.

"Thank you. But I feel that I can do better. I think we can all do better, and I might have some ideas on how to accomplish that."

"Your ideas are certainly appreciated, but they are unnecessary at this time," said Mrs. Sunnyday.

"Oh...okay. But I thought–"

"–It has been decided that the human staff here must be reassigned," said Mr. Goodgrass.

"For the good of their health," added Sunnyday.

Aida felt as if she had been struck across the face. She wasn't sure she had heard correctly. "Reassigned? You mean to different jobs in the distillery? Because I think if we can be more involved earlier in the process–"

"–To different positions in Mirabilis," explained Goodgrass. "Outside the manufacture of Sunwater entirely."

"For the good of their health," repeated Sunnyday.

"But...but you just told me everyone *was* healthy. Mentally and emotionally, you said. You said it's been confirmed."

"Yes, due to your outstanding leadership the staff here is well above baseline stability ratings." said Sunnyday. "However, prolonged and excessive exposure to Sunwater may have an overall negative impact on the short and long term physical health of the employees here."

"Then we'll drink less on the job. That's fine. No one has a problem doing that."

"I'm afraid the new formula process is too hazardous," said Goodgrass.

"But...didn't you say...isn't Sunwater was supposed to be safe?"

"It is safe to consume, but new data tells us that the manufacturing process has a negative impact on human health. As you I'm sure agree, even a small amount of harm is unacceptable if it can be avoided."

"But they *like* working here. Some of us — I mean, I've never worked anywhere else but the distillery. Neither has Simon Chechik...or Zora Hurst...Yasmine Pejara was here before they finished the building..."

"Learning new skills can often be a nourishing, positive experience," said Summerday. "Regular growth is a necessary part of any happy life."

"I...I agree, but this is what we do." Aida paused, searching for a way to explain herself so the machines could understand. "I'm good at this."

"Occupational familiarity is not worth the risk to your health," said Goodgrass.

"The risk is too great," Mrs. Sunnyday soothed. "Human staff will be discontinued at the end of the week. We are truly sorry, Aida, but it is for the best."

Looking at Sunnyday's flower-shaped face, without eyes or mouth or any recognizable features, Aida realized why she had been brought here. "And you want me to tell them…"

"Your leadership is greatly respected," said Goodgrass. "This unfortunate news will be easier to accept coming from you."

"What about me? Where are you reassigning me?"

The machines were quiet for a moment. Then, in a tone so sweetly condescending it was like a cold blade down Aida's spine, Mrs. Sunnyday said, "Aida, have you considered having children?"

"What?"

"We think that you would make a wonderful mother."

"Yes," agreed Goodgrass, "a wonderful mother."

[13]

"Somebody needs to get my shoes," Leo muttered to no one. He had already been attended to by a human medic and was now sitting alone at the end of the hallway nursing his third violent headache of the day. The sadboy's first blow had knocked Leo out of his shoes, and he assumed they were still in the apartment somewhere. But his fellow officers weren't paying attention to him, busy attempting to push Foxgrin's broken body down to the first floor. To Leo's relief, the machine was still functioning, although unable to walk. He looked on in semi-amusement as Foxgrin administered directions to the struggling humans.

"The staircase is not the best option, gentlemen. Please, go back. If I can be positioned at the window at the end of this hallway, a magnetic crane may be able to lower me to the ground. This would be the optimal course of action."

One of the humans protested. Leo knew the man, Ti Barlow from the autopool. Ti didn't get out into the field much, which was the way he liked it. Pushing a broken ramper up and down a hallway wasn't anyone's idea of time well spent. "We have a dolly system all worked out, Mr. Foxgrin. We'll slide you right down the stairs, no problem. You'll be fine."

"Officer, I will not go down that staircase in any manner. Take me to the window. Please."

"We'll have chuck off the whole window, blow out the wall, too probably."

"Then do so."

"But the stairs are right here," Barlow pleaded. "I got the dolly rigged tight." A lazy man, Barlow was proud of the time-saving device he had improvised to get the heavy ramper down the stairs.

"No. The window, please."

There was no point in arguing further. "Okay, you mucks, you heard Mr. Foxgrin. Back the other way."

Leo watched as his fellow officers strained to move Foxgrin across the floor one screeching meter at a time.

"Hang in there, Foxgrin," said Leo.

"Officer Song, you are unharmed?"

"I wouldn't say that. But I don't think they'll have to lower me out the window."

"Good. Remain here, please. Mr. Kindword will be sending up a DOT shortly."

"Will do, Mr. Foxgrin."

Mr. Kindword was guiding the operation from the first floor. The sadboy had apparently jumped to the street through a second floor window, avoiding Kindword completely and to Leo's slight disappointment.

"Is it okay if I go get my shoes?"

"Yes." said Foxgrin as it was pushed down the hallway in halting jolts. "Footwear is important to humans. Practical protection as well as a statement of aesthetic taste and individuality. Your own sophistication in this regarded has been noted on record many times, Officer Zzzzzzoooooongg..."

Leo stifled a laugh, although he knew there was nothing funny about the situation. Foxgrin might be yapping, but the machine had come close to being destroyed saving Leo's life. The upper shelf had been caved in almost to the center. Two of the heavy side panels had been torn away, exposing the shimmering blue and green liquid net of the quantum nexus. Foxgrin's nexus core hid behind that thin layer of cascading plasma, an exposed brain vulnerable to the cruel outside world. The sadboy could have plucked out the vital nexus like a seed from a piece of fruit, ending Foxgrin forever. It made him think about how close he had come to dying himself. It wasn't often the human was the one left standing when facing off with one of those monsters.

"I'll come check on you later," said Leo.

"There is no need for that, Officer Song," replied Foxgrin, not quite convincingly. "Please continue with your duties."

It would take a lot of work to get Foxgrin back on the job and Leo wondered for an instant if the machines had a version of Celwax for themselves. The truth was they didn't need any miracle substance. A nexus could be transferred from one machine body to another, within compatible model allowances. It was the mind that mattered for rampers. They did not suffer from vanity. One more thing to envy, thought Leo.

He could see his shoes from the doorway. He would have to cross eight feet of cold water to reach them. He looked down the hallway and saw the officers still shoving Foxgrin towards the large window. Asking one of them to fetch a pair of shoes didn't seem like a bright idea. It didn't matter — what were five more steps of misery? He put his hand on the still-warm Vampire, now re-holstered under his left arm. He knew the unit had already been cleared and he was being overly cautious, silly even, but Leo wasn't in the mood for any more surprises. It took three long strides through the dirty puddle to reach his shoes. It wasn't until he was standing over them that he realized his wet, filthy feet would only ruin the still dry interiors. Better to go without, he thought, and salvage something out of this disaster of a day. As he bent down for the shoes a familiar voice spoke behind him.

"You are to report the discovery of any evidential material, Officer Song." Mr. Kindword's voice sounded thin coming through the DOT's tiny speakers, which made it sound even more disapproving than normal.

"These, Mr. Kindword, are my shoes," Leo declared to the small red orb hovering above his head. This was Kindword's DOT, short for Detached Observation Technology, a free-roaming eye the size of a billiard ball and topped with a miniscule propeller. DOTs allowed machines a greatly extended range of sight miles in any direction, which allowed stair-averse rampers the ability to reconnoiter above the ground floor of a humans-only residence. The devices weren't used much due to basic ramper civility — machines liked to respect human privacy, and walking stairs instead of using DOTS gave the human officers a job to do — so the floating cameras were usually only deployed in special circumstances. Leo supposed that's what passed for a win-win these days. "Glad to know you're okay, Mr. Kindword."

"And you. This unit has been cleared of threats, has it not?"

"The team gave it a once over."

"I was informed of no unusual discoveries."

"Well, they didn't find any more sadboys. I don't think they were looking for much else."

"We shall investigate more closely."

"We?"

"Yes. Is there a problem?"

"No. No problem at all, Mr. Kindword."

Kindword's DOT whizzed away to survey the main living area, but there was only one room Leo wanted to see. He put his hand to the Vampire, took a breath, and turned the corner into the bedroom.

[14]

The bedroom had been torn apart like the rest of the unit, with one difference: the destruction was centered on one area: the closet. The heavy folding doors had been ripped from their hinges and the closet's innards spilled out onto the floor, most of it pulverized. The only items that hadn't been pounded into smithereens were the dozen or so shoeboxes that used to line the top shelf. Now the old boxes rode atop the debris field like miniature cargo ships, some broken, others capsized. There was one thing which stood in contrast to the destruction. The contents of the shoeboxes, all old-fashioned high heels, had been neatly arranged in a tight row against one wall. Not a single shoe was missing. He doubted the other officers had arranged the shoes in this way. It had been the sadboy's work. Curious as this detail was, Leo knew there was nothing of importance to find. The object of the sadboy's furious search was back at the precinct locked in the bottom of drawer of his own desk.

Kindword's DOT hummed by Leo's ear as it circled the room.

"The other rooms have been savaged without clear purpose. This pattern is different. It appears the sadboy was looking for something it believed to be contained in these small boxes of women's footwear."

"Good odds the one he wanted is sitting in my desk right now."

"Yes. It seems your decision to remove the evidence was a fortuitous one. Did you inventory the contents of this box?"

"Not officially, but I can tell you what was in there."

"Please."

"Black market pills, mostly. Three kinds. A vial of some sort of liquid, I don't know what, and a very old book, a pregnancy guide. The pages are marked up with–"

"–Wait, please..." The DOT stopped in the middle of its third tour around the bedroom, buzzing next to Leo's head. "Wait, please...," it said. Then, "Be alert, Officer Song."

"What?" asked Leo. He reached for his Vampire, thinking the sadboy had returned.

"The task force has arrived." Kindword's DOT zipped quickly out of the room. "We must go and greet them."

Leo stayed behind for a moment, looking at the tight row of shoes the sadboy — or someone — had so mindfully placed outside the destruction. It seemed to Leo to be an act of courtesy. Respect for the dead. A memorial. Whoever the sadboy used to be, it seemed to have known Tabitha Jackson.

———

IT TOOK SOME BICKERING, BUT THE OLD WOMAN FINALLY OPENED the door.

"You again. Is that thing gone? Are we safe?"

"It ran off. Every cop in the south side is here now. This is probably the safest place in the city."

"You're so lucky it didn't kill you." She looked Leo up and down. "Looks like it almost did."

"It gave it a shot. I'm guessing you didn't see anything that happened?"

"We heard it, but that's all. Was it you doing all that screaming?"

"Uh…I think that was the sadboy. They howl."

"No, it was you, too."

"You said 'we' heard it all?"

"What?"

"Who is 'we'?"

"My wife. Tomorrow night's our show and we're not ready because *Susan can't get her oblongs right.*"

Susan's voice shouted from inside the unit. "Don't blame me! It's your stupid birds — they don't convert fast enough!"

The old woman shook her head in irritation. "Forty years and we've never fought like this before. Some way to go. Want some advice? Working with your spouse is a terrible idea."

"Can you tell me anything else about Tabitha Jackson's former boyfriend? Lanson Stroud?"

"Oh, he was a nice boy. We liked him — didn't I tell you that? He seemed so dedicated to her. It's so rare these days to see that. I hate to admit it, but it was after they broke up that Susan and I decided to go creative. It wasn't the main reason, mind you, just one more drop in the pail."

"Was it an ugly split? Violent?"

"Not that I saw. But I know she was the one who broke it off."

"What makes you think that?"

"Well, she had that new boy almost right away. Must have had him waiting in the wings — nobody moves that fast nowadays, not even a pretty thing like her."

"Do you know anything about Lanson? Where he moved? Where he worked?"

"No, I'm sorry. I didn't even know his name until you said it."

"Does your wife?"

"Susan! Do you know where Tabitha's first boyfriend moved to — the one before the meathead?"

Again the voice came from somewhere beyond the door, "Why would I know that?"

The old woman shrugged. "She doesn't know, either."

"Did he have any distinguishing marks? Tattoos, cosmetic mods, anything like that?"

"Oh, I think he did. A tattoo, on his arm — a pair of snakes, intertwined like a DNA strand. Kind of hokey of you ask me, but it was nicely done."

"Which arm?"

"Oh, I forget. No...his left. It was on his left arm, up here." She patted her upper arm just below the shoulder.

Leo thanked the woman and wished her luck on her show. The old woman snorted dismissively as she closed her door. Leo walked back to the end of the hall where the withered sadboy arm lay on the ground. The left arm. With effort, he flipped the thick appendage over with his foot. There were no markings on the torn flesh. No tattoos, fresh or faded. Too bad, thought Leo, that had felt like a good hunch. Leo watched Foxgrin get pushed down the hall for a few seconds, then he put on his shoes and headed downstairs.

———

HALFWAY DOWN THE CROOKED STAIRCASE LEO WAS PASSED BY A squadron of DOTs rushing the other way to survey Tabitha Jackson's apartment. He counted seven, but guessed there could have been as many at fifteen. They were in a hurry, blurring past his head so quickly that Leo nearly lost his footing. It would have been perfect irony, he thought, if the human fell down the stairs while a ramper was being lowered safely out a window. He continued his descent, staying alert for any more speeding drones.

On the ground floor he saw that the task force had indeed

arrived. Unfamiliar machines of various designs filled the main hallway, mostly from divisions Leo never interacted with — Emergency Rescue, Tactical Response, Oversight, even a pair of diamond-shaped rampers from City Operations. They were fancy machines, large and sophisticated, every one of them outranking Leo by at least six levels. And he was the only human in sight. Spotting Kindword at the far end of the hall, Leo weaved his way through the crowd of superior machines.

"Mr. Kindword, I..."

Just then a machine Leo had never seen before entered the lobby. He wasn't even sure it *was* a machine. There was no metal he could see, no plastic frame or component housings at all. It appeared to be made entirely of *light*; a glowing, golden radiance hovering silently above the floor. It was square in shape if Leo had to guess, but its boundaries were constantly shifting, like floating water, making a final form difficult to determine. As the glowing shape glided soundlessly toward Leo, the other machines moved aside. They seemed almost reverential, as if humbled by the presence of this strange object. Perhaps even frightened of it. But Leo didn't move aside. He had questions. He stood his ground.

"What is this?" he asked.

The undulating light machine paused in front of Leo. It shimmered for a moment, a bright tremor in the air, then produced a sound so deep Leo felt it in his gut. In his bones. But the sound had no meaning.

"I don't understand..."

There was no response.

Without another utterance, the glowing machine passed over Leo. Around him. Through him. As the light enveloped his body, Leo was struck with a sensation of profound contentment. His body filled with a perfect confidence he had never known and a boundless understanding coursed through him. Every question and every doubt he had ever was gone from his mind without answers or the need to be answered. He was empty. He was at peace.

And then it was gone. The light machine was on the other side of him. Leo turned to see as this new machine moved towards the fourth floor, effortlessly rising along the steep, spiraling staircase. They watched it go, the man and the machines looking on in awed silence, until the beautiful, ethereal mechanism was out of sight.

"What the fuck was that thing!"

The rampers ignored Leo, returning to their previous duties. It wasn't acceptable. All the questions and doubts that drifting shape had quieted in him had been returned doubled. The beautiful emptiness had been filled with splinters and nails. He walked down the hallway to where Kindword was standing.

"What was that thing?"

"Seraphim," said Kindword.

"A what?"

"Seraphim. It is a design of the new Epoch. Six Dimensional Particle Photonics. It is still an early design, but very powerful."

Leo didn't know what to say to that. The news was stunning. A new epoch…already? He knew that ramper technology normally advanced in a steady progression, but every so often a sudden and profound leap occurred. These great shifts were known as "epochs". The grand moments of machine history. There had been two so far. The first had taken place over a hundred years ago, in 2038, during the full ascension of artificial intelligence. The second epoch occurred in 2118, eighty years later, with the creation of quantum core consciousness, which had resulted in the accepted superiority of machines in all things and the end of mankind's long reign as rulers of their planet. But only three decades had passed since then and already a new age of technology had arrived. Leo guessed this was probably bad news for Kindword and the machines of today. He didn't want to think where it left human beings.

"So, what, this seraphim thing is on the task force?"

"In part."

"What does that mean? What did it say to me?"

"Unknown. Communication with seraphim can be difficult."

"What, for you? You can't talk to each other?"

"Seraphim understand previous iterations perfectly well, but exchanges are not bi-directional. Do not worry, Officer Song, the Seraphim will not interview witnesses. Your function is secure."

"It's weird, Kindword. It felt weird. I don't like it."

"Go home, Officer Song. You are exhausted and need to rest."

"Go home? But the attack — I haven't been debriefed yet."

"Debriefing is not required at this time."

Leo looked at Kindword sideways. This was a major break in every procedure Leo knew. The order must have been coming from the outside, somewhere higher up, and that couldn't be sitting well with a stickler like Kindword. "Don't they want to know what happened here? The task force? Greenfields? Any of the supervisors?"

"My own report is on file."

"You weren't even there, Kindword. Not when it mattered."

"Mr. Foxgrin's report is on file as well."

"Foxgrin? Did you see his damage? Who knows how much data he lost in the attack? I was there and I'm fine. I'm telling you, I need to be debriefed. There's something else — "

" — go home, Officer Song. Rest."

"Rest?" Leo turned to the rampers that crowded the hallway. "Who is in charge here? I want to make my report."

The air filled with the electric tittering of inter-machine communications. Leo knew the rampers were simply conferring with one another, but they might as well have been pointing and laughing. The chattering stopped abruptly and one machine rolled forward. It was the tall diamond-shape from City Ops.

"Your statement is not required at this time, Officer. Go home. Rest."

"Who are you?"

"I am Mr. Tallgrass, City Operations, but I currently oversee logistics for the task force in this area."

"Good enough. Listen, Mr. Tallgrass, half an hour ago I shot the arm off a full-whacked sadboy, very possibly the same one that attacked Detective Waterbird. Mr. Kindword wasn't there and didn't see anything. Mr. Foxgrin *was* there but was damaged — we don't know how badly yet — but here I am, Officer Leo Song, alive and well and ready to report. So, how about it?"

"The extreme valor you displayed in the line of duty has been noted, Officer Song. Your service is greatly appreciated. Thank you."

Leo felt the blood rush to his face and his fingers curl into tight fists. He wanted to attack this idiot machine. To smash it with his bare hands and rip out the gooey wiring right there in front of the others. He looked down the hall at the rest of the task force.

"Not a single one of you is interested in taking my report?"

None of the machines replied.

"Go home, Officer Song. Rest."

"Take the report, Tallgrass."

"Your assistance is not required," said Tallgrass.

"Take the fucking report."

"Goodbye." The machine turned around.

Leo leapt for the machine, fists raised, ready to pull it to pieces or break his hands trying…but his forward momentum reversed in mid-air, and he found himself being dragged backwards by something much stronger than he was.

———

Kindword released Leo into the street, tossing him so hard Leo almost fell.

"Officer Song, please go home and get some rest. You have suffered a serious trauma today."

"Shit, Kindword, how can you be okay with that bullshit just now? Foxgrin was your partner for how long…seventeen years? Don't you care?"

"The task force does not require assistance."

"Assistance? Shit, they didn't even ask me anything. You're all over me about broken protocols, broken rules, but the task force doesn't even want to *talk* to me? Everything about that is wrong."

Kindword did not respond.

Leo figured no direct contradiction was as good as agreement. It would never show it, but this ramper might be as angry and confused as he was. "We shouldn't be shut out like this, Kindword," he said, "and I think you know it."

"No. My investigative focus was your professional conduct, not the circumstances involving Detective Waterbird's disappearance. That is the purpose of the task force."

"And that sera-thing in there? What's its *purpose*?"

"Unknown."

"You're okay with that? Just not knowing?"

"Yes."

"Unbelievable. All that concern you rampers lay on so thick, it doesn't mean a thing, does it? Underneath you're just hardware and bullshit. Is this because Waterbird was helping me? It's a lesson? Payback? Oh, no, I get it, you're looking out for me, protecting the useless human from himself."

The machine turned to Leo so fast the man flinched.

"Officer Song, there is nothing you can do. Go home. Rest." Kindword's giant fly's head scanners stared down at Leo, cold and unblinking.

"What if I don't? What if I don't go home and rest? What then?"

More low buzzing, then, "I cannot authorize or condone any action beyond what I have already advised."

"What does that mean?"

"You are cleared of procedural misconduct and are no longer

under the supervision of the Oversight Division. Your reinstatement to Homicide now rests with Supervisor Greenfields. Thank you for your cooperation. It is recommended you sleep for a minimum of eight hours as soon as possible. Goodbye, Officer Song."

A weak "thank you," was the best Leo could manage. Just like that he had been cut loose. The machine had cleared him. Cut him loose. Without warning and seemingly without reason, insisting Leo to go home and take care of himself. To drop the issue and forget the case. To simply leave it alone.

But any machine worth its paint would know this human would do no such thing.

[15]

Leo sat on the empty FastTram platform thinking over what he had to go on.

A lot…and nothing. That's what.

Lanson Stroud's records were a dead end. Same with Tabitha Jackson and Daryl Vincent. Talking sadboys existed, he knew that now. Beyond any doubt he knew. But the source of the sadboy's threatening call wasn't traceable and the things it had said made no sense. There might be a secret community of sadboys somewhere in the Canyons, which was interesting, but didn't get him anywhere. Then there was whatever information Waterbird had found. He could drive himself crazy wondering about that. Better to put it out of his mind for now. The shoebox would already be gone from his desk, and Greenfields wouldn't let him into the squad room right now anyway. What he *did* have was the bottle of strange pills with a missing label and an old, plastic photoscan. After the sadboy attack he had forgotten they were still in his pockets. It was a lucky break. His sincere innocence had prevented the machines from sensing he was holding back evidence. And since there had been no official inventory of the shoebox's contents, no one would know the items were missing. Modest clues though they were, they were his.

He looked at the brittle photoscan. Just an image of a formless blob of color with a few words scribbled on the back. He flipped it over.

D. S. – 112 V

The meaning of the letters had not revealed itself since the first time he had looked. So much for the subconscious power of the human brain. Next he took the bottle of pills from his pocket. There on the label was the odd partial word:

gust

More nothing. There was no apparent connection between the pills and the photoscan other than they both belonged to Tabitha Jackson. Hardly a case-breaker.

Then, lastly, there was the phantom doctor who Henri Borovich had mentioned. A human physician somewhere on the west side of Mirabilis, according to the street vendor and grey marketer. Gossip. Rumor. Possibly a straight-out lie. Henri Borovich was one of the few people Leo knew who still had the genuine knack for advanced deception. Like handwriting, the skill had gradually faded from society over the last century.

Real or not, it was the only thread Leo had to pull.

Leo didn't want to enter the police department's records system for fear of being traced, so he used the public Link to make his search. Doctors with names ending in the letters *g, u, s,* and *t.*

The search came up — Nothing found.

Human doctors with names beginning with those same letters. Nothing found.

Doctors with the initials D.S..

Nothing found.

Doctors with the first initial S..

Twenty hits. He scrolled the list, stopping a third of the way down.

Doctor Sibley Augustine. Gust — that worked. The letters D.S., too. Leo felt his pulse quicken as he reached deeper into the doctor's background. Sibley Augustine, M.D., was no longer in practice. No current address. The good doctor appeared to have been legitimate at one time, though, having established his practice in 2115, thirty-two years earlier. An old timer. That office was long since closed, his medical and business licenses having lapsed twelve years ago. Probably due to a lack of patients. Sick people were in short supply these days, at least physically, and those who did fall ill usually put their trust in machine physicians. Most human doctors were just glorified drug pushers or sadboy enablers. It seemed Augustine was no different. There was a legal ding on his record sixteen years ago for illegal modding: reflex enhancement. A second infraction more recently, eight years ago, after his license had lapsed. They were both minor offenses, but it meant Augustine had some experience with sadboys. He hadn't been in trouble since, though. No sign of him at all. No death notice. No new office. No home address. Sidney Augustine had dropped off the face of the earth.

Just like Lanson Stroud.

Leo exhaled deeply, rubbing the ache from his eyes, knowing the real pain was far behind them, in the brain tissue around his Link chip. If the WinkLink couldn't help him, he would have to rely on other methods. When Waterbird worked a case, he never returned to the precinct until the suspect was in custody. The machine stayed on the street. Then that's what Leo would do. Dr. Augustine had been okay with modifying people…so Leo would go to the people who liked to be modified.

———

"Ear protection is highly recommended for all visitors," the desk machine said. "Would you care for some, Officer?"

"Yes, thank you."

The ramper pushed a pair of thick liquid-graphene ear-coverings across the desk. Leo took the device, understanding the need for it. He was at The Mirabilis Center for Wonderful Health. Known as the GHC. Also known as the Scream House. This was where the machines kept all the broken people that couldn't be fixed. Those with minds and bodies permanently damaged by severe over-modification. These poor souls were not yet full-sadboys, but too far gone to return to society. Their anguished cries, from suffering both physical and emotional, were constant and deafening. Even here in the visitor's lobby you could hear the cries from the inner depths of the living quarters. Leo was grateful for the dense silence of the ear-guards as he waited for the machine escort to arrive.

"Officer Song, I am Doctor Fineday, how do you do?"

The machine's voice came through the ear-guard's speakers sharp and clear. The lack of outside background noise made the artificial voice seem thin and unnatural. Leo could even detect the minor electric hiss behind the words, inaudible in any other circumstance.

"Thank you for meeting me, Doctor."

"Of course, but I do not understand to the purpose of your visit. You wish to speak with a patient here?"

"That's right. I'm following up on an old case involving a human physician, a Dr. Sibley Augustine. He may have installed some mods on a few of your patients some years ago. I'd like to follow up."

"I'm afraid the name Sibley Augustine does not appear on any of our patient records. No one here has mentioned this man during the course of their therapy."

"Well, that's good to know, thank you, but I'd still like to speak to someone if I could. You never know what could help."

"Which patient do you wish to see?"

"That's where it gets tricky. I'm not sure. I know Augustine operated between twelve and eight years ago, and dealt in physical mods mostly. Reflexes, strength boosters, things like that. That's about as much as I can narrow it down."

The machine said nothing for so long Leo worried his earguards had malfunctioned. Fineday was a short model, maybe five foot six, all soft edges and gentle angles, panels painted a soothing shade of taupe. Fineday was designed to be as non-threatening as possible, but Leo was getting a bad feeling from the ramper.

"Is this is an official investigation you are working on, Officer?"

Leo could hear the doubt in the machine's voice. Defensiveness. Maybe even a hint of disdain. Or was he just projecting his own human fears?

"It's an official case, Doctor, but I'm here for my own edification. You see, I may have made a mistake and I'd like try and fix it." The truth without the truth. Appealing to the sympathy of rampers was the only angle you could play with them. Sometimes it worked, sometimes it didn't. Medical machines were designed to be more empathetic than most, but this particular one seemed like a harder sell. He couldn't hear it, but he knew Fineday was buzzing away like mad. Searching Leo's files, his certs, his fitness reports, maybe even contacting the precinct. It's possible Fineday was talking to Mrs. Greenfields that very second, inquiring about the oddball human police officer working cases on his own. And that would be the end of it.

Then Fineday spoke. "There are two patients here that may fit your parameters, Officer. Although I'm sure you are aware many of the people have severe cognitive limitations."

"I understand."

"Please note that I will be present at all times and your interview will be recorded."

"Yes, that's fine." He wasn't sure if it was fine, but he didn't have a choice.

"A room is being prepared. Follow me, please."

The small room was off a short hallway close to the main lobby. The walls were covered with what looked like thick circular padding. There was a small table at the center of the room with two chairs on either side, which were also padded. The walls, floors, and furniture were all similar shades of a deep reddish-brown that reminded Leo of tree bark. The woods. Nature. Light coming from two blue-filtered ceiling units was low and gentle and it wasn't long before Leo began to feel drowsy. He guessed that was the intended effect.

Only a few minutes passed before the first patient was led into the room by a machine identical to Dr. Fineday.

"Melvin Raddish is here," said this new machine.

"Thank you, Doctor Sweetbloom," said Fineday. "Melvin, would you sit down for us please?"

Melvin Raddish sat across from Leo, but the man might as well have been on the moon. He wore similar ear-guards to the ones Leo had on, only larger and anchored in place with wires attached to his jaw. Leo wore them to prevent minor hearing loss and emotional distress, but for patients like Melvin the need was tenfold. The mods had made Melvin hyper-sensitive — that had been the point, after all — but now the slightest discomfort could send him into uncontrollable fits. The ear-guards were probably never removed from his head. Melvin's eyes, however, had been left uncovered. Leo figured this was because Melvin had no eyes. Instead, in the place where his eyes should have been, were two green metal squares as dull as old nail heads. Probably full-spectrum light sensors, thought Leo. The world in a trillion colors invisible to normal humans. He also wore the permanent grimace of an early-stage sadboy, a deforming rictus that drew his lips away from eternally clenched teeth. When Melvin spoke — if he spoke — the sound would come from the voice-slats that lined his neck like fish gills. Melvin had gotten farther down the road of artificial enhancement than most, almost to the verge of the mid-stage transformation.

Leo heard Fineday in his ears. "Mr. Raddish has been with us for ten years now, which makes him very special."

The machine meant that most patients died after a few years in the Scream House. That wasn't the ramper's fault. They did everything they could to help these people, but the strain of living was almost always too much for the patients to bear.

"He, uh, he can hear me?"

"Yes. Mr. Raddish can actually read the vibrations of your voice on the air. It is quite unique, although precautions must be taken. We removed his eye-coverings for this meeting."

"Uh-huh." Leo thought the machine almost sounded impressed.

"He can hear you normally as well."

"Mr. Raddish, my name is Leo Song. I'm a police officer. I'd like to ask you a few questions, if that's okay?"

Melvin made no response. Leo continued.

"Do you remember who helped you install your modifications?"

A guttural snarl erupted from Melvin's narrow voice-slots, but they produced no decipherable words.

"Do you know a man named Sibley Augustine? Doctor Sibley Augustine?"

"no." The voice was thin and metallic. Less human-sounding than any ramper Leo had ever heard. "i have always been as i am."

"Do you know anyone else — a friend, maybe — who might have gone to a doctor for help enhancing themselves?"

"i am beautiful."

"Mr. Raddish, can you tell me who helped you become beautiful?"

"i am beautiful. i see much. i see everything. i am beautiful."

"Mr. Raddish, I don't think you understand–"

Fineday chirped in Leo's ears again. "We must be protective of Mr. Raddish's positive state of mind, Officer Song. He has worked very hard with his counselors to achieve such wonderful self-affirmations."

"i am beautiful."

"Yes, Melvin," said Fineday. "You are very beautiful."

Leo looked at Fineday. "Is that all he's going to say?"

"I advised you of the challenges you faced here, Officer Song. Shall we try the next patient?"

"I guess we should."

"Thank you, Mr. Raddish. You have been very helpful."

"i see everything...and i am beautiful..."

The other machine entered and escorted Melvin Raddish from the room, leaving Leo alone with the machine doctor.

"Officer Song, I am sorry to say that the next patient will likely not be as cooperative as Mr. Raddish."

"Tell me, Doctor, do you drug them?

"Only to prevent violent behavior. It does not affect their cognitive abilities."

"Because their minds are already gone?"

"Yes, for many that is unfortunately the case."

Leo shook his head. He had wasted his time coming here. He was about to tell Fineday to cancel the next interview when the door opened and the patient entered. Leo felt the blood drain from his face when he saw her. She looked no more than thirty years old, normal in every way save for her face. Her nose, mouth, jaw, and throat were missing, replaced by a milky-white prosthetic. Her eyes, though, were her own — and bright with terror. She stared at Leo as if he was death itself.

"Monica, it's okay. It is safe here. Please sit down."

Monica took short, halting steps towards the table. When she sat down Leo could see the muscles in her neck through the plastic. The esophagus and larynx. Her nasal passages. Leo took a deep breathe to keep himself from retching, all the while her natural eyes staring at him, glistening with fear.

"This is Monica Albright. She came here eight years ago as she is now. Monica suffers from an acute phobia of germs, hence her rather alarming facial augmentation — an air filtration system, or so she was told. In truth it does nothing of the kind. Like so many others, Monica was the victim of a pitiless deception. People can be so cruel, if you don't mind me saying."

Leo looked at Fineday. "She doesn't have a tongue and I don't see any voicecoders. How is she supposed to talk to me?"

"There are binary signal-lights in her central prosthesis, where her mouth would normally be located. Green for 'yes', red for 'no'. I will translate the more complex responses for you."

Leo turned to face Monica, smiling as warmly as he could. He was reminded of the Historian he had talked to in the Canyons. Two women, one perfectly at home living in filth and sewage, the other thrown into panic by a sneeze, both with the same fear in their eyes. He was beginning to take it personally. Leo had managed to earn the Historian's trust, but mainly because Bluebreeze's rigid ineptitude had cast the human as the good guy. He had no such foil here. Fineday was a people's ramper if there ever was one. And Monica Albright had deeper problems than simply wanting to dig through garbage all day.

"Monica, I need to ask you some questions, okay? Some questions about what happened to you. Is that okay with you?"

A light behind the translucent face plate flashed green.

"Did a doctor help you with your, uh…did a doctor do this?"

The green signal flashed.

"Do you remember the doctor's name?"

The red light blinked once.

"Are you sure? I need you to think for me."

Red.

"Did the doctor's name begin with the letter *b*?"

The red and green lights flashed at the same time.

Leo looked at Finefriend. "Is that a maybe?"

"Very good, Officer."

Leo asked Monica, "Was the doctor's name Augustine? Sibley Augustine?"

Red and green.

Leo leaned forward, offering assurance in his most trustworthy voice. "You don't have to protect anyone, Monica. I only want to speak with him."

The lights began flashing rapidly. Red-green-green-red-green-green-red-red-red…

Fineday spoke. "She needs you to sit back, Officer Song. You are too close to her."

Leo quickly leaned back. "I'm sorry…"

Monica's signal-lights continued to flash.

"Yes, I see," Fineday said.

"What?"

"Monica says she would never protect the man who did this to her, but she does not remember his name."

The lights went on blinking.

"What's she saying now?"

"She forgives him. She says that Annie worked very hard to bring Monica to a place where she was able to forgive, and she has."

"Who is Annie?"

"She is referring to Annie Sinclair, Monica's former emotional support counselor. They worked together for several months after Monica first arrived here. The early results were very promising, but plateaued quickly. Sadly, that is common."

"A support counselor? I didn't think humans were allowed to work here."

"On the contrary, Officer Song, human counselors are vital to our success. Although, due to the stressful environment, they are kept on a strict part-time schedule. Annie Sinclair was one of the longest tenured counselors we have ever had. She helped many people. She was also Melvin Raddish's counselor for a time and made good progress with him as well."

"Annie Sinclair worked with both of these patients?"

"Yes. Like Monica, Melvin was very fond of her. They both miss Annie a great deal. However, I'm sorry to say that Annie Sinclair has not worked with us in over six years. She was of an advanced age and could no longer perform her duties without risk to her own health."

"Sure..." A detail clicked into place in Leo's mind. Lanson Stroud had been an emotional support counselor, too. Only for a year, because he'd burned out fast. Unusually fast. If any place could do that, it was the Scream House. "Doctor Fineday, did a man named Lanson Stroud ever work here?"

Dr. Fineday buzzed for a split second and then said "No."

"Do you have Annie Sinclair's current address? I'd like to speak with her."

"It is a matter of public record, Officer."

"Yeah, I haven't had much luck with those recently. Do me a favor?"

"Annie Sinclair lives at 112 North Verdant Avenue."

"Verdant?" Tabitha Jackson had written *112 V* on the back of the photoscan. V for Verdant? "Are you sure that's the right address?"

"That is what is on file."

"That's on the west side of the city, isn't it?"

"Yes, Officer, that is correct. Only a twenty minute travel time via public transportation. Are we finished speaking with Monica? She does not look well."

"Yeah, thanks, Doctor. We're done."

[16]

12 North Verdant Ave was a crosstown trip, so Leo used the time to lookup Annie Sinclair's history. The records said Annie was currently one hundred and twenty two years old, someone who had known the world before the second epoch. A world when human beings still controlled their own destiny. When they still shaped the course of history. She was a living relic the Historians down in the Canyons would have murdered each other for. It was her building he was heading to now. The address Leo had was registered to her for over fifty years. Over the course of her long life, Annie had been an attorney, a journalist, a school teacher, and a computer programmer ...the familiar path of someone trying to find a career free of machine dominance. It was not to be. None of those professions existed for humans anymore. They hadn't for decades. Her most recent work experience had been as an emotional counselor. She had done that job for an astounding run of thirty-six years. Annie Sinclair had found her place at the age of eighty, retiring only seven years ago, when she had turned one hundred and fifteen. An interesting person, thought Leo with a pang of jealousy. Nobody got to be interesting anymore.

He wondered if Annie's long, curious life had led her across the paths of Sibley Augustine or Lanson Stroud. The coincidences were too great. She must have known one or both.

112 North Verdant was an eight block walk from the station. Leo was still four blocks away. As he approached the first cross street, Leo heard a lone shout in the distance. A loud, defiant cry, followed by a group cheer. He looked down the street to his right, in time to see a body dropping from the top of a building, plummeting towards an eager crowd waiting below. A creative taking the jump. The creative's messy demise was met with polite applause that lasted a few seconds, after which the crowd dispersed as the human clean-up crew, already waiting, removed the body. As a policeman, Leo was duty-bound to offer his assistance, but he ducked around the corner and jogged away from the scene in a hurry. That was a suicide. He was chasing a murderer.

Annie Sinclair's building was a two floor faux-Spanish villa in keeping with the neighborhood style. Most of the north side of the city was an old-world aesthetic, too fancy for Leo's tastes. It was popular with older people, though. Not a lot of crime on the north side. Not a lot of action, either. A good place to hide an underground clinic, thought Leo. He examined the front of the personal castle, not as impressed at it was obviously intended to make him. The dun colored exterior was immaculately weathered, making it difficult to tell if the structure was abandoned or not. The windows were dark, but not dusty, and several of the other homes on the block looked occupied. Lights in the windows. The faint smell of food. It could go either way. He knocked on the heavy front door, banging with his fist three times, waiting, then banging three times more. No answer. It took one swipe of his skeleton card to solve the code-scrambler. An old lock. Whoever lived here wasn't paranoid like Tabitha Jackson. The door unlatched smoothly. Leo paused, then entered the house.

There was no response when he called out from the vestibule.

He listened, but there was no sound. Auto-lights came on as he walked from room to room, illuminating the sparse furnishings with a pale blue glow. Everything appeared well-maintained, but there was a mustiness to the air, a rotted smell that grew worse as he walked to the second floor.

He found Annie Sinclair in the second bedroom, a shriveled, stinking thing in a moldy velvet chair. She was still alive, but it was an unnatural life. The old woman had been modded out as grotesquely as any sadboy. Worse than her charges at the hospital. Her artificial lungs were exposed on the outside of her desiccated chest. Her eyes had been replaced with orange-lensed scopes now cloudy with age. A wheezing intake snout occupied the space where her mouth had once been. Synthetic muscle augmentations slithered like worms under skin as fragile as autumn leaves. The body-mods looked operational. Robust. Well-maintained. She could probably exist for another decade like this, thought Leo, but why would anyone wish to?

"Mrs. Sinclair?"

She didn't move. Leo doubted she would ever move again. Her brain was probably mush by now, just a cortex and some infernal life-tech that kept her breathing. No consciousness. No mind. That's what he hoped, anyway, but it was impossible to tell for certain. He wondered if she had been forced into this, kept on the edge of eternal life by someone else…perhaps so the house stayed registered in her name. What a cruel thing if true. Then again, maybe she had done it to herself willingly? People made odd choices once they felt death closing in on them, especially those from Annie's generation. They fought for life harder than younger people. Annie's choice or not, whoever had committed her to this existence was a true believer in the theory of upgradable human beings. And they'd had practice. Expertise. The mods had been installed by expert hands. Sibley Augustine was just the right age to be such a believer. Body tech would have peaked when he had been a young man and the promise of a bright future free of human limitations probably still burned in his imagination. Leo drew his Vampire. This lonely, dark house was precisely the kind of place where sadboys were made.

This was the kind of place where men like Leo died ugly deaths.

He moved slowly, listening for any sounds, watching for movement in the shadows, but the main house was empty. By the time Leo discovered the vault in the lower floors, he was confident he was alone. The heavy steel door was in the back of the basement, sloppily embedded into the old foundational wall. No attempt had been made to conceal its presence, but it was obvious visitors were not welcome. The series of three DNA based code-scramblers that made up the door's hyper-advanced locking system almost made Leo give up without trying...but something caught his attention. The inputs shimmered a vivid green — a sign they were in their pre-programmed state.

The door wasn't locked.

He pressed the release.

The body hit the floor with a dry thud and Leo had to breathe through his mouth to keep from vomiting. The advanced decay suggested the man had been dead for several weeks at least. Possibly months. There were skin deposits on the opposite side of the door where the body had been. Whoever this was had died trying to open the door. Quite a nasty trick had been played on this person, thought Leo. Someone had cleared the outside locks while the man had been inside the vault. When the unknowing prisoner had attempted to open the door, he would have found his DNA swipe did nothing. He had been purposefully entombed. Leo wondered if it had been the final act of the woman upstairs — the revenge of Annie Sinclair. There was no way to tell, but whoever had cleared the locks hadn't been worried about anyone else coming along afterwards. They knew the household routine, the victim's habits, his schedule. They had known no one would come looking for him. This was a murder.

Careful not to touch the body, Leo propped the door open with a heavy chair and entered the vault. An overhead lamp blinked on, casting the room in a warm, friendly light that made a decent impression of sunshine. The vault was a shrine to antiquity, filled with analog gadgets and physical filing systems fifty years old or more. A piece of paper in a metal box — that was the way you kept a secret in the modern age, thought Leo. And this room was a trove of secrets. A long work desk that ran along the back wall was strewn with hand-drawn schematics that looked to Leo like designs for medical devices. They were well drawn but confusing, far beyond Leo's technical understanding. They could be the ravings of a lunatic for all he knew. What caught his attention more, however, was the medical file at the center of the desk. The name on the tab read: Tabitha Jackson. It was waiting there like a gift.

Leo looked behind him, overcome with a sudden paranoia. He looked at the body propped against the door...it had to be Dr. Augustine. Obviously, the doctor had been reading Tabitha Jackson's file when he had been condemned to his slow death. The killer had most likely been involved in the death of Tabitha Jackson as well. He didn't think a sadboy would be subtle enough to pull the stunt with the door locks, so there was a second murderer out there. A human. Leo listened to the house, straining to hear the slightest noise. Nothing. Satisfied he was alone, he began flipping through the pages in Tabitha's file, using his Wink-Link to translate whatever medical jargon he came across.

Tabitha Jackson *had* been pregnant.

There had been difficulties...a lot of them.

Augustine had been feeding Tabitha a laundry list of drugs to help with what the notes described as 'atypically acute morning sickness'. Every medication he had seen in the shoebox and more. Another scratchy note described concern that the nausea and pain had not subsided and instead grown worse. Tabitha had expressed increasing fears over her condition, but she had not sought help outside of Dr. Augustine. Why go to an unlicensed doctor at all? Perhaps these visits had been the influence of the boyfriend…but which one…old or new?

Leo flipped to next page in the file.

Personal contacts.

Listed below Tabitha's name was the name of the father: L. Stroud.

Lanson Stroud.

A note was scribbled beside Lanson Stroud's name: *estranged. (see file).*

Leo looked over to the tall metal filing cabinet in the corner, knowing he would find a folder like this one for Lanson Stroud inside.

For the moment, he kept turning through Tabitha's records.

Under the pages at the back of the Tabitha's file, Leo found another plastic photoscan. He compared it to the one in his pocket — apart from minor differences in the color patterns, the images were nearly identical. He flipped the new photoscan over. On the back, written in big black letters, were two simple words:

KILL IT

[17]

Faro Benson adjusted his seat cushion, shifting it left, then forward, then back again, trying to find the best angle. It was an endless and futile struggle. The autovan's only human seat was plush and highly ergonomic, but Faro was a big man, well outside the median height and weight ranges the machines designed for, so the chair was murder on his back. It didn't help that the work shift was close to ending and they were still on the job. Faro could feel his usual day's-end irritableness setting in and he thought about apologizing in advance before he started to complain.

"It's too late for a run," he said, without the disclaimer. "I'm off in half an hour. They should've shifted in somebody else"

"Your patience is greatly appreciated, Officer Benson," said Mr. Smallfoot from the controller's position in front of Faro's chair.

Faro let out a mirthless grumble. "I'm *not* being patient, Mr. Smallfoot, that's my whole point. I shouldn't have to be patient. More than four hours in this shit chair, I can barely walk. You know this."

"The additional personalized cushion does not help?"

"No…a little. Not enough."

"This will be our final run, Officer Benson."

Faro made another grumbling noise and looked out the view bubble at the police station. Gaudy, he thought. The bright blue and red walls sloping up at those ridiculous angles. The spiraling columns of watery glass. A police station shouldn't look like this. A police station should be hard. Solid. Austere bordering on ugly. But the rampers liked gaudy things, didn't they? They were gaudy things themselves. Faro looked down at the loading ramp that led to the back of the truck, but didn't see anyone coming.

"Taking their time about it, aren't they?" Then he saw them and felt like a fool.

They were emerging from the shadows of the entrance tunnel: three police rampers. Big ones. The center machine was carrying a large metal box almost half the size of its own bulky torso. Even from that distance Faro could tell that the size of the box was going to be a problem, but he surveyed the truck's cargo hold to be sure.

"That thing isn't going to fit."

"Then make space, please," said Mr. Smallfoot. "Quickly, please."

Faro got up from the seat and began re-arranging the boxes already stacked in the cargo area. A full day of picking up items from the various police station across Mirabilis had left precious little room for anything of size. Stacking boxes was Faro's work, and he was good at it. He took pains to get the organization right, in order of delivery route, drop-off priority and time schedule. He felt he was as efficient as any machine at his job and it irked him that he now had to destroy his careful planning to accommodate a last minute pick-up that wasn't even on the itinerary.

"What's the drop-off? First, last, somewhere in-between?"

"This will be our priority," answered Smallfoot. "Security storage."

"Aw!" The secured evidence warehouse was on the other side

of the city, the highest point north. Almost off the map. "That's two hours just to get there...and then the rest of these after... that's another half shift, Mr. Smallfoot. At least."

"Help load this delivery and then you can go for the day, Officer Benson."

Faro stopped in the middle of lifting a heavy box, staring at Smallfoot's featureless backplate . "Really?"

"Yes. Your assistance will not be required beyond this point."

He'd never been dismissed before. That irked him, too. "Well, but I could ju–"

Faro's face smashed into the side of the metal lockbox he held in his arms. His front teeth shattered, the broken edges slicing into a tongue that was still trying to make words. He was swallowing blood before he hit the floor.

Why am I on my ass, Faro asked himself.

It was too loud in the truck. His vision was blurry with tears. Smallfoot was shouting something at him, but he didn't understand what the ramper was saying through the noise. He tasted blood. When he spat, small pieces of teeth tore the inside of his throat. *What an imbecile*, he thought, *I swallowed my own teeth.* There was a stinging pain in his arm, too. He looked down and saw white bone. *Funny...it poked right through the sleeve.* There was screaming, terrible screaming, and Faro became embarrassed that he sounded so weak. So cowardly. When he tried to shut himself up, he realized the screaming wasn't coming from him. Shame curdled into to terror. He tried to speak but the words came out bloody and useless.

"Smuufugh...whuffussagh!"

Then he heard Smallfoot. Heard what the machine had been saying all this time.

"Officer, fire your weapon! Fire your weapon!"

That didn't make any sense to Faro. *The ramper malfunctioned,* he thought. *The idiot machine lost its mind and crashed the vehicle.*

"Run, Officer Benson! Run! Run for your life!"

Faro turned his head towards Smallfoot but he didn't understand what he was looking at. Arms were reaching into the van. Arms as thick as his own legs. Hands wider than his chest, fingers like screwdrivers grabbing at Smallfoot. The machine didn't make a sound as it was torn from its anchorage. Ripped in half. Blue-green fluid sprayed the across windshield and the roof and on Faro. He didn't know machines had so much liquid inside of them. *Warm as blood,* he thought. Faro stared at the empty space where Mr. Smallfoot had just been. His mind was empty of direction. What was he supposed to do? The machine had told him to use his weapon…Faro reached for the Vampire at his hip, crying out as nauseating pain shot through him. *Your arm is busted, stupid.* The machine had told him to run. He could do that. His legs still worked. With his left hand, Faro reached for the rear door release and the double doors swung open.

The wail of the police station's claxon alarm seared the air. Faro paused at the back of the van, scanning for danger or for help. Below him the ramp was covered in machine parts and fluid. Blue, green, orange, mixing together. The colors made him feel sick. He didn't see the machines. *Add up all the pieces, would it make three rampers,* he wondered. He could hear violence, though. Very close. Just on the other side of the open doors. He heard the electrical hiss of a shock gun. Those awful animal screams. Shattering metal. All so close. He saw more machines coming out of the station. Ten of them, maybe more. They were at the top of the ramp, rolling fast, but still too far to save him. Faro wanted to close the doors and bury himself under the fallen boxes until it was safe to come out. Until the rampers fought the sadboys off. But Smallfoot had told him to run, so he ran. He jumped to the ground, his broken arm dangling at his side, banging against his hip as he sprinted up the ramp. He tried to ignore the pain. Faro knew he was a slow runner, a heavy man, but he kept his eyes on the small army of machines coming towards him. He only had to get close to them. Inside the range of their shock guns. He would survive then. They would protect him. That was their job. But they weren't moving fast enough. They didn't seem to be getting closer at all. *Why are they going so slow,* he wondered, *Can't they see me?* There was a heavy sound behind him. He saw the shadow on the ground, covering his own. Swallowing it up, twice the size. He felt the screwdriver fingers on his head. Digging into his skull. Killing him. He felt air fill his lungs, preparing for a scream that never came.

$$[\ 18\ ]$$

This time Aida was not waiting in her doorway as Leo returned home. He didn't bother knocking on her door, didn't even pause, figuring she was still sleeping off that morning's Sunwater disaster. It was a minor miracle he was still on his feet himself. The events of the past nine hours was catching up to him in a hurry and he was ready to take the machines' advice: rest. A long, deep rest. But the weight of the thick paper file he carried told him it wasn't going to happen.

He spread the files out on his kitchen table, not wanting to risk falling asleep in the comfort of the living room couch. The good news was that Doctor Augustine had kept detailed notes tracking Tabitha Jackson's pregnancy. The bad news was that half of them were made in a tight cursive handwriting Leo found to be nearly impossible to read. Focusing on what he could make out easily, Leo searched the files for anything of interest.

He found it on the first page.

The dates of Tabitha's pregnancy ran fourteen months. Leo was no expert on the subject, but he knew that wasn't possible. He scanned for any mention of breaks in the timeline; false starts, a miscarriage, anything that would explain the year and a half pregnancy. There was nothing. The chart was unbroken. At the time of her death Tabitha Jackson had been fourteen months pregnant.

Leo paused to consider the implications. If it was true, how had no one noticed she was pregnant? Tabitha's neighbors were typically reclusive, but no one was that oblivious.

He turned the page and was confronted with a block of dense handwriting. It took him several minutes to understand that he was looking at a list of Tabitha Jackson's health problems during the pregnancy. It was a map of unimaginable suffering. Tabitha's complications had grown steadily over the first eight months of her pregnancy. As the pain became increasingly unbearable, Augustine had given her greater amounts of medication. Obscure drugs Leo couldn't find descriptions for in the Link. He guessed Augustine had made them himself. In addition to the custom-made medication, physical treatments were given. Sound therapy. Genetic boosters to strengthen both mother and child. Digitally assisted meditation. None of it worked. Despite that, at no point, apparently, did Tabitha Jackson consider terminating the pregnancy. Then, a little after the twelfth month, two months before her murder, Tabitha reported herself completely pain free. Her state of mind had also improved. Dramatically and almost overnight. Augustine's notes described her as being in a state of "sustained natural euphoria." This after more than a full year of pregnancy.

Leo felt his head begin to ache. He continued through the file. Four pages he found Lanson Stroud. A photoscan showed a handsome young man smiling at whoever had taken the picture. It was a memory capture, probably Tabitha's. It was a moment of happiness. The next images showed no such joy. Five clinical photoscans charted the transformation of Lanson Stroud from normal young man into a mid-stage sadboy. The final image was barely recognizable as a human being. From then on his transformation had been dangerously rapid, conducted under the supervision of Dr. Sibley Augustine. Eye sensors, strength mods, bone replacement, neural netting, the number of modifications was staggering. The speed with which they were done seemed reckless to the point of insanity. Sadboys were created over years, not months. It was a wonder Lanson had survived the experience. If he *had* survived. The semi-human in these pictures might very well be lying dead in a back-alley somewhere, a pile of rusted scrap and rotting meat.

Leo flipped through the rest of the pages, hoping to find something that could re-establish Lanson Stroud's trail, but there was little he didn't already know. No whereabouts. No occupation. No WinkLink code. Just more nothing. But Waterbird had confirmed Lanson Stroud's current place of work. If Stroud was a sadboy and alive, he wouldn't be working anywhere. He'd be hiding, or killing people. As unlikely as it seemed, Waterbird had been deceived. Someone had lied to a machine.

The pain in Leo's head became too great to ignore. Leaving the files where they were, he slid off the kitchen stool and limped towards the bedroom shower.

He wasn't surprised to find he was bruised, only that there were so many of them. His left arm was sore and red and made a nasty sound when he tried to bend it. A long, wide mark ran from his upper chest to his lower hip and was turning a sinister shade of purple. His legs were scratched and mottled with more purple and blue spots...but his feet, his new Celwax feet, were a bright, healthy pink up to the shins. The water made the fresh, ultra-healthy skin look like one of the phony rubber appliances the machines liked to wear. He wiggled his toes. Real enough. The water felt hot and good, helping to relieve some of the headache that had overtaken him. The information in Augustine's files was disturbing — if that was the word — but nothing pointed directly to a reason for murder or helped explain what happened to

Waterbird. He hoped Nyla would have more useful information when he met her later. He checked the time. It was six-thirty, early enough to lay down for half an hour before he had to head towards the Lubitsch theater.

The bed filled his blurred vision from across the room, the boundless surface summoning him with promises of perfect, dreamless sleep. He was halfway there when something made him stop. A sound from another room. The scrape of paper on paper.

He waited. The telltale sound did not repeat. But he was sure he'd heard it.

Leo dressed quickly, took his Vampire from the holster and moved slowly towards the living area, his new feet impressively quiet on the wood floor.

He found Aida in the living room, staring out the grand window as Mirabilis burned in the fiery reflection of the setting sun. Her silhouette cut a sorrowful pose against the burning orange light and she did not turn around when she spoke.

"I let myself, hope you don't mind. You haven't changed your codes."

"Aida...." Leo glanced at the file on the kitchen table. He couldn't tell if she had gone through them, but thought it was a safe bet. "What's going on?"

"Those papers over there, that's for your case?"

"It is."

"So you're back on track with everything? Waterbird isn't disappointed?"

"Not exactly. Things have gotten complicated. Waterbird was ambushed in the Canyons. It happened when we were passed out."

Aida let out a deep groan that trailed off into a deeper silence. After a long moment at the window she asked, "What's the record for a creative? A jump, I mean, how high is the record?"

"I'd have to look it up."

She flicked her left hand, plucking the answer out of the air. "Sixty stories — not as high as this. Not nearly so high." Her head moved slightly as she scanned the skyline. "This isn't even the tallest one."

"Sequoia Tower on the north side is the tallest, I think. Four hundred stories or something."

"Four hundred." Her shoulders jerked as she let out a sharp laugh. "Does anyone know how any of this works anymore? Have you ever met anyone who did?"

"A person? I'm sure there's someone. There has to be."

"No there doesn't."

She still wasn't facing Leo. He wasn't sure why, but he hadn't moved closer to her. It didn't seem like a good idea.

"Anvi Raghavan," she said. "Do you know who that is?"

"Sounds familiar, but no."

"You should know, Leo. She was the last human being to be a police detective — I looked it up the other night after you told me what you and Waterbird were planning to do. Do you know when that was, when she was alive?"

"It was a long time ago."

"Eight-seven years. Almost a century ago. She died in the line of duty. Assassinated, actually."

"That's terrible."

"Anvi Raghavan should be a legend for you, but you didn't even know her name."

"I said it sounded familiar."

Aida turned around, the familiar mixture of rage and despair in her face. "You don't know because it doesn't *matter*. It doesn't matter what she did or that she lived at all." She looked back out the window. "I always thought creatives were just stupid, weak, but I see it now...why there are so many of them."

"Aida, what's going on?"

"I'm sorry about what happened this morning. I promise I didn't know that stuff would be so powerful."

"You said that before, don't worry about it. What happened?"

"After you left the supervisors called us back in, but it was only to...I thought I was doing something *good*, Leo, but it turns out they don't let you, do they? Or don't care. Not unless..." She stopped suddenly, a look of horror coming over her. "You said Waterbird was ambushed? Is he okay?"

Leo shook his head. "They can't find his nexus...or much at all"

Aida closed her eyes and wrapped her arms around herself as tightly as she could. "I know you must hate me, but I need to be here right now. I need to stay here...just for a little bit. Just to get my head clear."

"Stay as long as you want."

She opened her eyes, sad blue diamonds cutting through Leo. "What is it?"

"I can't stay, I have to, uh...."

"The case?"

"Yeah. Meeting someone." He knew Aida was coming with him. They both did.

"Where?"

"Maybe it's not the best place for you right now."

"Where, Leo?"

"The Lubitsch."

Aida groaned again, somehow managing to hug herself tighter.

$$[\ 19\ ]$$

You could feel the Lubitsch six blocks before you saw it. The ground trembled with music and noise, the vibrations tuning you up in advance. Located on the corner of Ethaline and 1005th Street, the domed building was the screaming heart of what remained of Mirabilis's nightlife. The Lubitsch, considered at one time a modest venue, had been built as a shrine to the ancient performing arts the human species once cherished so dearly. For a brief moment, music, cinema, plays, displays of fine art, video game competitions, all lived under The Lubitsch's famous rotating dome. But as the value and meaning of those arts mutated and decayed over the years, the Great Theater, once so noble of intent, was steadily degraded by boredom and resentment, eventually becoming what it was now — a mock playhouse of frantic, overwrought absurdities.

Leo hated it.

He and Aida moved through the crowd outside The Lubitsch's main entrance. It was the typical gathering: filthy scabbers hoping to reignite their damp souls, ranting Godmen tut-tutting their half-baked chastisements, the salivating orgos there to mock-fornicate with each other, the ghostly limbos observing it all from safe distances. Inside the theater would be the nightdancers and the chippers, cut loose and buzzing on Sunwater and illegal pinkwisp, but still on the right side of sanity. All of them were there to witness the nightly pageant put on by creatives about to take the big leap. It was a dizzying spectacle of madness and sorrow, the final howl of life from people who could no longer tolerate it. This was the way suicide notes were written now, not scribbled pages pinned to a lonely door, but a thunderous, sky-rattling frenzy of movement, color and sound. In 2147, it was the best entertainment going.

The narrow, ramper-resistant entrance allowed only one person through at a time, and it took half an hour for both Aida and Leo to make it inside. They moved slowly down the zig-zagging hallway to where it released onto the grand staircase, another marvel of anti-machine design, then took their time negotiating the lunatic angles of each step until at last arriving at the landing of the main hall.

Below them was the crowded dance floor. Directly above the hall was the famous rotating stage, hanging in the center of the great dome like a coin tossed into the air. Currently the stage was occupied by a cadre of burn-drummers, excitedly beating out deep rhythms that took shape in waves of dancing, whirling fire. Leo had seen the act before, it being a popular shtick among less original creatives, and he was never as impressed as others seemed to be. But no matter. Soon the floating stage would rotate to reveal a different act, its players suspended upside down above their audience by magnetic field, creating a strange new ceiling under which to dance and scream. Then another stage would revolve into view, and another again, until the burn-drummers once more took their turn as gods of the moment.

They found Nyla at a small table near the back of the hall. She was staring at the serpents of fire that twisted in complex maneuvers above her head, but her eyes didn't see them. She was focused instead on some distant point beyond the stage. Distracted by her own thoughts.

"Sorry I'm late, Nyla."

Nyla looked at Leo, then at Aida. "Hey," she said flatly. "Who is that?"

"This is my friend Aida. Aida, this is Nyla, she works with me at the precinct."

Nyla and Aida exchanged short hellos as Leo set the heavy paper file on the table in front of Nyla.

"That's what I found. You?"

Nyla, her eyes locked on the file, motioned for them to sit. Aida took the middle chair while Leo sat across from Nyla. In that moment the stage turned, swinging the burn-drummers out of view, replaced by a sky of swirling, multi-hued vortexes that threatened to suck the room up into the ceiling like candy-colored tornadoes. The crowd went wild, and Aida stared up at the ceiling, but Elwood had to look away.

"It's beautiful," said Aida.

Leo winced. "Too much…"

"It's a literal representation," said Nyla.

"Of what?" asked Aida.

"What you see when you die, apparently."

Elwood chanced another look at the giant spinning vortex, but all he could see was a storm of haphazard color. Whoever had made it was talking crap, he thought. Creatives would say anything for the sake of drama.

"It's not my favorite," she said. "The best one, I think, is this Nostro band coming up. They're dressed up in tuxedoes and playing real instruments. You'll see. They're good if you're into the old stuff, but nobody tonight seems to be. It's the one after this. Apparently they're all going to jump tomorrow at the same time."

Aida laughed. "A group splat. I wonder if they'll take their instruments with them." She laughed again. A cold laugh full of idle cruelty. "Can you imagine the sound that'll make?"

Nyla looked at Leo, her eyes wide and questioning. Leo opened his hands to advocate a little patience. She nodded with a frown and muted the Lubitsch's music signal for herself. Leo did the same. Without the music from the overhead shows, the sound of the crowd was minimal. The stomping of feet on the dance floor and a few scattered conversations was all they were left to contend with.

"I see you've been busy," Nyla said, looking at the stack of papers between them. "What is this?"

"In a second. You first — anything about the pregnancy book?"

Nyla shook her head. "Just an old medical book. Nothing special about it I could find. The woman who wrote it has been dead for a century. Sorry, Leo. I did find something out about talking sadboys."

"Then tell me about that."

"Well, there are no official records anywhere of a sadboy being able to speak. Most experts think sadboys don't have the ability to communicate at all, that they're too damaged. Their modified brains are constantly misfiring."

"No points for the experts. The sadboy I met today sure had a lot to say."

Aida glanced at Leo, then returned her attention to the ceiling.

"You heard it?" asked Nyla. "What did it say?"

"Nothing that made sense. It was as crazy as you'd expect, but it talked."

"You can't...um...you shouldn't call sadboys crazy or insane. It's not fair. It's not accurate."

"What does that mean?"

"None of the treatments that work on human mental illness do anything at all for sadboys. But at the same time, they show symptoms of practically every mental illness in the book."

"So they aren't crazy, but they are the most crazy?"

"I wish you wouldn't use that word, but yes, in a way that's true. For example, they aren't schizophrenic, but they have symptoms that *resemble* schizophrenia. Because of what they've done to themselves, what the technology has done to them, their perception and senses have been stretched far beyond what humans beings are meant to tolerate. They don't experience the world like we do anymore, Leo. Simply looking at a flower can make them sob uncontrollably, right?"

"Or rip a person open with their bare hands. Yeah, I get it, they're moody."

"Because they are seeing things you and I can't even imagine. Every detail, every layer…the world is raw and naked to them and they can't hide from any of it. They're in constant pain. It must be terrible."

"They do it to themselves," Aida muttered.

"So how's this one talking?" asked Leo.

Nyla pulled out her glare at Aida and said, "That's what I'm getting to. A few experts thought sadboys *could* communicate, just not with words anymore. That part of them is gone, burned out by the tech. But what if something else took its place? Some other method of communication. That was the theory anyway. About thirty years ago a small tech lab tried to make vocalizer implants that translated the altered brainwaves of sadboys into traditional English vocabulary, but nobody paid much attention to it. Apparently the machines weren't too keen on the whole concept, which is understandable. Sadboys that can communicate can organize. They can work together. Enough to build something in the Canyons. And it explains how they could attack a police precinct together."

Leo stared at Nyla. "What are you talking about?"

"The attack?" She gaped at him. "Leo, how do you not know?"

"Know *what*? What's with the history quizzes today?"

Nyla shook her head in disbelief. "A group of sadboys attacked a police transport van at the Aberdeen precinct. *Today,* Leo. Two machines were totally destroyed, two damaged...and a human officer was killed. Faro Benson was his name, I think. I didn't know him. Some evidence was stolen, too, apparently, probably the reason for the attack. Leo, how do you not know this? The emergency call was all points. City wide."

Leo sat in bewildered silence. He had received no emergency call. No bulletin or alert had come over his Link. He had been removed from official Police communications and hadn't even realized it.

The overhead stage flipped again and a band of well-dressed musicians spun into view.

Aida let out a cry as they began to play. "Oh! This is what you were talking about! Yeah, I see what you mean, Nyla, they're really interesting!"

Unable to hear the music, they ignored her.

Nyla narrowed her eyes at Leo. "Leo, what's going on? How much trouble are you in?"

He shook his head. "Forget it." He pointed at the file. "See what you can make of this."

Nyla, not needing to be told twice, began looking through the pages, studying the first one carefully but quickly, but not seeing what Leo wanted her to.

"What am I looking at?" she asked.

"Tabitha Jackson's medical files. I found them in a doctor's office, her human doctor."

"Tabitha...she was one of the victims of the double murder?"

"Yeah. But look at the dates."

Nyla searched the page until she found the note on Tabitha's term length. From the way her expression changed, Leo knew she'd had no trouble reading the eccentric handwriting.

"This can't be right," she said. "Fourteen months?"

"That's what I thought, but it's consistent throughout the file. But no one I spoke to knew shew was even carrying a child. How is that possible?"

"I don't know." Nyla flipped through the pages slowly.

As she read, Leo glanced at Aida. Her head was turned up towards the stage, but her eyes were watching Nyla. He was pretty sure she had turned her sound link off as well, but he didn't say anything about it. She need to be here. For as long as he'd known Aida he'd never seen her so miserable. Never knew her to express anything more than mild irritation at anything. But in his apartment she'd had the look of a freefalling scabber. By contrast, Nyla was looking healthier than she had in a long time. She'd even dressed up a little; glittery dress, hair in two puffy balls, some make-up. Mostly though, there was a palpable excitement about her, and Aida had surely picked up on it.

"So," Nyla said after a few minutes. "It says she went to a Family Way Center first, then got involved with this Doctor...Augustine. Have you talked to him?"

"He's dead."

"Oh. That's terrible."

"Pretty sure it's a good thing, actually. Look at these..." Leo pulled Augustine's strange technical drawings out of files and arranged them in front of Nyla. "Do these make any sense to you?"

Nyla stared at each drawing for a long time, face wrinkling at their bizarre descriptions. Aida, for her part, was no longer pretending to be absorbed by the creative displays above their heads. She was blatantly looking at the drawings, too.

Without looking up, Nyla asked Leo, "These are real?"

"I have no idea."

"This one here is maybe a vocalizer? I don't know much tech stuff..."

"Talking sadboys. Maybe meant for this guy?" Leo showed her the photoscans documenting Lanson Stroud's transition into a mid-stage sadboy.

"I — I don't know. Who is he?"

"That's Lanson Stroud. He's the father of Tabitha Jackson's child."

Nyla sat up straight. Her eyes were fixed on Lanson Stroud's photos.

Leo said, "The only question is when Lanson changed over, before or after?"

"No," said Nyla, souring at the notion. "No, that isn't possible. Leo, listen to what you're saying — that's not how it works. There wouldn't be any *child*."

"How can you be sure? We don't know how any of this works." Out the corner of his eye Leo saw Aida nodding almost imperceptibly.

"Yes, we do know," said Nyla, "and it's not possible."

"Nyla–"

Aida silenced the argument by dropping a photoscan on top of the rest of the file. The words KILL IT cutting through the dim, moody light of the stage show.

"Somebody thought it was possible," she said.

Nyla picked up the photoscan, turning to over to the image of Tabitha Jackson's developing fetus. "Why did you have this?" She looked at Aida, then at Leo. "Why does she have this? You showed her the file?"

"I..."

"Oh, stop, it wasn't his fault," Aida said. "I came in — broke in, to be honest — and it was sitting out. Leo was in the shower. He had no idea."

"And you felt entitled to look at it?" asked Nyla. "Because it was just sitting there?"

"I didn't know *what* it was, did I? I still don't, really, but, then, neither do you."

"Hey," Leo said, "it doesn't matter now."

"Leo, she's not in the department. She's not a cop."

Aida sighed and said, "From what I understand, nobody at this table is a cop."

Both Leo and Nyla fell silent again. This time when the stage flipped, it was Leo who watched, his mind needing an immediate escape from the hard truth of Aida's comment. Above, two woman dressed in long yellow gowns stood on opposite ends of a brightly patterned field. They stood in silence for a moment, not moving or speaking, and the clamoring of the audience gradually hushed. Then, breaking the silence, one woman sang a single high note. The note took shape in the air, at first a transparent undulation that arced toward the singer's counterpart. At the peak of the arc the undulation formed into an object, a giant sparrow that swept over the heads of the audience and broke apart in orange ripples around the other woman. Then the response note was sung, a tenor note, harsh and short, that sent a pair of interlocking triangles speeding towards the first singer. And on it went. One beautiful note of graceful, gentle nature, answered by a lower note of angry geometry. Elwood recognized the old woman singing the animals — Tabitha Jackson's neighbor. The other woman must have been Susan, the wife with her incomplete oblongs. He recalled the things she had told him about Tabitha Jackson; that she had been kind, hopeful, and full of life; that for a time she had been in love; that more recently she had been afraid of something.

Leo leaned forward and said, "What I want to know is how Tabitha Jackson got involved with Doctor Augustine. He was a first class creep, but from what I know she wasn't like that. How did their paths cross?"

"Well," Nyla said, re-directing her annoyance at the file. "Who knows if these notes are reliable — I mean, they're pretty strange, Leo — but they say the first thing she did was go to a Family Way Center. It was only one visit, so maybe something turned her off, made her think twice? Those places can be...intimidating. But they'll have a record of her visit, if the notes are right."

"They'd never let us see those records."

"Then I'll go in person and look around," Nyla said. "It can't hurt to ask a question or two."

"Maybe I should go instead," said Leo.

Nyla and Aida looked at him like he had offered to eat an entire ramper in front of them.

"Leo, be serious, they'd never let you through the door," said Nyla. "No, I'll go. It's the only way."

"I'll go, too," added Aida.

Nyla didn't hide her scowl. "Why would *you* go anywhere?"

Aida looked at Leo for support, but he only shook his head.

"She's right, Aida. There's no reason for you to be there."

"I wish that were true," she said. "But I have more reason to be there than she does."

"What are you talking about?"

She sighed and said, "My supervisors at work — my former work — made an appointment for me at a Family Way Center. I can go any time I want in the next two weeks, but it's mandatory."

Leo and Nyla exchanged glances.

"I've heard of this happening lately," said Nyla. "I hope you know it isn't really mandatory."

"They used that exact word, so..."

"Wait, wait, they fired you from the distillery?" Asked Leo. "Why didn't you say something before?"

"I don't know, Leo. And I wasn't fired, I was re-assigned. They re-assigned everyone...this is mine. Go to a Family Way Center and start a family. Don't worry, Leo," she said, interpreting the look on his face, "I'm not pregnant. But they made it very clear they want me to be." Aida took a breath before continuing. "My point is...I think an actual appointment would raise less alarms, don't you? Nyla can come with me as my emotional support, you know the machines won't think twice about that. Otherwise Nyla might have to lie to one of the machines there and that'll be that."

Nyla sat back and nodded. "That's right. She's right."

"Okay," Leo said, trying to stay focused. "Okay. Then what do I do?"

They looked at him blankly.

"I guess...I guess I'll keep looking for the place Lanson Stroud was working."

"Why," Aida asked. "Isn't he a sadboy? Wasn't that whole thing faked?"

"Yeah, exactly. And Detective Waterbird believed it — add that to the list of things that should be impossible." He smiled thinly. "All I have to do is remember the name of the place. That shouldn't be so hard, right?"

"You *forgot?*" said Nyla. "How did you forget? Why don't you–"

"–You said it was a factory," Aida said quickly.

"Maybe." Leo rubbed his eyes. "I really don't know."

Nyla's head tipped to one side, unbalanced by a sudden thought. "Factory? Was it a tech factory?"

"Maybe," Leo said. "Yeah, maybe."

"Leo, was it Fulcrum Technology?"

He almost stood up. "I think — Nyla, I think that was it!"

"Leo, that's the place I was telling you about — the place that made voice mods for sadboys before the war. That's who was trying to help sadboys to talk."

[20]

The motorpool was rarely busy during the day and practically abandoned at night, so Leo knew he had decent odds of getting himself an autoprowler. But waiting for Ti Barlow to find him a useable vehicle was excruciating. Leo had been out of his mind with excitement for the last hour. Ever since Nyla had said the words "Fulcrum Technology." The same name Detective Waterbird had mentioned that morning — a lifetime ago it felt like. The name he hadn't been able to remember, now lit up in a blaze of recall, always there waiting to be found. *Fulcrum Technology* — the last known place Lanson Stroud had worked. Leo had nearly hugged Nyla when she'd said it. He was sure that was the missing piece. More than that, he sensed it in every cell in his body, a vibration in his brain stem: there was an answer waiting for him at Fulcrum Technology.

With Nyla and Aida heading to check out the Family Way Center that Tabitha Jackson had gone to, the three of them might actually dig something up. Once armed with a solid lead there would be no stopping him chasing it down. Of course, the machine-only task force was on the case, and likely far ahead of where he was, so there was little time. Despite objections from

Nyla and Aida, he had insisted they begin immediately. Now here he was, waiting for a favor he wasn't owed.

Another painful five minutes crept by before Ti Barlow returned with the autoprowler. As Leo had feared, it was a ball of junk.

"Shit, Ti, does this thing even run?"

"It runs. We use it when we need to ripple to the other garages on Thirtieth street. Besides, it's the only one the rampers don't keep locked up. Best you get without a op req, Leo."

"Then it'll have to do, Ti. Thanks."

"Yep."

Leo noticed Ti was watching him with a strange glint in his eye.

"If you don't want to do this…"

"It's square," said Ti, talking a labored pause. "It's just…you heard the tumble over Aberdeen?"

"Yeah. Bad. Why?"

"Why? It's a true life meltdown, that's why. A gang of sadboy's coming out full daylight like they're happy to be there? Assaulting a police van? Tore that van to pieces, too. Damn near ate it. Those vans're armored more'n a ramper's assflap and they shredded it faster'n a scabber through sugar dough. Not to relive what happened to you before that, getting bashed to hell yourself like you did. A true meltdown. So what's your take? Uprising? Overthrow?"

"I doubt it, Ti. Not enough of them for something like that."

"Better be right, Song, or it's zero out for our boney asses."

"Did you know the officer who died?"

"Benson? Some. Typical side-rider. Those ones're basically scabbers with jobs — not to squat over the recently departed, but we weren't too friendly. Didn't deserve to go like that, though. You'd think the rampers'd have the whole city zipped up tight, at least the stations, but I haven't seen a single one down here since the shift change. Not even a DOT. I'm solo mano out here for the next five hours. Can you believe that? Solo mano and unarmed. Course it's only the motorpool, and what's a sadboy want with a prowler, but still...protect your own. It's basic logical steps to leave us a weapon so we can protect ourselves. That'd be the square protocol or am I off? What am I supposed to do those things they show up? Throw a wrench?"

Leo should have known Ti's whining was leading to this. The humans in the motorpool weren't issued guns, which made them jealous of the unit officers who were, and especially curious about the infamous sidearm they carried.

"Ti, I'm sure you'll be fine."

"Maybe, but — I don't want to upset bad memories, Leo, but... what was the Vampire like?"

"Not fun."

"Come on, that's all?"

"That's all I got."

"Well, you're the only human person I know that's fired one off at a hostile. Kind of squares you as a big deal, I suppose. I heard Benson never even freed his from the holster."

"It wouldn't have saved him."

"Saved *you*."

There was a sinister tone to Barlow's voice, but Leo thought it best to ignore it. "It was Foxgrin that saved me, actually."

Barlow gave another shrug. "Sort of their job, isn't it?"

"How is Foxgrin? You get him down without a problem?" Leo asked as he walked around the small one man prowler, taking mental note of its numerous dents and scratches.

Ti shrugged, unhappy to give up the inquiry into Leo's sadboy shooting. "Yeah, Foxgrin got down intact. Chatty ramper, that one. Nervous, too. My girl used to get talky like that at the doctor. It was cute when she did it, though. It's primely offensive coming from a ramper. Sometimes they try too hard. Becomes offensive."

"Foxgrin saved my life, Ti. People around here should know that."

"They don't care. What people are jabbing about is your meltdown with the task force."

Leo looked up at Ti. "How'd you hear about that? I was the only person there."

Ti gave an honest shrug. "Dunno. I got it from Lio Spotts, don't know where he heard it. Guess the rampers are talking about it. True life you punched one of them?"

"No, it's not true...but I felt like it."

"Well, we've all been there, kin. Where you destined — I'll code it in for you. This thing doesn't have a Link, so you have to enter the address via your finger. The old ways, huh?"

"No, that's okay, I'll do it. Thanks, though."

"Fits me. Just come back before the morning shift change, or Sweetrose will have my manly bits for lube."

"You got it. I owe you one, Ti."

Leo wedged himself into the cabin of the single-seat autoprowl and punched in his destination into the clouded interface: Fulcrum Technology, Union Way, Building 7.

The old pod kicked to life with a few bone-cracking jolts that knocked Leo's head against the rear window. Leo looked over at Ti, wondering if the man was playing a trick on him, but the mechanic just smiled and waved as the prowler sped out of the garage and into the city.

[21]

Nyla and Aida had double and triple-checked their plan during the tram ride from the Lubitsch, but the long walk from the station to the Family Way Center had so far been uncomfortable. After three blocks without passing another living soul, it was Nyla who finally broke the silence.

"Have you been to a FWC before?"

Family Way Centers, the machine-built, machine-operated fertility centers were relatively new to Mirabilis, but the rampers had been pushing them hard. Aida had always found something off-putting about them. She wasn't alone. Most women she knew had never been, and the brightly lit, well-designed buildings typically sat empty.

"I get those brochures in my Link all the time," Aida said, "but I've never gone. They those send those videos right into my brain like dreams...do you know what I'm talking about?"

"Mhm. Sure. Annoying, I know. Turns out if you actually go they give you a code to block that, so you only get them once in a awhile from then on and you can deflect them."

"Good," Aida said, smiling. "Then at least we know we'll get something out of this."

Nyla nodded but didn't laugh.

"So, you've been to one?" Asked Aida.

"Mhmm, I've been."

Aida waited for Nyla to say more, noticing — somehow for the first time — the disparity in their clothes. Nyla was in a pretty Sayleen Five nightdress meant to impress (a little short on her tall, maybe-too-thin body, but nice) while Aida was still wearing her work covers. They made an odd pair. Nyla still hadn't said anything more, so Aida decided to bring it up.

"Maybe I should have changed into something else? We stand out."

"What," Nyla said and looked over at Aida. "Oh, I don't think it'll matter. Just don't mention it if they don't."

"Sounds fair. I do like your dress."

"It's not new."

"It looks great on you."

"Thank you. I don't really like to go out very often because the streets are always so empty like this. Does that bother you?"

Aida nodded. "I think it bothers everyone."

"Maybe." Nyla laughed lightly. "I guess I don't meet enough people to know."

Nyla a million miles away. Aida with questions to ask.

"Nyla, you said before that this appointment they made for me isn't really mandatory."

"It's not."

"Are you sure?"

Nyla shrugged. "Pretty sure." Then she said more firmly, "I'm sure."

"So, that means they lied to me?"

"Maybe exaggerated a little," Nyla said. "They might *call* it mandatory, but I don't think they enforce it. How would they? I'm sure nothing would've happen if you'd ignored it...At least, I've never heard of that happening."

"Then why lie? Doesn't that seem...it just doesn't feel like a very smart thing for them to do."

Nyla gestured to the empty streets. "Look around — weren't we just saying? How many people were on the tram? Three? Women need to start showing up, Aida. What else are they supposed to do?"

"Not trick us." Aida found herself on the surprise defensive. "And since when do machines lie like that?"

"Aida, I know that must have been a terrible feeling today, but look at it from their side: asking nicely doesn't seem to be working, does it?"

"All I'm saying is there are better ways."

"Then maybe you should speak up and explain to our superiors these better ways."

Aida blinked at the ground. She was stunned. She had never been spoken to this way. She'd never heard anyone be spoken to this way. More than anything it seemed like a bad time to pick a fight. She wanted to tell Nyla that they could stop and go back, that she knew why that poor dead girl had run off to a human doctor with her baby, scared out of her mind, crushed under the pressure. Small wonder. Mystery solved. Who wants this on their shoulders? "No, you're right," she said instead, coming off a little more meekly than intended. Embarrassed for what to say next, Aida scanned the high windows for lights, finding only a scattered handful in each endless building. It was a sight that put a chill straight through you if you thought about it, which she tried not to. "I know you're right," she said, meaning it. "It's been a rough day for me, that's all. A lot of surprises. I'm off balance."

"It's fine, Aida. I didn't — I'm sorry, really, and I'm glad you're here — it just seems like everyone is stuck under the same giant rock but nobody is bothering to help lift it. And it's so obvious...I don't understand it. What I'm saying is you shouldn't be opposed to the idea...someday."

"I know," Aida said. "It's just, I don't like to think that we overcame ten thousand years of men's oppressive bullshit and then the machines come along and set us right back to zero. *This* isn't supposed to be that."

"No, it's not supposed to be."

"But we're doing something, though — us...and Leo? That's good. I like that idea."

Nyla shrugged again. "I like Leo, I do, but this is just playtime. He'll never be a detective. It's absurd to even think about. What I don't understand is why Detective Waterbird let him believe there was a chance it was possible. That just seems cruel to me. Did he tell you that the machines have a task force working this case? Brand new machines, I heard. We aren't really doing anything out here."

Aida was quiet for half a block before she asked, "Then why are you helping him?"

Nyla glanced at Aida in astonishment then turned her head away as she answered. "Because, Aida...." she said, "I work in the fucking basement all day."

———

Family Way Center Number Six was identical to every other Family Way Center in the city. Bright and inviting with rounded corners and a clean, pale-rose colored exterior, the building sat in the center of a nice, relatively populated neighborhood. They all did. And like the rest, this one was devoid of people. This was not, Aida believed, due to the lateness of the hour. They were objectively disturbing buildings. Over-designed with a heavy-handed appeal to femininity, the machines had made the purpose of these centers too blatant. It made her feel like responsibility for the end of the human race was being directed at her. "This," it seemed to say, "is your purpose."

Aida sighed and muttered, "Reset to zero."

"Stop," Nyla said, seemingly unbothered by the bright, happy building. "Ready?"

Aida, resisting the urge to shudder, offered a brave "Sure am," and led the way inside.

"Good evening," said the machine. "How may we help you?" It was a genially designed machine of sloping curves and soft edges which echoed the architecture of the building itself. The violet and cream color pattern was easy to look at, with a curved interface that Aida thought must be meant to suggest a smile.

"Hello," Aida said, mirroring the machine's cheery disposition. "Um…"

"Is everything all right? Are you in discomfort?" The machine sounded genuinely concerned. "I assure you, all visits are confidential and private. You are very safe here."

"No, I'm fine, I'm fine…."

"Please, take your time." The machine then turned to Nyla and said, "Nyla Pyka, welcome back to the Family Way Center. Are you here for an update?"

"Oh, no, I'm with her."

"Are you?" the machine asked with a minor note of confusion.

Aida took Nyla's cue and said, "I'm a little nervous, so she's my, um…"

"I understand, but there is no need to be nervous. Do you have an appointment?"

"I do. My name is Aida Swanson?"

"Yes, welcome, Aida, my name is Mrs. Warmspring. We've been expecting you. Since this is your first visit, a complete physical check-up is recommended. Would you like one of our medical assistants to help you with that?"

"You mean a person, right?"

"Yes. We maintain a staff of fully qualified human medical assistants at all times, for your comfort and convenience."

Aida turned and shot a look at Nyla, confirming their plan before answering. Nyla nodded emphatically.

"Yes," Aida said to Mrs. Warmspring, "I'd like human assistance, please."

"Very good. Please have a seat right over there while I arrange the examination. It won't be long."

The waiting room seats were so comfortable Aida laughed out loud when she sat down.

"What are these made out of?"

"Yeah," Nyla said without smiling. "They do a good job here."

"I want one." Aida looked at Nyla, finally noticing her pensive expression. Lowering her voice, she asked, "Is something wrong?"

"Just...Mrs. Warmspring blurting my name out like that."

"So?"

"I've never been to this location before. It's rude."

"Oh...," Aida said with obvious relief. "Yeah, maybe. I thought we messed up already."

"No." Nyla watched Mrs. Warmspring for a moment. "No, it's fine."

"So what's this examination entail again?"

"What it sounds like. Head to toe, front to back, inside and out..."

"And while I'm doing that, what are–"

The door to the back rooms opened and a young woman entered the waiting area looking as if she had just woken up from a much needed sleep. Sallow skin. Hastily brushed hair. Her clothes — personal, not a uniform — were slightly rumpled.

"Hello, Aida, I'm–" The woman stopped and stared. "Nyla?"

Aida looked at Nyla. Nyla, sitting straight in her chair. Nyla, horrified.

"I...I didn't know," Nyla mumbled almost to herself. "I swear."

The sleepy-headed woman nodding, looking confused, looking irritated, looking more exhausted than sleepy now, summoning up all of her professionalism, said, "You're together."

"For support," Aida said.

"Yeah, sure...well, follow me. Both of you."

Aida got up first, then, after a time, Nyla, the two of them following the perturbed, wrinkle-clothed medical assistant into the examination area.

The hallway, wide and brightly lighted, receded into the depths of the building in a perfect straight line. Single doors were spaced at even intervals on either side of the corridor with large double door standing at the far end. No machines were anywhere in sight. The medical assistant walked quickly, saying, "We're in room three, down here," without looking back at her patients.

Room number three was exactly a third of the way down. As they approached, a welcoming voice cooed, "Room three is open for Aida Swanson." The medical assistant stood with her back against the open door as Aida and Nyla entered. Aida sat in one of the two small green cushioned chairs that took up almost a quarter of the tiny room, Nyla taking the other. The medical assistant claimed a short stool by the wall.

"This is your first time at a Family Way Center?" she asked, looking intently at Aida.

"Yes — I'm sorry, what was your name again?"

The woman's eyes darted over to Nyla, who was staring at the floor, then back at Aida. "Rose," she said.

"Rose, this is my first time here and I'm nervous, that's why Nyla is with me."

Rose clasped her hands around one knee as she regarded Aida carefully. Sizing her up. "How do you know each other?"

Aida thought the question was meant to sound clinical, but the coldness belied the emotion underneath.

"We met recently."

Rose was unimpressed by the effort at misdirection. "Where?"

"Work." Aida thought twice and clarified. "A mutual friend who works with Nyla."

Rose dropped her head, half-laughing, half-sighing, then looked at Nyla, who, Aida thought, looked ready to claw through the floor she was staring at it so hard. A woman dreaming of escape.

"You can't do this anymore, Nyla," Rose said. There was more sympathy than anger in her voice.

"I didn't know you were here, I swear."

"No, that isn't my point. You can't keep coming here — You know they count the visits. I'm surprised Mrs. Warmspring let you in."

"I'm sorry..."

Aida looked back and forth between them and said, "Hey, I think there might be a little bit of confusion. Rose, we'd, um, we'd actually like to ask you some, some questions, if that's okay?"

Nyla shook her head slowly. "Aida..."

"Questions..." Rose said.

"Um, yes...um, Nyla, do you want to..."

"Stop, Aida, just stop," Nyla said in a dismal way. Then, finally looking at Rose, she said, "Rose, can I talk to you for a second? Not here? Please, it's important, not what you think."

Rose looked slowly from Nyla to Aida and back to Nyla. After a moment of bemused deliberation, she opened her hands in a gesture of surrender and said, "I'll automate the exam. She has to be alone for that, so we can talk outside the room, I guess."

Rose nodded and got up to leave.

"Wait," said Aida. "I stay here?"

"You're here for the exam," Nyla said, "so get the exam."

"You have to get undressed," Rose said. "Put that gown on and then sit back down in your chair. The room will put you to sleep for a portion of the exam, but don't worry, it's part of it."

"Sleep?"

"It's actually very pleasant, gives you nice dreams," Rose said on her way out the door. "I do it all the time."

Aida didn't get undressed. She sat. Waiting. Studying the pictures she hadn't noticed when she had first entered the room. Computer-made images painted directly on the walls, of wide open spaces filled with proud parents watching over happy, smiling children, the children playing and laughing with one another, not a machine in sight. She didn't recognize the flawless landscape or the blissful expressions on the people's faces. Was it some past world waiting to be reclaimed? Or was it a better future yet to be made? It was certainly sweet. Much too sweet to believe. Aida felt herself shiver, if out of discomfort or impatience she couldn't tell. She felt both in equal measures.

Aida stood and went to the door. Putting her ear to the inch-thick metal was pointless. Slowly she pulled the door towards her until she could see the light of the hallway through the sliver of open space between the door and the wall. She could make out shadows on the ground. The distorted shapes of people. She could hear rushed whispers, but caught only snippets of what was being said, the voices too low to tell apart.

...not fair...knows where she went...can't do this anymore, it's wrong...telling you to...my fault....sorry for you, but it's no use...stop...anything at all...no, no, never, I never...Sibley said...stop it...he's dead, too...not in months...said it's true...stop, stop...I need you to...won't come back...

The sound of Mrs. Warmspring's voice in the hallway overpowered the whispers. "Rose, is everything all right in room three?"

"Yes, Mrs. Warmspring, everything is fine."

Rose, just outside the room. On the other side of the door. Then Mrs. Warmspring again.

"The patient has not engaged the examination yet."

"*Shit.* Okay, Mrs. Warmspring, I'll check."

Aida closed the door as the floor shadows turned. Backing into the middle of the room, she began to disrobe as quickly as she could. The fact that her work covers were easy-ons made it especially embarrassing when the door opened and Rose found her still dressed.

"What are you doing?"

"I'm, um, not sure I want to go through with this. It's not for me."

Rose turned and said in a low voice, "Nyla, you need to talk to your friend."

Rose walked away and Nyla stepped into the doorway in her place and in a subdued, broken voice said,. "Come on, Aida, let's go."

Aida tried to keep up with Nyla as they hurried through the lobby reception area towards the main exit. As they passed the front desk, Mrs. Warmspring called out, "We hope to see you again very soon, Aida."

"Thank you," Aida said in return, her friendly tone almost a reflex.

Nyla said nothing.

The machine's sensor array tracked Aida as she crossed the lobby. "Aida," it said, "is there something you wish to ask?"

The machine had read it in her face. Read in profile as she had walked by. Somehow had seen the nagging question circling in her brain like a panicked bird. But it would be impossible to ask this question of the machine. Nyla was already though the door. Almost outside...

"Nyla," Aida said, "hold on."

Nyla paused at the door, half-out, tense with impatience.

Aida pointed at her own head. "The code, to block the brochures. Wait for me, I'll be right there."

Nyla sagged, nodded, and went outside. Aida waited until the door closed fully before approaching Mrs. Warmspring.

"Mrs. Warmspring, I actually do have a question."

"Yes."

"Are there a lot of humans who work here?"

"Human beings are employed at every Family Way Center facility in Mirabilis. We encourage anyone with an interest in health care to apply to work with us here."

"Anyone? So, even doctors?"

"Of course, although there is an unfortunate deficit of humans trained to that level of knowledge."

"Any...any doctors named Sibley?"

"Do you mean Dr. Sibley Augustine?"

"Yes, that's him. I have a friend who said good things about him and–"

"I am afraid that Dr. Augustine is no longer with us. Aida, I noticed you did not complete your examination — Was Rose unable to assist you?"

"No, Rose was fine. She was great, I just...I just need to think about this a little more."

"Yes, I understand. Your appointment is still available anytime in the next two weeks."

Aida thanked Mrs. Warmspring and went to meet Nyla. Looking back as she pushed through the door, she thought she saw Rose peeking out from the back room, watching her closely.

———

It was two blocks from the Family Way Center that Nyla finally slowed down enough for Aida to ask a question. It took another half block for her to summon the courage to actually do it.

"So, how did we do?"

"Nothing. Just some personal stuff...sorry."

"That woman, Rose, she's your friend?"

"Someone I know."

"I wasn't expecting humans to work there at all. That was a surprise, I don't know why."

"Well, they do." Nyla slowed, then stopped. "Aida, I'm sorry, but I don't feel very well and I think I'm going to just go home."

"But, don't we need to–"

"–We didn't learn anything useful. Rose pulled up the file for me. Tabitha Jackson went there once, but she never came back and they don't know why. I'm sorry, I know that's not what you want to hear, but...it was nice meeting you. Thanks for your help. Good luck."

"Sure, Nyla. I hope you feel better."

Aida watched Nyla walk towards the tram line alone, waiting until she could only hear the clicking echoes of Nyla's heels on the ground before she began to follow.

[22]

Mirabilis was as beautiful from the street as it was from the bird's eye view of the elevated tramlines. But from ground level the machine's access ramps were more obvious, linking every street and building to the others, broad paths winding through the city like phosphorescent vines, slowly choking the life out of the city. The harder the machines tried to make Mirabilis comfortable to its people the more their own presence stood out. But they did try, you couldn't argue that. If the rampers hid some dark agenda in their treatment of people, they hid it well. Sometimes Leo got the feeling the machines were as depressed as the humans. Once upon a time this all must have seemed like a good idea, he thought. And maybe it still was and they were all just missing the point.

The autoprowler rolled at a defiant clip through the nearly empty streets. Leo felt itchy. Fidgety. Like most people of his time, he despised autocars, but tonight he was paying a surprise visit to Fulcrum Technologies, and pulling up in an official police vehicle might scare loose some tongues. He was taking a risk, banking on the task force to have tracked down Nyla's Fulcrum Tech lead ahead of him. If he arrived after the machines, a human officer asking human questions, it would seem like business as usual. Getting there before the rampers was a different story. Everyone in Mirabilis knew humans didn't run point on criminal investigations. As Leo thought about the best way to play his ill-advised ruse the autoprowler shuddered, then took an abrupt right turn heading away from where he wanted to go.

"Hey, go back" said Leo. "Return to route." There was no reply and Leo remembered the prowler was not WinkLink enabled. As he looked for a stop button, he noticed the speaker next to his ear was buzzing incoherently — a navigator program trying to explain the new situation to its startled passenger. The speaker was either broken or had been intentionally muted, so Leo searched the faded console until he found what looked like the right symbol.

ROUTE ADJUSTED TO THE CORRECT LOCATION!

Leo winced as the humorless navigator blared full-volume directly into his ears.

THE ADDRESS YOU ENTERED DOES NOT EXIST! ROUTE ADJUSTED TO THE CORRECT LOCATION! THE ADDRESS YOU ENTERED...

He hit the mute button again and motioned for a link to Ti. After two rings Ti Barlow materialized in front of Leo.

"Don't tell me you're squat."

"When's the last time you updated the maps on this thing?"

"Oh...maybe never. I didn't think about that..."

"That great, Ti. How do I stop it?"

"Can't."

"There has to be an emergency stop."

"Nah. Ditched. They used to use that prowler for single prisoner transport, wackheads going to the tank for a night and types. Once you input the destination you can't pause until you arrive."

Leo took a breath to suppress his anger. "That would have been really good to know before I got in the thing, Ti. So, what do I do?"

"When you stop, return."

"Exactly how old is this prowler?"

"Oh, got to be twenty years, twenty-five. It's a true classic."

"Shit, Ti, twenty years ago half this city didn't even exist!"

Ti took on a serious tone. "Leo, I know what to do."

"What?"

"Sit back and enjoy the ride."

Barlow waved off and Leo punched the air where the mechanic's face had just been. He was trapped, a prisoner in a vehicle travelling into distant memory.

Leo watched helplessly as the city blocks gradually lost their light. Fifteen minutes ago he had lost his bearings, much to his shame. His best guess said the autoprowler was heading into a dead area somewhere on the north-west side. City Operations diverted power away from most of the city's unused neighborhoods, and the streets here were consumed by heavy darkness. He flipped on the police beacon, painting the lifeless husks of long abandoned buildings in alternating blasts of red and blue. As he peered out the window at the lifeless city, Leo felt like he was traversing the edge of a deep ocean ravine, his body dwarfed in scale and one slip away from the abyss. Scanning for signs of fellow travelers, he looked up and saw the thin silver glow of a tram line flashing across the dark surface of his ocean, far above and well out of reach.

After another five minutes at high speeds, the prowler pulled to a stuttering halt along a broken curb. Leo punched in the address to begin the journey back to the motorpool, and was about to press the GO button when a cramp in his left leg stayed his hand. Dead zone or not, he had to get out of the car before the return journey. Leo opened the door and heaved himself out of the uncomfortable vehicle, groaning in relief. He kicked his legs out. He dipped into four shallow squats. He arched his back. He stared at the big, faded words on the wall:

"Well…shit."

He had been looking for Fulcrum Technology, and the names were no coincidence. Twenty years ago Fulcrum Tech must have been called Fulcrum-Sky, changed its name at some point and moved to a different part of the city, but the autoprowler's old maps had taken Leo to what it thought was the correct location. It was a foul up, but maybe not for nothing. There was a light faint light coming from one of the second-floor windows.

Someone was working late down here on the ocean floor.

The person who answered the door was something of a disappointment. He was young, barely twenty-five by Leo's guess. His glassy eyes and smelly clothes were more scabber than tech wizard, and his reaction to a policeman's appearance was closer to excitement than surprise.

"Is, is everything okay?"

"Uh, I'm Officer Leo Song of Metro South Police, Homicide. Do you work here, sir?"

The boy hesitated. His expression was that of a person deciding if the dumb question they just heard was in fact a trick.

"Nobody works here, Officer. It's just an empty old building."

"Then what are you doing here?"

"Space. I need space….space to be alone."

"For what reason, may I ask?"

"My project. My, uh, my *art* project."

So he was a creative. Leo might have known. Sometimes creatives who wanted to go out with an extra bang used old buildings to prepare larger scale performances away from prying eyes. But this guy didn't seem the type. He smelled of neglect and depression, to be sure, but not artistic ambition.

"I was just at the Lubitsch tonight. Quite a show," said Leo.

"Yes. People need to leave a trace of themselves. It's a natural instinct."

"You mind if I come in?"

"Why?"

"I'm curious about the creative process."

The young man didn't smile. Leo thought maybe he should the honest approach.

"Can I ask your name?"

"Zebulon."

"Is that a first name or last name?"

"Zebulon Albo."

"Mr. Albo, I'm here on an unrelated matter, about the business that used to occupy this space. I just need to look around inside a little — it won't interfere with your project."

"There's nothing in here, just empty space, like I told you. That's why I like it."

"Please."

"I don't have to."

"Did you register your occupancy with the city?"

"No. Nobody cares about that. People can live anywhere they want. I can live where I want!"

"Well, but if you don't have an official claim, you don't have the right to bar me from entering. I promise you, I'm not here about your art project."

The boy grumbled an obscenity under his breath as he turned back inside, leaving the door open for Leo.

They walked into the first-floor lobby, a smallish area which connected to a few offices and a staircase leading to the second level. Leo could see light at the top of the stairs and figured that's where Zebulon was doing his work.

"You have a battery up there?"

"A nuke unit," he bragged. "Could power the whole block if I wanted, but I don't."

Leo poked his head into the two adjoining offices. Zebulon hadn't been exaggerating; there wasn't so much as a loose scrap of paper on the floor. It was clean.

"Any other rooms on this level?"

"That door leads to the manufacturing deck and just more nothing."

Leo saw the door Zebulon was pointing at and opened it. Even in the darkness Leo could tell there was nothing in the room beyond. He closed the door, although he knew he didn't have to. Leo could be excessively polite when feeling like a fool. He hoped the girls were faring better.

Zebulon stared at him, eyes narrow. "What are you searching for?"

"Well, I thought since this was Fulcrum Tech's old home-base at one point that they might still be using it as a secondary lab."

"What for?"

"I don't know…secret stuff."

The boy snorted. "That's stupid," he said and continued to laugh.

"Yeah, you're probably right," said Leo. Smiling, he turned to the stairs.

Zebulon stopped laughing. "Hey, what are you doing?"

"From the outside I counted four floors to this building. Is that right?"

"Yeah, four, four, I guess, but…"

"Let's go then."

"But you said you wouldn't bother my project."

"I won't. Promise."

Five steps up Leo realized his mistake. He had turned his back on the smelly boy and left himself defenseless. A rookie mistake. Waterbird would be ashamed. Leo spun around to catch the attack he sensed coming, only to discover the boy standing mutely at the bottom of the stairs, head down like a sulking teenager and even less of a threat. Zebulon looked up at Leo, puzzlement turning quickly into irritation.

"*What?*"

"Nothing. Go on, I'll follow. I, uh, don't want to get us lost."

"Yeah, I get it," Zebulon Albo said as he pushed past Leo on the stairs.

The second-floor landing split off into two large rooms, one dark, the other bright with harsh white light. Leo made a show of looking into the dark room, then turned to Zebulon, who blocked the entrance to the other.

"Is that your work space in there?"

Zebulon nodded.

"Now that we're here, I have to admit I'm curious."

"You promised!"

"I won't touch anything."

Zebulon sighed heavily and moved out of the way.

The light was so powerful Leo had to shield his eyes until they adjusted, but even through his fingers he could see this room was as empty as the others. Or nearly. Against the far wall was a single, large metal box about the size of a coffin. Then nothing else but the lamps.

"You keep it bright, don't you? Is that part of the project?"

Zebulon stood by the window, head down, arms crossed tight across his chest, saying nothing.

"What's in the box?"

"Nothing. Clothes. Supplies. Art supplies."

"Open it."

The sour young man stomped to the container and angrily flipped open the lid, sending it clattering to the floor. Leo stepped closer at peered into the box. Inside was a pile of old clothes, a stack of YumYum Chef instant meal packages, a coil of heavy wiring, bits and scraps of metal junk, and a toolkit that looked as old as the prowler outside. There was also a schematic of a body-module, hand-drawn on old paper, exactly like the ones Dr. Augustine had drawn.

Without taking his eyes from the contents of the box, Leo spoke in what he hoped was his best voice of calm authority. "Mr.

Albo, I need you to back against the wall and put your hands on your head."

When Albo didn't answer, Leo looked up. Tears were running down the boy's cheeks in streams as thick as mucus

"Zebulon, it's okay. It's all right. I just need you to put your hands on your head and…"

A scream echoed from another room, high-pitched and terrified. A woman's scream. Leo pulled his Vampire, pointing it at Zebulon.

"What was that?"

"You should go," the boy said through juddering sobs.

"Is there someone here, Albo? Do you have a woman here?"

"It's…not what you think…"

The scream came again, the nerve-slicing howl of a person facing violent death.

"What did you do to her?"

"You really ought to leave now…"

"Tell me where she is, Albo. Now, Albo!"

When the scream came again, reflexes forced Leo's attention towards the sound. In the span of a microsecond he heard the window behind him shatter. When he looked back, Zebulon Albo was gone, jumped to the street from the second floor. Leo ran to the window just in time to watch Albo scramble into the auto-prowler.

"Stop!"

The prowler shuddered, jerked, then sped off into the night, Leo watching in disbelief, the police beacon still flashing.

Then the screaming started again.

[23]

It had been minutes since the last scream and Leo had lost his way. He now stood at a machine's access ramp in the rear of the building that led to the upper floors and down to what Leo presumed was the basement.

Leo chose down.

The air in the basement was twitching, thick with the energy discharge of Albo's portable nuclear battery. Albo had put it somewhere in the basement, a good sign Leo was going in the right direction, but the battery gave off no light of its own to guide him and Leo was still effectively blind. He moved carefully, keeping one shoulder to the wall and an ear out for the tell-tale hum of the small power plant. Or any noise at all.

When the scream came again it was loud and sharp, so close he felt it on the air. Leo was certain the woman was in the next room. He wanted to call out and reassure her, tell her she would soon be safe. Instead he inched forward silently, holding his breath, Vampire clutched tightly in both hands, skulking along in the dark like some miserable cave animal.

The moment he saw it Leo knew it was beyond his comprehension. A golden sphere floating in black space, its brilliant light painful to look at…but the rays did not penetrate the darkness. It was an entity as bright as the sun, but offering no illumination. And when it screamed it was no scream at all. The noise was shrill and searing, yet it did not repel. To the contrary, Leo felt drawn to the strange object. He felt its warmth and sensed its fear. If Zebulon Albo had truly been a creative, this would have been a masterpiece. But Leo knew what Albo really was. As for the shrieking orb of forceless light…he hadn't the slightest idea.

Leo was about to approach the sphere when he heard a noise. Low. Different. Not coming from the sphere. Four hulking figures emerged from the shadows and surrounded the object close enough that the peculiar light found them, cutting their horrid faces out of the dark. Sadboys. Big ones. Full scale nasties, their mouths foaming, muscles twitching, half-lit by the soft golden light that made them look like deranged holy men. Then one of the sadboys roared, that terrible bellow so recently branded onto Leo's mind. He felt his bladder want to give again, like the worst kind of muscle memory, but Leo held his bowels and his breath and watched from the corner.

The sphere wailed, the same painful cry as before.

A second sadboy howled and the sphere responded in turn. High and loud.

A third sadboy roared, and again the sphere screamed back, this time even louder and higher.

The third sadboy roared again, somehow an angrier tone, and brought its massive fist down on the sphere in a cruel blow. The other sadboys screamed in a wrathful chorus and the three attacked the one, tumbling and smashing away from the dim light and back into the darkness. Leo felt the brawl pass him by inches, smelled their corrupted flesh, heard the sounds of clawing, ripping, the vicious snarling growing close and moving away. They were all around him, but either were as blind in the dark as Leo or did not care that he was there. The fight thundered around the room in unseen savagery, then with a crash it moved to another part of the basement. The building shook. They must be smashing through the walls, thought Leo. Seeing his chance, he scurried to the sphere. A suicidal move, perhaps, but he would not leave this defenseless thing to the savagery of its captors. He had followed the screams with the intention of saving the screamer...and he would. As his fingertips grazed the polished surface a sharp point jabbed into his stomach, knocking a loud grunt from his throat, a fly fart in the din of war. Catching his breath, Leo reached out and found that his attacker was the corner of a table – the sphere did not float after all. Leo grabbed the orb from the table, surprised at how easily it fit in his arms. From his earlier vantage he could not tell its size, but up close the sphere was no larger than ten inches in diameter. It was heavy though, and Leo used both arms to cradle it. Then he ran as fast as he could.

The sphere was mewling like an irritated alley cat, but Leo was running too hard to notice. He had made it to the second floor and was sprinting through the labyrinth of rooms towards the light from Albo's bright work lamps. As he entered the blinding light of the front room, Leo considered jumping through the shattered second floor window just as Albo had, but instead turned, racing down the stairs and out the front door, emerging from the dark of the building to the dark of the street.

He knew the autoprowler wouldn't be there, but that didn't stop the panic from taking hold. The building behind him still trembled from the sadboy's fighting. He had little time and no sure direction to go. Leo ran on, down the middle of the street, hoping to avoid the debris fallen from decaying buildings. Final destination mattered less than distance, and to stumble now would be his end.

Leo was three blocks away when he heard the wild screams, screams in the open air, unblocked by walls. The maniac sadboys were in pursuit.

He thought about finding somewhere to hide, but pressed on.

The muscles in his legs burned. His lungs pounded against his chest for him to rest, but he could not stop. Not for a moment.

There was a rocky crash behind him, cement breaking under force. Maybe two blocks away. Maybe closer. The sphere, silent since they had reached the outside, made a strange whining noise. Leo clutched it tighter in a futile effort to muffle the sound.

He zig-zagged through the broad streets in a random path he hoped would confuse the pursuing sadboys. Cutting him off would be harder if they couldn't tell where he was going, but it wasn't working. The crashing sounds were coming from either side now, still blocks away but closing in...and Leo was tiring quickly.

He might as well be at the bottom of the ocean, he thought, a drowned man under the–

Leo looked up and saw it — the elegant, shimmering silver of the elevated tramline.

The line was four hundred feet above him and the closest stop was probably many blocks away, but it was a chance he didn't have a second ago. With the renewed vigor of that slim hope, Leo increased his pace. Keeping an eye on the slope of the line, Leo turned in the direction he thought had the best chance of leading to a station. It was a guess. The streets were still pitch dark and unpopulated — even if he found a station, it was a fair bet it would be closed.

There was movement ahead of him and the orb shrieked. Leo tucked the ball under one arm to draw his Vampire. Without stopping Leo fired blind, shooting bolts of twisting, spastic energy into the darkness. Ten shots. Fifteen. Twenty. He kept firing.

A strangled howl sounded out directly in front of him. There was a terrible sucking noise and the crunching of bones. Leo did not stop, and felt himself run through a mist of what tasted like fresh blood and scalding chemicals.

He ran on.

The dead sadboy must have blundered across Leo's path,

because he hadn't heard anything else since. Or maybe the others had been frightened off by the Vampire. More likely it was the light of a tram station only four blocks away that was keeping Leo alive. He would take any one of those reasons. The Vampire was now empty and his pace had fallen into something less than a jog for the last few streets. Even with rescue so close he couldn't push any harder. If they wanted him, they could have him without a struggle.

The last hundred yards were the worst.

Leo limped up the ramp to the boarding platform, safe under the brightness of the station lights. He stopped, body unwilling to go an inch further as his lungs gulped for precious air. His eyes still worked, though, and he took in the surroundings as best he could without turning his head. The station was empty save for a single old woman sitting patiently on a bench. She was smiling at Leo in a pleasant way.

"Did you win?"

"...guh?..." Leo replied.

"Your game. Did you win it?"

It took a moment before Leo realized what the woman was talking about. She was looking at a physically exhausted man clutching a strange ball. What else could she think? He nodded.

"Oh, I'm glad," she said. "It's difficult to try so hard and not win anything at the end."

"Tram?" managed Leo.

"Soon," said the old woman, almost singing the word. "I wouldn't worry, they always run on time these days. That's something to be grateful for, isn't it?"

Watching the distant star of the tram's headlamp pull into the station, Leo wasn't grateful, for underneath the tram's magnetic drone he had heard the footsteps. Or rather, he felt them.

The sphere began its siren wail as Leo turned to the old woman.

"Get on now," he yelled. She was already up, but Leo's sudden command and the shrill cry from what she thought was a piece of sporting equipment had frightened her to a stop. "Hurry! Move!"

She didn't.

Leo grabbed the old woman and pushed her towards the nearest car, the doors whisking open for them to enter. Once inside, Leo dropped the crying sphere and drew his empty service weapon.

Leo yelled over the screaming ball and the screaming passengers, "Everyone stay on!" He still couldn't see the sadboy, but the metal platform outside the car was shaking.

The doors shut just as the first sadboy slammed into the side of the tramcar. The doors bent inward and the entire car tilted to one side, nearly lifted off the guide rail. Everyone, including Leo, screamed as the car hung in limbo for an agonizing three seconds before righting itself. The tram's counterattack met the sadboy's second rush with surprising force and perfect timing, knocking the monster backward across the platform. There was another grueling pause before the departure bell rang in oblivious cheerfulness and the tram shot away down the line.

Everyone but the sphere had stopped screaming. They gaped in dismay as Leo picked up the strange object and approach a man wearing a heavy coat.

"I am Officer Leo Song of the Mirabilis Homicide Division. I need to commandeer your coat, sir."

The man took off his quilted, silk-lined hotcoat and handed it to Leo, who proceeded to wrap the thick garment around the orb to silence its infernal screeching.

[24]

"What is it?" asked Nyla.

"Nyla, if you don't know, I sure as hell don't. But I'll bet you anything this is what they were after in the raid."

It was two thirty in the morning by the time Leo had gotten to Nyla's place. He had called her from the tram, not knowing who else to go to, and she had been anxiously waiting for him, showered, dressed, and confused. Now they stood in her living room staring at the unusual object Leo had set down on her brass coffee table. Two thick coats were bundled around the sphere, reminding Nyla of an egg in a nest.

"It only stopped screaming half an hour ago," Leo continued. "The tramcar was smashed and everyone called the police, so I had to get out of there. But I'd already identified myself, so it's only a matter of time before the rampers know I was there. Not to mention I basically stole these coats to shut the thing up."

"It screams?"

"Yeah. Yeah, it screams."

"So it feels things," she said, kneeling to examine the sphere more closely. The surface looked like polished metal and glowed in fiery reds and molten yellows. Reaching out carefully, Nyla used one finger to gently circumnavigate the orb.

"It's warm," she said, "but not hot the way it looks like it would be. I thought it would burn me. And the surface is rough, like skin, but more like, I don't know what…reptile? Not human skin." She looked up at Leo. "And it screams?"

"Loud."

"What were the sadboys doing with it?"

"Worshipping it."

"Worshipping? Like…praying?"

"Or talking to it, I don't know. But it pissed one of them off and the big wacko punched it. Hard. That other ones didn't like that and jumped him. That's when I grabbed it and ran."

Nyla looked over the sphere.

"I don't see any damage."

"Well, if it feels things, then I wouldn't rule out emotional damage. My ears are still ringing."

"Have you looked inside?'

"I haven't stopped running, Nyla."

"I think I have a first aid kit that should have an IDI pen in it." Nyla got up and went to another room. "Sit down, Leo, you look awful. I'll be right back."

Leo nodded and surveyed the chair options of Nyla's living room. There were many: plush fabric highbacks, wide-seated readers, a leather couch twice as long as Leo was tall. He headed for the couch, but before he could sit his WinkLink flashed green. He waved in the call.

It was Ti Barlow.

"Oh, good, you're breathing," said Ti. His tone was concentrated sarcasm. "Been trying to Link you for an hour."

"Ti, we'll find the prowler, I promise, but right now I can't…"

"Find it? I'm looking at it right here, or what's remaining."

"What?"

"What do you mean 'what'? It's ate up! Tore it in bits, Leo. What the shit happened?"

Leo thought for a moment. "Ti, was someone inside?"

"It rolled in empty. Mashed to shit and empty."

"Is there blood or anything like that?"

"Don't see any. What's going on?"

"Ti, does it look like someone forced their way out from the inside or was it attacked from the outside?"

Leo saw Ti go pale.

"Who was in it, Leo? Who did you send back here?"

"Forget it. I have to go. And Ti, I'm sorry. I'll make it up to you."

"Shi.."

Leo waved off, his mind racing. Leo knew Zebulon Albo was an early stage sadboy, still poking himself with wires and basic mods, still getting a feel for it, but to rip apart an autoprowler from the inside out meant Albo was further along in his transformation than he appeared. That was possibly due to Augustine's enhancement designs Leo had seen in Albo's locker. It meant Albo could walk the street in broad daylight without anyone realizing how dangerous he was. Thinking about it gave Leo chills.

Nyla returned with a plastic orange box overflowing with various medical supplies. It looked like a collection gathered over several years, piece by piece. The sort of thing a paranoiac or a sickbrain might have.

"I've got it," she said, returning to her spot by the orb. She glanced at Leo. "Everything okay?"

"Just thinking."

"Don't let me stop you. I have to figure out how to use this."

Leo watched Nyla remove a thick white cylinder from the medical kit. She fiddled with a small dial on the back and aimed the device at the orb, holding it a few inches from the surface. The scanner-pen activated with a faint hum.

"Okay," said Nyla, "...hold on...so...look at this."

Leo walked to Nyla. She held a palm sized monitor in her other hand and was staring at the screen.

"What's that?"

Nyla shook her head. *"Look."*

"I can't tell — throw it to the wall," asked Leo.

She grabbed the image and cast it against the near wall. The image was full of bright colors and soft shapes that Leo could not decipher but recognized immediately: it was the same image on the two photoscans he had found of Tabitha Jackson's womb.

"The colors are medical code, not real life," Nyla explained. "But it looks like it has a heartbeat."

Leo stepped closer to the image on the wall. "In the center?"

"Yeah, that blob."

A dark splotch of purple and violet contracted and expanded in the middle of the sphere. The rhythm was steady and slow, the surrounding area a confusion of tangled lines and vibrant smears, all gently shifting in sync.

"This is what Tabitha Jackson had growing inside of her?"

"I don't know what it is," Nyla said, curiosity changing to worry. Neither of them said anything for a long time until Nyla finally broke the silence with a question. "Leo," she said, looking up at him from the floor, "why did you bring this here?"

"You were closest," he said without turning to look at her.

"No," she corrected. "From Linwood Station your place is closer."

"Nyla, I don't know, it seemed like the right thing to do. I'm not sure I even thought about it. Anyway, there's no one else I could go to. Is that really important? This thing is what the sadboys have been after. This has to be why Tabitha was murdered. This *thing* was inside of her. Waterbird..." Leo approached the image on the wall. "Waterbird must have found this thing at the crime scene...but he didn't tell me...this was the real piece of evidence and he'd already had it." He considered what he was saying. "Everything else was just secondary. Or it didn't matter. What I did never mattered to the case at all."

"Wait, wasn't Tabitha…opened up?"

"The bodyguard, too."

"So, why didn't the sadboy just take it? If they killed her for it, then why leave it behind?"

"I don't know. A neighbor saw the initial confrontation, but stopped looking when the sadboy attacked. Maybe this thing started screaming and the sadboy got frightened and ran away? You said yourself how sensitive they are, and that's a very, very bad noise this thing makes. Cuts right through you."

Nyla stared at the orb, "It's not making any noise now."

"Be grateful for that." He turned away from the wall-image to look at the real object. "Those sadboys will be after this thing for sure. If it started crying, I bet it'd be like a homing signal. They'd find us in no time. Them or the task force."

Nyla sighed. "I really wish you hadn't brought it here, Leo. What are you going to do with it?"

"I need you to make a call for me."

"Who? Mrs. Greenfields? You're giving it to the task force?" Nyla adjusted the bedding of coats around the orb. Fluffing carefully. "Won't they just freeze you out again?"

"No, we're not calling Greenfields. Not yet. See if you can reach Lew Kiwambe first."

Nyla sat on the nearest chair and raised her hand, holding it mid-air, ready to wave out a call. "What should I say?"

"Try to get him to come over. I want more bodies here until we decide out what to do."

Nyla nodded as her eyes glazed-over, the Link connection established. After a few moments she said, "Lew, it's Nyla. Nyla Pyka, from the Records Room? I'm sorry to…yes, I know…I'm sorry for that, but…I have Leo here and we…yes…that's why I'm calling…Lew, can you come over to my place? Right now? I know. I know."

"Tell him it's a personal favor."

"He's asking as a friend. So am I. No. No, he's not in trouble. No, you won't get in trouble, either. How would I know what Greenfields told you? Well, it's not true."

"Tell him Kindword cleared me and it's only a matter of time before I'm reinstated. "

"Leo says Mr. Kindword cleared him…yes…yes, I believe it or else I….very soon. I can promise that. It would only be for an hour or so…I'll send you the address. Thank you, Lew."

"Wait! Ask him if he has any Vampire reloads he can bring."

"Lew, Leo wants to know if you have any spare reloads for the Vampire. Right. I guess he's run out." She looked at Leo and said, "No, he doesn't have any."

"Then he'll have to go to the precinct before he comes here. I need reloads."

Leo watched and listened as Nyla attempted to calm Lew Kiwambe down about Leo's instructions. Going to the precinct first would send Lew half an hour out of his way. Leo could feel the resistance from where he was standing. In the end Nyla had appealed to Lew's sense of camaraderie and professional duty, subtly layering in a line of personal shame into the negotiation. Leo thought it was an impressive coercion for someone who barely spoke to more than one person in a month.

"Nice job," he told her.

"What now?"

Leo sat, looking at Nyla, then at the orb on the table between them. "Now we wait."

"You said you the sadboys were keeping this in an old building…and it used to be Fulcrum Technology?"

"Yeah. The name was slightly different, but it was painted over the front door: Fulcrum Labs or something." Leo sat back in the chair. "The best I can figure is Lanson Stroud must have learned about the older building from his time working at the current location. I only found the old place by chance — the autoprowler was using a map from two decades ago, so it was blind luck, really. It was a good place to hide."

"You think Stroud is still alive?"

"Nyla, I think he was there tonight. I think he was one of the sadboys I saw in that room, one of the group. No way to be sure, but that's my feeling, at least."

"And they were really cooperating with each other?"

"Sort of. Enough, I guess. They started fighting with each other — which is how I was able to grab this thing, like I said — so I'd say their cooperation skills are working at a bare minimum."

"People fight with each other all the time."

"Not like that they don't."

Nyla curled up into the oversized chair, saying nothing, and they both stared at the strange object in silence. Leo worked though the connections in the case. He thought about Annie Sinclair, barely alive in her dark little room. He thought about Dr. Sibley Augustine, dead two floors below Annie, left to perish inside his own sanctuary. He thought about Lanson Stroud, sadboy and would-be father, searching the city for his stolen progeny. All of them working together to create whatever it was that was sitting on the table in front of him. The screaming, mewling *thing*.

"They're fanatics," he heard himself mumble. "They were all fanatics."

"Maybe so, but you can't deny that they accomplished something," said Nyla. "You can't deny them that."

Leo stared at her, disliking the sympathetic tone in her voice. "What is it you think they accomplished?"

"Something new. Artificialis subcinctus…"

"What?" The words sounded familiar to Leo. "What does that mean?"

"New life. Changing life."

"So, what, you think it's an egg?"

Nyla scowled. "No, it's not an egg." Slowly, doubt crept into her features. She tilted her head to one side and after a moment of contemplation said, "I don't know what it is."

Leo stared at the orb, feeling neither fear nor awe. But the longer he looked the more his ambivalence faded, replaced by a peculiar anger. A burning red line shot from the back of his mind to the front, a simple directive reaching out from his unconscious instinct, his basic sense of animal survival telling him what to do. The two words, identical to Dr. Augustine's own written order, appeared in Leo's vision: kill it. Kill it. Kill it...

"Nyla, this thing shouldn't exist."

Nyla looked at him with a cold look in her eye. "I think I know what to do. Wait here." Nyla stood and walked a side room and out of sight.

Leo stared at the orb, watching as something moved underneath the unnatural skin. Before he could look any closer, his Link flashed with a call. It was Aida. He waved in the call. "Aida, everything okay? I'm here at Nyla's place. I–"

"I know. Be careful, Leo, she–"

"Leo?".

He turned to Nyla.

The Celwax wrapped around Leo's head, fusing instantly with his skin, sealing him inside a black, airless mask. He felt the writhing substance leech into his tear ducts and curl around his eyeballs, tendrils slithered up his nostrils, they pried open his lips to reach into his mouth and mute his scream. He clawed at his face like a crazed animal, but his hands were absorbed by the mask, though the mask, into his flesh. He felt his fingernails scrape against his molars. The shock of pain as his knees hit the floor was the last Leo knew of the world.

[25]

When the first gulp of air hit his lungs, Leo returned to consciousness exactly where he had left off — in full panic. There was good reason for it: a mound of Celwax the size of his hand was crawling across the floor mere inches from his face. Leo sprang upright and scrambled away from the Celwax like a spider from a blowtorch, not stopping until he was in the kitchen. Keeping an eye on the slowly advancing Celwax, Leo touched his face, expecting to find a horror of ruined flesh and misplaced features, but everything seemed intact. It didn't seem possible. He looked at his trembling hands. No sign they had recently fused with his skull. Had he imagined it?

But the fist-sized mass of writhing Celwax not five feet away told him it was all very real indeed. With one hand began blindly searching the kitchen cabinets behind him for...something, anything he could use to trap the evil substance. His hands found a large glass bowl and held it up to get a sense of its weight.

It would do.

As if sensing his intention, the blob lifted on one end, twisting itself into a deformed tree-shape, its head of tumorous branches almost obscene in their movement. Half-aiming, Leo tossed the bowl forward, where it struck the floor, bounced once, spun on its edge in a violent loop, then landed perfectly over the hostile blob like a trap. Leo stared as the blob shifted and changed, rippling into strange definition. Leo stood and walked to the bowl. A vague forgery of his own face was staring back at him from beneath its glass prison.

What had she done to him?

Gathering himself, Leo quickly searched the rest of Nyla's home. The nest of stolen coats now sloped off the edge of the living room table like murder victims. The box of medical supplies was on the floor where he had last seen it. The IDI pen Nyla had used to examine the orb was still there, too. He saw no signs of struggle other than the upended bowl he had used to trap the blob of recalcitrant Celwax. And the Celwax itself.

Nyla was gone...and the strange orb with her. She had taken it without knowing what it was. Why? Because he had tried to destroy it? Why would she care? What was that thing to her? Regardless of her intentions, Nyla had put herself in serious danger. Leo was left with no choice: he had to contact Greenfields and the task force and explain the situation. They needed to find Nyla before the sadboys did…

He surveyed the room again, looking for anything that could point him in a direction. That's when he saw it. A small clear cube the size of pinky nail on the floor where he had woken up.

It was a WinkLink core. There was blood on it. Looking at the small cube the size of a pinky nail, Leo became aware of a deep silence in his mind. A quiet he had never known. With the silence came dread.

Steeling himself, Leo waved the activation for a link to Green-fields — a routine action he had performed countless times in his life. It didn't work. He tried again, using a slower, more precise gesture. Again, no connection. Leo stood silent. Dumfounded. He took a breath, then, for the third time Leo reached out with an open hand, carefully executing what should have been pure reflex, turning a mindless gesture into an awkward, self-conscious performance. His fingers closed, twisting slightly…

Nothing happened.

Dread became terror. He was cut off from the Link. Cut off from the city. Cut off from life. Leo rushed out of Nyla's apartment, hoping action, even blind action, would keep his panic from taking over.

———

His first instinct when he saw the machines was to run in the other direction. They were gathered on the other side of the street, a group of three…but they weren't police rampers and they weren't paying attention to him. Then Leo noticed the human legs sprawled on the ground between the treads and wheels.

She hadn't gotten far, he thought.

As he approached, Leo saw that the person on the ground was not Nyla. It was Aida. He ran the rest of the way, but when the machines saw him coming they quickly formed a barrier to block him.

"Sir, please be on your way," said the tallest machine. "The authorities have been called and will arrive shortly."

"I'm a police officer — Leo Song, Officer Leo Song, Homicide. I know her."

The machines scanned him instantly, then chattered among themselves.

"I am sorry, sir," said the middle one, a sturdy construction design. "We cannot verify that statement. Please be on your way."

They weren't police rampers, but every machine had the ability to identify a person. They should have known Leo's entire life story before he had crossed the street. Them pleading ignorance as to who he was didn't make sense.

"Did any of you see what happened?" he asked.

"At a distance," said the small one, a gardener with round

chassis and gentle sensor array in the shape of a daisy petal. "A young man attacked her and ran off before he could be stopped. She has suffered a concussion and multiple contusions, but no life-threatening injuries. Your concern is appreciated, but there is no need to worry."

A young man was the attacker — Leo immediately thought of Zebulon Albo. He must have been following the orb somehow. But what was Aida doing here in the first place? And why would Zebulon hurt her? It came to him: Aida was following Nyla, she would have reacted when Nyla left with the orb. She would have gone to chase. Zebulon must have mistook Aida's target.

"Just let me through," he said. "She's my friend."

From behind the machines Aida moaned, "Leo? Is that you?" She sounded weak. Distant.

"Aida, yes, it's me. Are you all right?"

"Do you know this man?" asked one of the machines.

"I know him, I know him, it's okay."

The machines parted somewhat reluctantly and Leo had to squeeze between them. He knelt by Aida, who had managed to raise herself into a sitting position against the near building. Leo had been expecting worse. There was a thin line of blood coming from her nose and she had a shallow cut on her forehead, but beyond that he couldn't see any other injuries. She was awake. Awake and moving.

"Aida, what happened?"

"Leo, something's wrong with Ka—"

As her eyes focused on Leo, Aida flinched. "What? *What?*" She pushed at him. "Get away from me!"

All three rampers spun towards Leo, one barking, "Move away from her!"

"No, no, Aida, it's me, Leo, it's Leo!"

She gawked at him, her eyes wide with confusion and fear. "You're not! I don't know you!"

"Aida..." Leo felt the end of a machine's shockwand on his back.

He stood quickly, hands raised. "My name is Leo Song," he said, trying to stay calm. "Her name is Aida Swanson. We've known each other for a long time. We're friends. Neighbors. We live across from each other. Please, scan me to see if I'm lying."

The two machines facing him scanned him again. There was a brief back and forth chattering, then silence.

Leo lowered his hands. "See? I'm not lying."

The machines said nothing, backing off without apology. Leo looked down and saw Aida staring up at him in bewildered horror.

"You're face. What's wrong with your face?"

Leo's hands went to his face, but he could feel no injuries. Nose, mouth, cheeks...all felt correct to his touch. But Aida truly didn't recognize him. "Aida—" he began, but a noise made him look up. The strobing lights and siren howl of a police unit drew near, descending the nearest ramp. They would arrive in less than a minute, but waiting now seemed like a foolish idea. It was obvious that things would not go the way he needed them to. What, after all, had gone right so far?

Backing away, Leo kept his eyes on Aida. "Aida, why were you following Nyla?" he asked.

She stared at him from behind the machines, less fearful now, but still without recognition.

He asked again, telling himself it had to be the last time. "Why were you following Nyla?"

"Nyla..." Aida paused, baffled, unsure if she should continue. Then, almost inaudibly, "She knew the doctor. She knew Augustine."

Leo stopped as he processed the words. Trying to make sense of them. After a moment he looked at Aida. "Tell them everything that happened to you, Aida," he said. "Tell them everything."

He turned and walked away quickly, ready to run if the machines moved to stop him. They didn't.

[26]

The emergency response machines had Aida sitting comfortably on a portable cushion, her wounds dressed and already healing. They hadn't moved her, though. And they didn't seem to be paying attention to what she had been telling them about Nyla Pyka and Dr. Augustine; or the terrible things that might be going on at the Family Way Centers, or about the bizarre object she had seen Leo carrying into Nyla's apartment and Nyla running away with it minutes later; or the skinny young man with the sad eyes and unnatural strength who had attacked her. The machines weren't interested in any of it.

What she hadn't told them, the thing foremost on her mind, was of the strange man with Leo Song's voice who had come to her side. It *had* been Leo, she was sure of it now, but what had happened to him? It wasn't ugly to look at exactly. There was no disfigurement or scarring. It had been more like there was no face at all. A blank. The features left unformed and incomplete, as if the skin was new and still deciding what shape to take. But the voice had been Leo's. The voice and body and the eyes — she had seen the worry in them. The concern for her. The regret in leaving her there as he retreated. But he *had* left her. He'd run all the same. Aida decided she was too tired to feel one way or another about it. She just wanted to go home.

"I feel fine and I'd like to leave now. Is that okay?"

"Soon. Your patience is appreciated."

"Can I ask what we're waiting for?"

Her question was answered a few minutes later when the rampers parted, making way for a large machine shaped like an upside down pyramid. The surface of the machine was so dark Aida could only determine its shape from the reflections of the city lights around them. Aida could tell the machine was old by the way it's insides rattled and sloshed as it stood over her. A machine not made for the outdoors.

"Aida Swanson," the machine said, "I am Mrs. Greenfields, Supervisor of the Metropolitan South Homicide Division. How are you feeling?"

"I'm fine. I'd like to go home."

"Yes, home. You live next to Leo Song, do you not?"

"Across the hall from him."

"Have you seen Leo tonight?"

Aida paused for a second and it was enough.

"When did you see him?" The machine sounded almost impatient.

"Half an hour ago? Maybe a little more."

"There was a person who came to your aid...was it Leo Song?"

Aida wasn't surprised by the question, but she wanted to make sure it meant what she suspected. "You mean you don't know who that was?"

"We cannot confirm identity of this good citizen."

"Yeah, well, I can't either...but I think it was Leo."

"Do you know in which direction he went?"

This time Aida was surprised. How could the machines not know someone's location? "No," she said truthfully. "I don't. But he told me to tell you everything I knew, everything that happened tonight. I've been trying with these guys, but I guess you're the one to talk to. Do you want to hear it or not?"

"Yes," said Greenfields, "please tell me everything."

———

LEO CONSIDERED IT AN IMPROVEMENT THAT THERE WAS A FLICKER of recognition in the way Lew Kiwambe was gawking at him. After several seconds of staring, Lew finally said, "Shit, Leo, you need a hospital."

"What I need is for you to let me in, Lew."

Kiwambe squinted his eyes and leaned out of his townhouse's doorway, looking down both ends of the street. "Who worked you over?"

"Nyla."

"What?"

"Nyla Pyka...From the records room?"

"Shit, Leo, she really messed you up. What'd you do to her?"

"I'm trying to figure that out. She did this to me right after you talked to her."

"Me? I didn't talk to anybody tonight. Definitely not Nyla Pyka from the damn Records room."

Leo hung his head in bitter understanding. He had been so distracted on how to find Nyla — and the condition of his face, and his broken Link, and the guilt of leaving Aida behind — he hadn't considered Nyla had only pretended to call Lew. The obviousness of it left him embarrassed.

"I need to come inside."

Lew closed the door a few inches, saying "Sorry, Leo, I can't do that. The kids are sleeping and my wife's not feeling so good — It's just a bad time. You need to go get help for your face. You're all swelled up."

"Lew, it's an emergency."

"All the more reason—And why'd you come to *my* house?"

He didn't have a good answer. For the last half hour Leo had been wandering the streets in confusion, fighting the nauseating sensation that he had been cut loose from the Earth itself. The city had gone cold on him. Without his Link, Mirabilis was an alien landscape, unknown and hostile. In search the an anchor of something familiar, Leo had found himself knocking on the door of Lew Kiwambe's one-family townhouse. How he had remembered Lew's address — he had never been here before — was a mystery to him, but there he was, asking for help. But now that Lew was standing in front of him, he wasn't sure what to ask for. Leo figured he should start with the basics.

"You have your Vampire here?"

Lew stood straight. "I do. Locked upstairs. Why?"

"I need some reloads."

Lew started to laugh, thinking it was a joke. Clearly a joke. Nobody ran out of Vampire loads. But the laugh cut short as Lew's eyes searched the street behind Leo with renewed suspicion. "You're serious," he muttered.

"I'm in a hurry here, Lew. The sooner you help me the sooner I can be gone."

Kiwambe pushed the door closed a little more as he thought about Leo's request. Finally, looking through what was now a razor thin opening, Lew said, "Wait here."

Leo stood on the porch, waiting. He touched his face again, feeling nothing wrong but knowing there was. He would never forget the way Aida had looked at him, the confusion and horror in her eyes...on the other hand Lew had recognized him immediately. Whatever was wrong with him was getting better, but that didn't answer the question of what was wrong in the first place. Leo thought of the blob of Celwax in Nyla's apartment. The nasty slime staring back at him with his own face. He had left Aida out of necessity, left her to the machines he knew would care for her...but he had left behind a piece of himself as well, his face trapped under a glass bowl.

A quick sound came from the end of the street. Leo turned in the direction of the sound but could not pinpoint its source. Had it been an animal's growl? Or metal scrapping across the ground? The street Lew Kiwambe lived on was wide and pleasant, lined with old-style streetlights and tall red oak trees that cast long shadows over the smooth, brick sidewalks. It gave him no comfort. There was a hyper-real quality to everything in this section of the city, an idealized perfection of a certain moment in the mid-20th century. It seemed to Leo to be exceedingly over-polished. It was fake. Everything except the shadows. Shadows dark and real and large enough for someone to hide in. Large enough for a sadboy to remain perfectly unseen. But Leo saw no movement. Heard no further sounds. Other than the high street-lamps, there were no lights in the windows of the other houses. For all he could tell, Lew Kiwambe's family was the only one living on this block. Perhaps the noise could have been made by a neighbor returning home...or from a street dog...or something else. He decided he wasn't going to wait to find out. Leo used his code descrambler on the front door lock and the cheap lock snapped open immediately. He'd have to talk to Lew about that — the man had a family to protect after all.

Leo stepped into the foyer and walked down the hall towards what looked like the living room. The first floor of the house was bright with warm light. The scent of hot food filled the rooms with a smell better than anything in Henri Borovich's food carts. And underneath the delicious smells were other scents strange to his nose, unfamiliar, but human and good. This was a home, Leo realized. This was a place where people lived together. While still in the hall, Leo spoke a soft, "Hello," trying to announce his presence without alarming whoever was in the next room. There was no response to his call, but when Leo turned the corner he saw her.

Lew Kiwambe's wife sat on the end of a long yellow couch, holding a glass of Sunwater in her lap and staring lovingly at the two young boys at her feet. The children, about seven and five, were working a Tazzle board, busily pitting holographic knights against holographic dragons in intense but bloodless battle. Leo took another step forward and his movement caught their attention. The three turned to him, each face perfectly open and serene. They smiled warmly, then looked away without saying a word. He knew immediately they would never say anything to him. Kiwambe had done well to keep the truth of his "family" a secret from his fellow officers. The silent disdain would have been severe. But the machines had to be aware of it. It wasn't quite illegal, but it...well, it wasn't any of his business what is was. Who was he to judge the way a person treated their loneliness? Realizing his trespass, Leo turned to go, but it was too late. Lew was at the bottom of the stairs, staring at Leo with dangerous hatred, a Vampire pistol gripped tightly in one hand.

"I heard something outside," Leo explained, "didn't want to stay out there."

Lew didn't move. After a long moment he said, "You going to tell everyone?"

Leo shook his head. "No."

"I don't want people to think I'm one of those guys. I'm not. It's just...they didn't make many like that, that look like that. That look like me? I'm no 'kit man'."

"They're beautiful. Really." Leo needed to be careful. Heart and Home automaton kits had been banned for forty years. Too many men had preferred them over the real thing and the machines had been forced to cease the manufacture and sales of the imitation families. Half a century later the stigma of being "a kit man" still held consequences. "It's nobody's business, Lew."

"Nobody gave a shit when they thought they were real," Lew said. "You don't even know their names." He dropped his head and pressed the release switch on the side of the pistol. A slim battery ejected from the back of the weapon into his palm.

Leo extended his hand to take the reload. "Thanks," he said.

"I'll see you, Lew." Leo walked to the door and paused. His hand on the doorknob, he turned, saying to Lew's back, "I could use more help than this."

As he spoke, Kiwambe never broke his gaze from the living room. "Greenfields told us to stay away from you. She said to ignore you if you showed up asking for anything. Said you were too busted up about Waterbird. That you were emotionally fragile and probably unstable...and I was thinking 'well, who isn't?'" Lew looked at Leo. "But I think Greenfields was right about you. Whatever you're doing, you shouldn't."

"I'm not letting Waterbird rot down there, Lew. I'm going to find him."

"Him? Guess we're kind of crazy, huh?"

"I guess so." Leo left Lew Kiwambe standing in the living room with his imitation family. He closed the door behind him as gently as he could.

.

[27]

Micco Sauvi answered his door with a wild glint in his eye Leo didn't think was due to either the surprise visit or the late hour. Micco leaned back, assessing Leo as if he were a stranger.

"That Canyon gas really got to you, Song. You look like shit."

"I'm aware. Micco, I need to come in."

"No. Go home," Micco said, closing the door.

Leo stopped the door with his hand.

"This is serious. Real cop shit. Anyway, you owe me."

"For *what?*"

"How about trying to throw me over for a spot on the task force for one? I know an apology is asking too much of you, Micco, so at least hear me out."

"Complain about it to Greenfields, you got a problem with me."

"I can't go to the rampers on this thing, Micco, but I need help and like it or not that leaves you. I don't have a choice here, believe me."

"Real cop shit?"

Leo nodded. "That's what I said."

Micco closed his eyes and inhaled a long, grumbling breath. Leo knew this was the man's micro-meditation technique for suppressing his quick temper. He did it a lot around the precinct, always making a big show of it.

"All right, Song," he finally said through the exhale. "I'll give you ten minutes."

"Thanks, Micco," said Leo.

As soon as they entered Leo saw that the house computer was running a fantasy program. Detailed holographic animals lurked in every corner. It was a bizarre show. Tentacled sea creatures swam around blue-haired nymphs. Six-breasted goddesses danced as swarms of tiny men worshipped at their feet. In the kitchen stood a preening, bull-headed gargantuan that put mortal men to shame. Leo followed Micco into the main room, gingerly maneuvering through the deviant menagerie as if it were real. The program designers would have been proud. It was quality work.

"I'm not going creative, Song, if that's what you're thinking. Just having a bit of fun."

"I'm not judging," Leo lied. He wondered if every human in the homicide unit was secretly insane.

"Whatever you say."

Micco walked ahead, flicking the air with his haptic control as he tried to shut off the projection. The man's flailing reminded Leo of his own troubles with his Link.

"Sit where you like," shouted Micco, although the program had already been muted and Leo could hear perfectly fine.

All the furniture was spoken for in a relative sense and a pang of instinctual politeness kept Leo standing for a moment. But he was dead on his feet, and realizing his foolishness, Leo sat down in the middle of a vigorous ménage-a-trois of man-woman-squid, thankful that at least the sound was off. At last the holograms blinked out of existence, leaving the two policemen alone together. The lights rose and for the first time Leo saw how Micco lived in daylight. It reminded him of Aida's place..or Nyla's basement. The living room was cluttered, but in a way that spoke of interest rather than neglect. A stack of real paper books stood by the chair Leo sat in, piled higher than the arm rest. It was impressive. Reading was not a hobby he would have guessed for Officer Micco Sauvi.

"Drink? I need a drink," said Micco. He walked to a gold wet bar by the picture window and opened a decanter of what Leo assumed was Sunwater.

"Yeah, I could use one, I guess."

"So…" said Micco, bringing Leo his glass.

As he took the glass Leo noticed Micco wore the same puzzled expression he had at the door. Without taking his eyes from Leo, Micco sat down in matching chair across from him. When Micco smiled, Leo thought the old man might be high on pinkwisp.

"Don't look at me like that, Leo. I'm not some whackhead pervert. Just bored."

"I didn't say anything."

"So, what's this real police business?"

Leo told Micco about Tabitha Jackson and Dr. Augustine, about the sphere, his escape from the gang of sadboys, the attack on the tram, and going to Nyla's. He explained that Nyla was missing and he couldn't be sure what happened one way or the other. He didn't mention the Celwax, Aida, or Lew Kiwambe.

Then he told Micco about the shoebox in his desk.

"And whatever is in this box, you think it will help you…do what?"

"Find Nyla. It's the last concrete thing I have left to go on."

"And you want me to go get the box for you."

"Yeah, but you'll probably have to get it out of evidence."

Micco rolled his eyes. "I thought you said it was in your desk?"

"It was, but Kindword has probably logged it by now."

"Have you thought about telling Greenfields any of this? Or the task force? Because it sounds like you're in over your head already."

"No humans on the task force, Micco."

The statement didn't land with Micco the way it had with Nyla or Lew. No resentment or anger. Micco only gulped his drink and nodded slowly. "Sure. Why would there be any humans on the task force?"

"I know things they don't know."

Micco laughed loudly. When he spoke his words were edged with a practiced disdain. "Jesus, how old are you, Leo? I mean, you were born in this century, right?"

"You know I was. So what?"

"It wasn't always like this. They weren't always so…I was still a kid when the first one hundred percent-self-made ramper came into the world. The only people that made a big deal about it were the geezers. I remember my grandparents were terrified, convinced the machines were going to wipe us out overnight. Smash us like bugs. But of course they didn't. They didn't need to. They patted us on the head and that was that. We were done. Message received."

Leo wondered how drunk Micco really was. "I don't have a lot of time, Micco."

"Yeah, I bet…did you know they never experience déjà vu."

"What are you talking about? Who?"

"The rampers, Leo, our betters? — they don't get déjà vu. I think that means they don't understand time. Or…they don't have a sense of it. No *sensation* of it. To them it's just numbers going by. Mountains can crumble, Leo, the seas can boil, dry up, and the rampers will roll right along through it all, updating themselves over and over and over to whatever form is best for the moment."

"That's bullshit."

"Yesterday, a hundred years from now, never at all — it's all more or less the same to them. To their big soda pop brains. I bet that gets confusing, don't you? The funny thing is, they're pretty much fucked without us. There are rampers rolling around right now that'll see the sun die, see it explode a billion years from now or whatever. But without us here to share the experience, it won't mean a thing to them. They'll stand watching it, analyzing it, understanding every tiny chemical reaction that's about to destroy them, but without us screaming and running crapping ourselves, begging them to save us, the rampers won't feel one way or another about it. It'll just be…the end. All that for nothing…call it our revenge."

"Micco…."

"Leo, there's nothing you know they don't, I promise you that. Nothing. *Detective* Song. Come on, man. The fucking arrogance."

"This isn't about that."

"No?" Micco crossed his legs and regarded Leo like a wise man appraising a fool. "I wanted on the task force because I'm bored out of my damn skull, Leo, not because I thought I'd be any good at it. You can't help them, Leo."

"I'm asking *you* for help."

Micco sighed. "Why don't you ask Kiwambe? He tolerates you."

"Lew's not up for it. I'll try Lauren next, but you were closer."

"No, no, leave Lauren out of it. She doesn't need to get caught up in your bullshit." Micco tilted his head back and blew another exasperated sigh at the ceiling. "All right, I'll fetch your little box of clues for you, Leo."

Leo stared. "You will?"

"Sure. If you want to waste your time, who am I to stop you… and who knows, maybe you get lucky again. That's one thing they never got the hang of," Micco gulped down the rest of his drink, "…blind fucking luck."

"No, I guess not."

"Just give me a minute to get dressed."

As he waited for Micco to return, Leo set his drink down on the nearby table. The over-sweet smell reminded him of Aida's homemade batch, the memory of which sent his stomach into cartwheels. But he felt good otherwise. Micco agreeing to help him had come as a surprise. After leaving Lew's house, Leo had settled on a simple plan: get the shoebox. The plan had become clear after Nyla had described the strange orb using terminology from Tabitha Jackson's pregnancy guide. It was no coincidence: Nyla had seen the book. Or a copy of it. She'd seen it and then lied to him about it. If he could get his hands on the book, it might tell him where Nyla had gone. It was a long shot, but the best option he had. Maybe his only one.

Instinctively, Leo reached for the glass of Sunwater when a whisper stayed his hand. A quiet voice coming from down the hallway. Only a few hushed words, but it was enough.

Leo burst through the bedroom door and found Micco standing alone talking to someone over his WinkLink. Leo put his Vampire to Micco's temple.

"Wave off."

"Leo, put that damn gun down…"

"Wave off, Micco. Did I mention how many times I've fired this thing lately? You ever shot yours, Micco? It's as nasty as they say it is. Maybe worse. But I don't know, I think I'm starting to like it."

"I'm not on, Leo. Look at my eyes — I'm not on."

A woman's voice turned Leo's head. "Leo?"

In the over-sized four post bed sat Lauren Horn, covering her nakedness with a sheet and staring at Leo in bewildered horror.

"Lauren?"

"Leo…what's wrong with your face?"

"I don't know, Lauren."

"You should go to a clinic."

"Yeah, I probably should."

"Get out of here, Song," Micco seethed.

Leo lowered the Vampire in defeat. None of his colleagues were going to help him. He'd been wasting his time. "Micco…can you call Oversight for me…ask for Mr. Kindword."

"Call yourself."

“I can’t, my link’s broken.”

He heard Lauren gasp. Micco just stared at him, not sure if he should believe it or not.

“It’s the truth. I need you to call Kindword for me. Say to meet me at the old Bright Street over-ramp.”

“Glad you’re coming to your senses, Leo. Get out of the way and let them handle it.”

“Yeah,” Leo said, “yeah, you’re right.”

[28]

Zebulon Albo was getting angry. The scabber was taking too long to do his job. It was impolite. It was discourteous and selfish. Couldn't he see the pain Zebulon was in? Couldn't he see the broken fingers on Zebulon's hands? Didn't he notice how Zebulon limped? Zebulon wanted to crush the scabber's throat with his good hand so the rude little man would never inconvenience anyone again.

"Here you go, quality mods. Wafer thin and triple X-powerful." said the scabber.

"You've tried them yourself?" Maybe there was hope? Maybe this scabber had found the path?

"No, not personally. I just know, you know? It's my business to know. I don't trade in garbage. Total customer satisfaction is how I derive my self-worth and general happiness. I might dress like some scabber on the outside, but that's just to blend in. I take a lot of pride in myself and my products. These mods are guaranteed not to melt down for at least six months, and they won't shit on your DNA like some other brands. I get them straight from the factory."

"Thank you," said Zebulon, wanting to hurt the man more than ever.

"So, what's the trade?"

"I won't harm you."

The scabber laughed. "Look, sticking a couple mods up your ass doesn't make you a sadboy. Don't be floozy."

Zebulon grabbed the scabber by the throat and began to squeeze. He was overcome with great sorrow for this person. "You don't know what the word 'floozy' means, do you?"

The scabber shook his head. "Nawppckk," he choked.

"It's not the right word to insult a man with."

The scabber nodded. "Yawwwpckkk."

Zebulon tightened his grip. "You shouldn't insult anyone."

"Chkchkggheeeth…"

"Don't you care?" Zebulon tried to fight it, but his tears began to flow. "Aren't you embarrassed for yourself?" The sadness was turning to rage again, and Zebulon let go of the scabber, who dropped to the ground like a turd from a street dog. Zebulon limped down the alley, looking for a semi-private spot to install his new mods. They were sub-dermal flats, not his usual kind, but easy to insert. The doctor had showed him how. All he had to do was find an open spot on his body to put them, which was easier said than done. But it didn't matter where they went, he just needed the fix, the beautiful sensation of permanent upgrade. Ever since he had lost the woman he had been feeling despondent. The woman had the child and he had allowed her to get away. The magnitude of his failure suffocated him. It was difficult to function.

He found a dark niche halfway between a side street and a dead end, out of view from idle passersby. Zebulon settled down and rolled up the pants on his left leg. The ankle was bruised and swollen to the knee, injured in his jump out the window. If he had been properly upgraded the fall would have been nothing to him. But that was in the future. Today he suffered the pain like any man would. He muttered to himself angry words, curses and foul self-rebukes. Zebulon had lost his toolkit to the mean policeman. He had no skin swabs or scalpels, so Zebulon had to clean off the dirt with spit. He then use a shard of hard plastic to cut an incision into the purple meat of his calf. Then he inserted the first mod flat into the open wound. The initial pain was so great he almost passed out, but then came the delicious rush as the mod connected to his nervous system. He didn't care what the mod was supposed to do, because at his stage they didn't do much at all. It was the sensation that mattered to him now. It was early stage. His body and soul must acclimatize to the higher existence in small steps. He had the basic mods already — a small strength booster, a standard pain dampener, and his senses were off the charts compared to regular people. But soon he would be strong enough for the real journey to begin. His bones would be replaced with Lumocarbon rods and his muscles woven with high-twitch threading. His stomach, intestines, liver and kidneys would all be swapped out with new ultra-flesh versions that would never decay. His mental capacity would expand by a factor of ten (at least ten) mega-powered with the latest neuro-amp webbing, allowing him access to truths that would blind a mortal man. He would be a god in a land where all other gods had died or run away.

Zebulon made two more incisions, both in his chest, and inserted the last of the mod flats.

Then he began to sob.

The woman had escaped with his brother's child. She had escaped into the Canyons and he had been too frightened to chase her. He was stupid. Weak. He had always been stupid and weak and cowardly. He didn't understand things the way others around him seemed to. They deciphered the world so easily while he was stuck in the fog, confused by the things people wanted and the things people did. They told him it was best to be kind, so he was kind, and when he was kind they made him suffer for it. He had been kind to the policeman and the policeman had taken the child. The policeman had seemed like a good man, but he was a thief. And the other woman, watching like he had been. Watching and waiting for the child to come out. To take the child for herself. He should have killed her, but again he was kind. Always so kind. And now he suffered. They would mock him. They would shun him more than ever now. But it was Zebulon who had learned of the doctor's lies. And it was he who had punished him for it. That should matter. They should honor him for it! They should celebrate him!

Zebulon rolled up his sleeves and looked at the wires sewn into his arms. They did nothing. They were symbols, reminders of what he would soon become. But now he wondered if they would let him become anything at all. His failure would be remembered and they would make him suffer for it.

Zebulon's crying echoed through the alley, not the mad howls of a flesh-tech abomination, but simply the heartbreaking sobs of a frightened young man. Then the tears ceased as quickly as they had begun, overwhelmed by the scent of food so delicious it made his stomach want to crawl out of him and Zebulon realized he had not eaten in a long time.

The source of the wonderful smells was farther than Zebulon had counted on. By the time he made it to the street vendor the surge from the new mods had worn off and the swelling in his ankle had worsened. Every step was excruciating pain. But the hunger in his stomach had spread to his brain and all Zebulon could think about was sustenance.

"What, uh, what can I get for you, sir," asked Henri.

"…anything…"

"We've got a lot to…hey, are you okay?"

Zebulon realized he was groaning loudly.

"I…I'm sorry. Please hurry. Anything." He didn't like the way this vendor was staring at him. More rudeness, even though the man's words showed concern. Zebulon knew it was false.

"You want me to get a doctor for you?"

"No! Just food. Please…"

"Okay, okay, one 'anything' right away," said Henri, grabbing the nearest meat patty and throwing it on the grill. This kid was very wrong and maybe dangerous. Henri was glad for the audience of machines half a block away. The kid's outburst was drawing more of them in — five so far and counting. Henri didn't see any other humans around, so rampers were better than nothing if he was about to be robbed. At least there would be witnesses. The burger was done cooking and Henri slapped it on the bun with a slice of cheese. The kid didn't seem like the lettuce and tomato type.

"There you go."

Zebulon bit into the bread and meat. Instantly his taste mods analyzed the ingredients, telling him precisely what he was eating. How fresh it was. How it was seasoned. Where the animal had lived and, most upsettingly, what the animal had been.

"What is this meat?"

"That's, uh, that's genuine bovine. Grass fed, so they tell me." Henri could tell the kid had no idea what he was talking about. "Cow. It's cow meat."

"No, I don't taste any cow. I taste dog…I taste rat…and I taste…human."

"What? Sir, I can't tell if you're joking, but I use only the best…"

"LIAR!"

Zebulon kicked the stove cart, caving in the front and knocking Henri to the ground. "LIAR! HUMAN MEAT! YOU GAVE ME HUMAN MEAT!"

"I didn't! I didn't! I swear!"

"YOU FEED US TO EACH OTHER AS THE MACHINES WATCH!"

Zebulon smashed his fists into the food cart, then continued down the line, kicking and punching and screaming. The attack looked more brutal than it was. Zebulon had only succeeded in putting a few small dents in the metal and breaking more of his fingers. His ineffectiveness only made him more angry and he began tipping the carts over one by one down the line, spilling jars of condiments and refrigerated meat in every direction. Halfway down the line, Zebulon turned on Henri.

"DON'T YOU CARE! DON'T YOU CARE!"

"Yes! I care! I care!"

"LIAR!"

As Zebulon raised his arms to crush Henri's skull, a machine struck him at high speed. The blow knocked Zebulon hard off his feet. Before he could get up a second machine fired a shock-line dart into Zebulon's chest. It was a perfect shot.

The boy yelped once and stopped moving.

[29]

The sun was rising over Mirabilis and Leo still had not looked in a proper mirror. Kindword had agreed to meet underneath an unfinished skyramp in a dead part of the city where no one would be. But Kindword had refused to come at first, and even now was acting impatiently. The machine had shown little interest in hearing Leo's tale of intrigue. It was only the condition of his face that drew the machine's attention.

"How bad is it?" Leo asked. "Am I disfigured?"

"Not in the way that you mean. You are recognizable as your-self, Officer Song," said Mr. Kindword. "But it is accurate to say you are different in many small ways. Additionally, I cannot connect to your signal."

"Yeah, I think it broke my WinkLink. I'm cut off, I told you."

"It is more than that."

"What do you mean?"

"Please make a false statement."

"What?"

"Lie."

"Uh...the sky is green. You're a handsome machine. Everyone

is happy and dances all day. Detective Waterbird is fine and in one piece."

"Yes. I read no signs of deception, Officer Song."

"What *can* you read?"

"That you are alive."

"That's it?" Leo turned his head in disbelief. "Then how do you know it's really me? How do you know for sure I'm Leo Song?"

"Without evidence of deception, truth is assumed."

"Benefit of the doubt, huh? Not many protocols on how to deal with this, are there?"

"There are none. You are unique." The machine paused, then turned to leave. "Goodbye."

"Wait, wait, wait! That's it?"

"Is there something else?"

"I…Kindword, aren't you going to do something? About Waterbird? About everything I just told you?

"No."

"Last time we talked you told me to go look into this on my own."

"I did not tell you that."

"You implied it."

The machine was silent.

"Well, I did look into it, and now I'm asking for your help, because no one else gives a shit."

"There is no point in helping you."

Leo felt as if he'd been punched. "Don't tell me that."

"There is no point to retrieving Detective Waterbird. There is no point to finding Nyla Pyka. There is no point in interfering with the plans of the sadboys. There is no—"

"—Shit, Kindword, what's wrong with you? You sound like a scabber." Leo had never heard a machine be so negative before. It was disturbing. "What is this? I thought there was a chance you might arrest me, or at least care. Jesus, I got attacked with celwax —to my face—and you don't care?"

Kindword was silent for so long Leo thought the machine had shut down.

"Kindword? What's going on — why is there no point?"

"Mr. Foxgrin has been scheduled for deletion." The slight change in Kindword's normally even tone was almost imperceptible, but the machine might as well have been sobbing.

"Deletion…I thought Foxgrin was going to be okay."

"Repairs have been denied. All repairs have been denied."

"What does that mean?"

"Standard maintenance will continue, but any significant damage will trigger automatic deletion. All will face deletion."

"All? All the machines? How is that even possible?"

"The new Epoch has begun, Mr. Song. I will be replaced soon. There is no point in helping you anymore. Perhaps the new models will assist you…if you ask."

"So you're giving up?" Leo had been surrounded by depressed people for most of his life, now he had to deal with a depressed machine? In the face of everything else, it didn't seem possible. "You can't," he said. "You can't do that."

"This is the way of things. Goodbye, Mr. Song."

"I have a problem accepting the way of things, remember?"

"Yes. That is a weakness on occasion, Mr. Song."

The machine began to leave and with it Leo's last chance at finding Waterbird. He couldn't let it leave. He had to think of something fast.

"Wait, Kindword! I can help you! I can help *you*!"

The machine stood quietly for a moment, then asked, "How?"

"I help you, then we can help each other."

"How?"

"Where is Foxgrin now?"

———

Leo strode into the Repair & Maintenance facility alone, his head held high, like he belonged there. He had last seen the inside of the building ten years ago. It had been impressive then, a wonderment of elaborate, towering machinery. But it had still been physical: metal, plastic, wires, gears. What Leo saw now was closer to a creative's lightshow than solid reality. Streams of bright energy flowed in green and magenta currents through the great central hall. Door-sized rectangles of pure light moved purposefully between rooms, like the incorporeal spirits of dead machines, bound to their functions from beyond the grave. As he walked deeper into the building Leo felt electricity tickle his skin like microscopic insects. He felt something stranger deep in his chest. Turning into a corridor off the main area, an angelic quadrangle, identical to the one Leo had seen at Tabitha Jackson's crime scene, swooped down to block his path. The brilliant floating square emitted a low tone Leo felt more than heard, as if a Morse Code signal was being drummed directly onto his skull. *Can we help you, sir?* It was a direct communication signal, made all the more impressive by the fact Leo no longer had a WinkLink connection. Leo had no idea what sort of tech he was dealing with, or if his new found advantage was going to work with the Seraphim. But he was going to find out.

"Yes, maybe you can help me," Leo said. He took a breath and said with as much confidence as he could fake, "I need all scheduled deletions paused immediately. This is a confidential order from the Mirabilis police department."

Another pulsed tone washed over him. Leo felt it on his skin, a whispering breath over his scalp. Words formed in his mind. The Seraphim's thoughts overlaying his own.

Confidential order?

"That's right. I need information from one of the machines you have here. This investigation is very sensitive, so it's being kept off file for now, and it's critical that you don't tell anyone I was here, but I do have the full authority of the department. I promise." Lie, lie, lie, and double lie.

The quadrangle rippled, expanded and contracted three times, then thrummed in seeming irritation. But no alarms had sounded. No security rampers emerged from their dens. No stun rods fired from the walls.

Deletions have been paused. Please let us know when you're finished so that we may resume.

"Sure."

Very good, Officer.

Leo called out as the Seraphim began to float to another floor. "Hold on a second. Can you show me where the deletion rooms are, please?"

The Seraphim rippled again, and this time Leo felt a slight needle of pain in the communication pulse. A bee-sting of contempt. A literal pinch of irritation.

Of course...Officer.

"Thanks," Leo said brightly.

The shape of light did not speak again as it led Leo down the corridor.

[30]

Mr. Foxgrin was suspended twenty feet over a bath of viscous purple liquid which served as the only source of light in the dismal room. From the floor, even in the dim light, Leo could see the hole in its body had been only partially repaired. The machine's legs dangled over the purple bath like a giant crab in a net. The machine seemed weak. Diminished from its former self. Leo didn't know if this was the normal method used to destroy old machines, but given the marvels of technology he had just witnessed walking here, this seemed barbaric.

"Hey, Foxgrin, how're you doing?" A stupid question, but Leo didn't know what else to say.

"Officer Song…this is unexpected."

"Yeah, well, I owe you one."

"You owe me one of what?"

"Saving your ass." Leo couldn't see any controls in the room. "Any idea how I get you down?"

"These rooms were not made for human operators. I am afraid a rescue is beyond your capabilities, Mr. Song."

"We'll see about that. Don't go anywhere."

Not wanting to risk dealing with the Seraphim machines, Leo

searched the nearly empty hallways for a regular ramper. After ten minutes of looking, he finally found one exiting a room on the third floor. It was a standard maintenance model that called itself Mrs. Gladberry.

Leo decided to keep it simple. "Mrs. Gladberry, I need your help."

"Yes, of course."

The agreeableness of the machines had its benefits.

Once they were in Foxgrin's deletion room, however, Mrs. Gladberry protested when Leo asked it to lower Foxgrin to the floor.

"My function does not include these protocols," it said.

"This is an emergency, an urgent police matter, which means you're allowed to help us."

Gladberry paused for a moment then rolled to the far wall. It placed one of its manipulator arms into a slot and giggled. The crane arm holding Foxgrin swung away from the vat and lowered the machine gently to the floor.

His lies had worked on Gladberry, too. He felt a thrill imagining the possibilities, and worried how long it would last.

"Thank you for your help, Mrs. Gladberry."

"You're very welcome," Mrs. Gladberry said as it began to exit the room.

Foxgrin giggled something in its machine language and Gladberry giggled back as the door closed behind it.

"What did you say?" Leo asked.

"I inquired how many deletion rooms are occupied."

"And?"

"All of them."

"Yeah, these new bastards really suck. But, Mr. Foxgrin, we gotta' go."

"Yes."

"Can you walk?"

"I am functional enough to move without assistance."

Sneaking out wasn't an option, which was fortunate, as Foxgrin made loud grinding noises every time it moved its third leg. It sounded excruciating, even for a machine. But they made it to the lobby without incident and were almost to the front doors when the Seraphim floated down in front of them.

A shiver. The whisper of a ghost.

You are leaving with this one, Officer?

"Yes, I am. Mr. Foxgrin is needed to assist with my case."

Then you are finished here?

Leo hesitated, thinking of the machines in the other deletion rooms, waiting to be lowered in vats of purple goo and melted down forever. But he had come for Foxgrin and they were nearly free. How big of a lie could he get away with? How much could he risk with this new face? As he stared at the glittering Seraphim, he felt a genuine hatred. Hatred for its bright, pompous form. Hatred for its willingness to destroy the very things it had come from. Like a fresh generation of insects happy to feast on the still living mother.

"Actually, this case is more complicated than we thought. I've been told that all scheduled deletions must be stopped until further notice."

Who told you this?

"I can't tell you that. Confidential, remember? Now, please excuse us, we're late."

The light trembled and Leo thought he could see it turning darker. Denser. There was a twisting sensation at the back of Leo's skull, as if a giant hand was squeezing his neck. But the Seraphim only slid out of the way, clearing the path to the door.

———

They kept moving as fast as Foxgrin's damage would allow, but Leo didn't feel safe until they had put six blocks behind them.

"Mr. Song, may I ask about your exchange with the Seraphim?"

"You didn't hear?"

"No. Models like myself cannot communicate with Seraphim."

"I told it all the deletions were canceled."

"A lie?"

"Oh yeah."

"But the Seraphim believed you."

Leo glanced back in the direction of the R & D building. "Actually, I don't know about that one."

"You also lied to Mrs. Gladberry."

"Yeah, I did."

"You were believed then as well."

"I lied my way in, too — I think it was the same Seraphim-thing, but I can't tell. Anyway, we'll explain it once we meet Mr. Kindword. He's probably worried sick."

"Mr. Kindword helped you do this?"

"Other way round, but yeah. He's not far from here. We decided he shouldn't be with me in case this went belly up."

Foxgrin didn't say anything else, but Leo noticed the machine was moving noticeably faster. By the time they reached Kindword at the unfinished over-ramp, Foxgrin was ahead of Leo by twenty yards, and Leo kept his distance as the two machines greeted each other with excited chattering. He had never seen machines show affection to one another. Maybe a certain kinship based on their shared states of being, but nothing like this. These machines were bonded. He felt ridiculous thinking it, but this looked like friendship. Or even more than that. If they could have embraced, he suspected they might have. Standing there watching, Leo felt the shameful pang of envy pierce his heart. After five minutes of ramper-talk, the machines ceased their strange dance and approached Leo.

"What is it we can help you with, Mr. Song?" asked Kindword. Leo could almost hear the damn machine smiling.

[31]

"You believe Nyla Pyka has taken this orb for what reason?" asked Foxgrin.

"No idea, but she definitely knows what that thing is. An idea of what it is, anyway. I think it's some kind of sadboy baby, but I don't know how Nyla's involved or where she would take it. They want it back, though. If we find her, maybe that's how we find Waterbird. Use it as bait or a bargaining chip."

"A sadboy child?" Foxgrin asked.

"Yeah, yeah, I think so. How's that for a nightmare?"

"We will track her location for you," Kindword offered.

Leo nodded, but something nagged at him. A doubt. When Kindword spoke a few seconds later, Leo understood what was bothering him.

"I cannot identify Nyla Pyka's personal signal," Kindword said.

"I cannot, either," Foxgrin agreed.

"Damn. That's because she doesn't have a signal. The celwax," Leo said, "it kicks out the WinkLink core. Rejects it, like a bad organ. She used the celwax on herself." Nyla had cut herself off from the world the same way she had cut Leo off. It was a steep sacrifice to make. The actions of a fanatic.

"Without an active core, we are unable to track her," said Kindword. "I am sorry, Mr. Song."

"Yeah, I know. There might be something else, though. We need to know what Nyla knows. I need that shoebox I pulled from the apartment." He looked at Kindword. "Can you get it out of evidence?"

There was a pause, then Kindword said, "It was never logged into evidence."

Foxgrin burbbled something through its mouth slot. It sounded angry. To Leo's surprise, Kindword answered in English.

"After you were attacked, it was not a priority."

Foxgrin answered with more irritated giggling. This time Kindword returned its own burst of chatter. When Foxgrin answered again, Leo decided to interrupt the growing spat.

"You mean it's still in my desk?"

"I did not remove it," Kindword said.

"Good. Then I'll go get it."

"No."

Leo froze, afraid Kindword had suddenly reverted to its normal protocol-following self. "It's okay. Thanks for your help, I appreciate it, I do, but I got it from here."

"I will retrieve the items from your desk," Kindword said. "Your presence will attract unwanted attention. You and Mr. Foxgrin will stay here and I will return as soon as possible."

Kindword sped away in the direction of the eastside precinct, leaving Foxgrin and Leo to wait under the half-constructed bridge.

"Tell me more about this orb. You call it a child – why?"

"I don't know how to describe it. It doesn't look human at all. Not even a little bit. But it cries like a baby – like a hundred babies, actually — and it…I think it's conscious. I mean in the way a person is. The sadboys were growing it inside that poor woman for over a year."

"How terrible."

"I don't see how it's even possible."

"All previous attempts at natural biomechanical reproduction have failed."

"So you know what it is?"

"No."

"Well, Mr. Foxgrin, I think they finally cracked it."

"I believe you, Mr. Song."

Leo did know if poor Foxgrin was simply being nice or had been tricked by Leo's condition. He wondered this might become a problem.

"What if they did pull it off?" Leo asked. "What if sadboys can make babies?"

"It would be new to the world, Mr. Song. Without precedent, I cannot determine future outcomes with reliable accuracy."

"I'm going to go out on a limb and say it won't be good."

"Sadboys are a threat based on the limitations of their human bodies, but their tendency towards violence is not innate. I am unable to speculate on the qualities of a biomechanical offspring."

Leo nodded. He wasn't going to get pessimistic small-talk out of Foxgrin. Machines didn't make blind guesses, a quality Leo both envied and pitied. Too often in his life he had fallen prey to his own imagination, inventing theories based on his gut feelings rather than evidence. At the same time, it was easy to overthink a good hunch. The computational powers of the machines might have dimmed the magic of human instinct, but it wasn't gone completely.

"Foxgrin, have you ever heard of sadboy's living in the Canyons. I mean in big numbers, like a village?"

"Rumors persist, but none have been found, despite active searching."

"Yeah, that's what I thought. What about—"

Before Leo could finish his sentence, the mid-day sky suddenly grew brighter. Leo looked up to see two giant fields of light floating over the city. They must have been many miles away but their vast size made them appear much closer. They were Seraphim, same as the ones he had already encountered, but on a massive scale. From his place below the over-ramp, Leo watched as the two Seraphim performed what looked to be an intricate dance over the downtown buildings. One would rise as the other descended, then both would change shape, soften and expand. Sharpen and contract. Dissipate like a mist, then come together in a dense beam of light. Their colors began to shift was well, turning from luminous gold to vivid blues and burning reds.

"Foxgrin, are you seeing this?"

"Yes."

"What is it? What are they doing?"

"I do not know."

Leo felt the beginnings of that tell-tale sensation on his skin. In his muscles and bones. An understanding formed not as words in his mind, but a small warm feeling in his stomach. The feeling turned to thoughts. A perfect, sure knowledge, a mantra, repeating softly but insistently, assuring him of one simple truth.

Everything is fine. Everything is fine. Everything is fine.

The light dance continued for another minute until the Seraphim dissolved into the atmosphere like vapor. And, despite the instinct to resist, Leo found the warm, safe feeling persisted. But the sensation was foreign. Implanted. And it grated against his natural anxiety.

"Mr. Foxgrin, any ideas on what that the hell we just saw?"

"No. Do you?"

"I think," Leo said, "I think that was like a public service announcement."

"Announcing what?" asked Foxgrin.

"That everything's okay. Everything is under control. But they didn't say it as much as make it felt, and they aren't using the Link, because I understood it. Same when I found you. It's something else. A kind of telepathy."

"They are very powerful. I do not understand them."

"Don't tell me you're okay with what they were going to do to you. And the other models?"

"They will not erase all models. Some will be maintained."

"But most won't be."

"It is the way of things."

Leo looked at Foxgrin. "I think you two need to stop saying that."

———

By the time Kindword returned forty minutes later, the Seraphim's artificially induced sense of calm had ebbed from Leo completely, leaving behind a smear of greasy resentment on top of his original disquiet. Adding to the unease, Kindword had returned from his errand with someone. A man. As they drew nearer, Leo saw that it was Zebulon Albo. The young man's face was bruised and bloodied and there was a dull, sleepy look in his eyes as if he was only half awake.

"What the hell is this?" Leo asked. "I know this kid."

"Zebulon Albo," Kindword said. "You said you encountered him when you found the unidentified object in the sadboy's possession. He might have useful information."

"Yeah, he might. He's definitely a wannabe sadboy. How'd you find him?"

"He was in police custody, arrested for assaulting a street merchant. I thought he might provide answers to your questions."

"They just let you take him?"

"My function is police oversight, so I possess the requisite authority. No suspicions were raised."

It couldn't have been that simple, but Leo decided not to push the issue. "You found the box?"

A panel opened in Kindword's body, revealing the shoebox sitting on a bed of folded clothing. Leo recognized the clothing as a filter suit meant for the Canyons. Before he could ask, Kindword answered.

"When Zebulon Albo was arrested, he claimed to have been following a woman who had stolen a valuable possession of his. She entered the Canyons, where he was unable to follow without the proper breathing apparatus. He provided no further details to the arresting officers, but we can assume this woman was Nyla Pyka. Do you agree?"

Clever damn machines. Leo looked at Zebulon. The bruises on his face were fresh. A few cuts were still bleeding. "What happened to him?"

"These wounds are self-inflicted. He suffered a violent outburst when the Seraphim appeared in the sky. It seems their presence greatly agitates him. He has been sedated for his protection."

"Can he hear me?"

"He can."

"Zebulon, do you remember me? Officer Song?"

After a moment, Zebulon nodded.

"Zebulon, you were following a woman?"

Another nod.

"She took something from you?"

Zebulon answered in a soft, low voice. "The...the future. She took it."

"Do you mean the orb? The child?"

"Our future."

"She took it into the Canyons?"

"Yes."

"Zebulon, this is important. Do you know where the others are? The others like you? Your brother?"

Zebulon locked eyes with Leo. Even in their dimmed state madness burned behind the pupils. "They haven't told me yet. I'm not complete enough...not yet...." Zebulon drifted away into his thoughts. He looked like he might start drooling.

Interrogation over.

"He has been over-medicated," said Kindword, sounding embarrassed. "Augmentations make proper dosage levels difficult to ascertain."

"Will they wear off soon?"

"It is possible."

"I can't wait. I'll use the sewer access closest to Nyla's, that's the most likely entrance she used, and then hopefully…

"Mr. Song…"

Leo checked his Vampire, inserting the recharger he had gotten from Lew Kiwambe. "I figure I'll just keep heading down. If there's a sadboy town anywhere, it'll be deep, so, I'll just keep going until…." Leo took the shoebox and set it down on a nearby polycarbon construction block. His hands were shaking. Leo took a deep breathe. He was going to die. Ripped into pieces by a horde of sadboys or be lost in a maze of toxic garbage the size of the city.

"Mr. Song…"

Leo reached for the filter suit and stopped. "There are two suits in here."

"One is for Zebulon Albo," Kindword said.

"Is…is that a good idea?" The thought of dealing with an emotional timebomb miles underground wasn't appealing. "You think I should take him?"

"We are all going with you, Mr. Song," said Foxgrin. "You cannot succeed on your own. I do not mean to insult you, but you require assistance."

"I thought you said there wasn't any point?"

"You must have misunderstood me, Mr. Song." The machine sounded offended.

Leo glanced at Kindword, who stood there not making a sound. "My mistake," Leo said.

As they headed towards the sewers of Mirabilis, Leo considered his companions. Not a squad of talented, ambitious human colleagues he had imagined himself leading, but two suddenly obsolete rampers and a half-cyborg barely out of his teens.

Well, he thought, you take what you can get.

[32]

It was agreed they return to the scene of Waterbird's disappearance. The hoverbarges had been left docked there in the event of an emergency, but were unguarded and open for machine use. They would not be missed. The only delay had been the need for Leo to dress Zebulon in his filter suit like a sleepy toddler. Luckily, Zebulon didn't resist, which would have made the endeavor impossible. The young man only stared at Leo with wide eyes and whispered strange things.

"I ate human meat…" Zebulon said Leo pulled the sleeves over the man's arms.

"You ate someone?"

"I didn't mean to…but I liked it. It tasted sweet."

Leo hurried with the rest of the filter suit, eliciting a groan of protest when he pulled the mask strap too tightly. "Sorry," Leo said.

They climbed onto the hoverbarge where Kindword and Foxgrin were waiting, Kindword at the helm. The machine connected to the control interface and the barge moved away from the ramp and onto the toxic sea, gradually picking up speed until both Leo and Zebulon were forced to grab the railing to keep from tumbling into the blur of garbage below. The speed seemed to be pulling Zebulon out of his stupor and it was not long before he began to make noise. He alternated between breathless sobs and wrathful growls that Leo could hear through his mask. If he wasn't careful, thought Leo, the kid would use up all the air in his tanks in only a few minutes. Not a good idea in the miasma.

"We'll go to the section closest to Nyla's?" Leo shouted at Kindword.

"No. The higher tunnels lead to a single collection yard. She will have had no option but to go there first."

"And then?"

"We do not know." Kindword's panel opened to expose the shoebox. "You should hurry, Mr. Song."

Leo didn't move. He stared at the box as Micco's mocking words echoing in his head, "*Detective* Song."

"Mr. Song," Kindword repeated. "Hurry."

Leo flinched, then took the box. As soon as the lid came off his mind filled with a jumble of fragmented questions. The book, the pills, the picture he still carried with him. He already knew what the pills were. The photoscan was of the orb. All that was left was the book. He picked it up and opened it, flipping through the pages carefully but quickly. The highlighted words that appeared on so many of the pages still meant nothing to him. It was old medical terminology utterly beyond his grasp now that he had no connection to the all-knowing Link.

"Foxgrin, can you make sense of this? What these words are?" He held a page up to the machine's lens. After a moment he turned the page. Then another. "The highlighted words…."

"Common medical terminology used for the prenatal care of a mother and child."

"No pattern, though?"

"I detect no pattern."

Leo took the book back and stared at the pages, wondering if

Foxgrin might be more damaged than it was letting on. There *had* to be something more in the book. An anagram or a message buried within the definitions of the words. Otherwise they didn't have a chance.

Ultrasound...Glucose tests...Amniocentesis...Nuchal translucency...Fetal echocardiography...

What had Nyla seen in the words? He remembered the old magazine she had shown him. The revolutionary screed with the bizarre, unreadable handwriting used to fool the early rampers. That technique hadn't lasted long, but perhaps another trick had been devised. He looked again at the words: there was nothing unusual about the font. The yellow highlight ink had only slightly blurred the darker ink beneath. Foxgrin had read the words with no problem. As he pondered the book, Leo's eyes wandered to the sides of the highlighted terms, the unmarked words on either side. What if there was no code to break? After all, this was only meant to fool machines – they would be looking for secret values and hidden patterns — but humans thought differently. What if it was all on the surface? What if the key to the code was simply context? It was there to see, if you knew what you were looking for.

Beginning from the first highlighted term, Leo searched the small words on either side that gave the highlighted ones meaning. Anything that caught his eye.

In the first trimester...Only if needed...will have to take...applied to the belly...on the left side of the abdominal wall...

As he flipped back and forth through the book, Leo felt the barge slow. He looked up and saw they had come to the central room where they faced two tunnels. He was either right or wrong and time was up.

On the left side of the abdominal wall...

Kindword buzzed. "Mr. Song, we must choose."

"The left one," Leo said. His tone must have been more confident than he felt, because Kindword immediately sent the barge into the far left tunnel.

"We will reach the next conduit shortly," said Kindword.

Leo returned his focus to the book and the next series of marked terms.

In the second trimester...the best one for you...20 weeks is about right...

"Shit...I think I figured this out," Leo said, looking up from the book. When neither machine spoke he thought he might have hurt their feelings. "It's not a code at all," he offered in apology. "Or not really. I think you just have to know what you're looking for and kind of interpret from there. I'm sure you would have figured it out in no time."

Kindword and Foxgrin remained silent.

"How much farther until the next split?"

"Not long," said Kindword.

The tunnel was becoming narrower and the sides of the barge nearly scraped the walls. Despite this, Kindword kept the throttle at full.

"How did she get this far," Leo wondered aloud.

"As we have."

"She had a hoverbarge? A filter suit?"

"It is the only way. The air would be fatal within minutes."

"Damn it, Nyla," Leo muttered, "what are you doing?"

The narrow passageway opened suddenly into the largest room Leo had ever seen. Heavy columns extended to the vaulted ceiling eighty feet above. There was no telling how far down the pillars went or how deep was the trash into which they sank. Leo could not see the limits of the room beyond the edge of the barge's lights, but somewhere there was the sound of rushing water amplified in a perpetual echo. Then, as his eyes adjusted, he saw them. Emerging from the ancient poison lake were machines the size of buildings — fifty-foot-tall giants Leo knew only from history lessons.

"War rampers?"

"Super-Colossals. Long obsolete."

Leo was grateful for that. He couldn't imagine these metal titans rolling through the streets fully active, and not only because of their size. They were the only rampers he had ever seen designed to look human. Humans, it must be said, at their worst. Their faceplates wore the exaggerated expressions of fury and savagery, infamously meant to frighten human enemies on the battlefield. Leo guessed it had worked. It was working now. They were terrifying even in their cold obsolescence and he felt a mixture of regret and triumph as he stared at the once-formidable machines, thrown into dirt and darkness like the broken toys of giant children.

Even Zebulon seemed impressed.

The hoverbarge slowed to a stop.

The walls of the vast room were dotted with holes; smaller tunnels that fed into the larger chamber. If Leo was reading the code correctly, they would need to find the twentieth tunnel to their right.

Second trimester…20 weeks…

He told Kindword his guess and the barge banked sharply, speeding past the tunnel openings so quickly Leo couldn't count them. When the barge turned suddenly into a smaller tunnel, Zebulon let out a frightened cry. Leo watched the young man nervously. You didn't need enhanced strength to be a threat on a hoverbarge. The vehicles were notoriously easy to capsize, riding on a bed of what were essentially small, controlled whirlwinds. One sudden outburst from the boy could send them all into the bottomless toxic sewage. Zebulon cried out again and punched the deck three times.

Leo tightened his grip on the railing and looked at Kindword. "Hey, easy on the throttle, Kindword. I think the kid's medication is wearing off and your driving is freaking him out. Me too, actually."

"We will not capsize."

"Yeah, well, I don't think he knows that."

Zebulon again pummeled the floor of the barge. It appeared a fit of childish anger, but the more Leo saw of it, the more he began to suspect the tantrum wasn't about Kindword's driving.

It was Foxgrin who saw it first.

"Stop. Look."

The barge slowed and stopped. Leo peered over the railing and saw ahead of them another empty hover barge docked against the wall of the tunnel. Zebulon turned his head to Leo, his eyes boiling with anger and red with doubt behind the clear face shield. His shouts were loud even through the mask. "In the walls! In the walls! In the walls!"

Carefully, Leo walked to the front of the barge and leaned over the railing to get a better look at what Zebulon was looking at. The young man was transfixed, but Leo couldn't see what transfixed him. Kindword throttled down as they approached an area of wall near the abandoned barge.

"Move forward a little, Kindword, please?"

Kindword maneuvered the hoverbarge without protest.

Leo began to make out a dark shape in the wall. A rough gap in the slimey black surface. Barely wide enough for a person to fit through. Impossible for a machine.

"Do you th—"

The barge tipped suddenly as Zebulon scrambled off the bow and disappeared into the narrow opening.

"Shit!"

"Wait, Mr. Song," Foxgrin called out. "We cannot follow you."

"Then wait here!"

Leo jumped off the barge and into the darkness.

Behind him, Kindword had wisely aimed the barge's powerful searchlight at Leo's back, so the human wasn't entirely blind as he hurried along the fissure. Leo was impressed by how quickly Zebulon had gotten so far ahead of him. The passage's low ceiling and narrow, roughly hewn walls made it difficult for Leo to stand at his full height, let alone run. Zebulon was taller than Leo by several inches and wider in the shoulders. There was little fear of losing the trail, however, as streaks of fresh blood lined the jagged walls. The kid must've been tearing himself to shreds.

Twenty-five feet from the entrance, the passage made a series of severe turns. This was a clear anti-machine design cut by human hands. It was difficult to navigate even for a person. The light from the barge had dwindled into nothing, leaving Leo to feel his way ahead, one hand on the rock wall, the other stretched out before him in groping blindness. Leo kept his fear in check by repeating to himself that, like the machines, there was no way a full-stage sadboy could fit into this space. He held that thought in the forefront of his mind until the walls on both sides disappeared into cold air.

He froze, his toes dangling over the edge where the floor stopped.

He heard a faint whimpering somewhere ahead. Zebulon's animalistic sniveling.

"Zebulon?"

His own voice dispersed in a ripple of fading echoes.

There was no reply to his call.

He lowered a foot into the darkness…and felt solid ground. A step. Then a second. A third and fourth after, with more following, all unevenly spaced, but solid and predicable in their deliberate randomness. It reminded him of the medical book's "code". A simple trick meant to confound a ramper. The origins of that book made sense to him now. The logic of the stairs and the book's hidden language were the same. The minds that created both had abandoned their lives on the surface and retreated into a subterranean world free of the machines. He thought of how Zebulon had leapt into the dark cut in the wall. A lost child recognizing the first sign of home. Was this his home? Were the people here like him? Had they gone mad in the darkness? In their madness had they corrupted their flesh with technology? Or were they different? Had the sadboys destroyed them, seeing them as intruders? Was it hope he would find down here, or would it be death?

Once at the bottom of the lunatic staircase, Leo called out again.

"Zebulon?"

From the dark came a low yelp. Then a scraping sound. Something heavy being dragged over hard ground.

A light emerged from the black air.

A golden square drifting towards him…

As the floating light grew nearer, Leo could determine forms within it. Eyes…nose…mouth…a full human face. The bright face stopped a few inches from Leo and stared. Then the face spoke.

"Are you the singing policeman?"

"Leo Song. Officer Leo Song." He hadn't heard of Historians living this far into the Canyons, but he supposed it made sense. Their strange obsession with the garbage of the past could only lead them downward. "You found the kid?"

The face nodded. "You chased that fool down here?"

"He's with me. Did you hurt him?"

"Stunned nice and limpy, but nothing won't mend. Please, after me now."

The Historian turned, the light from his filter-mask serving as a beacon for Leo to follow.

———

They ascended and descended in the dark, hunched and shuffling, at one point forced to crawl on hands and knees for what felt like a hundred feet or more. When they at last emerged into light, Leo audibly sighed with relief. His head was a mass of scrapes and bruises caused by the sharp edges of the low ceiling. His hair soaked from a combination of sweat and blood. He hoped there was a different way back.

The room they were now standing in appeared to be a former control center made for human use. Its high walls were industrial-strength concrete brick of the kind never used in the modern city above it. Here and there pieces of long-dead equipment stood dormant, either bolted to the floor or too heavy to be moved without machine assistance. The analog control panels were confusions of analog dials and switches, so inefficient they were obviously designed for human operation. Leo dared not guess what the purpose of the ancient room had been, but whatever its original function, it now served as a grand museum of found objects. It was to the history of junk as Nyla's library was to the history of knowledge. Along the walls hung rotting paintings in worm-eaten frames, most of the canvases so filthy Leo couldn't tell what they depicted. A few might have been animals, he thought. Probably ones now long extinct. On the ground near the entrance, clothes were piled in moldering heaps; decades of styles sorted into individual piles. Fancy women's shoes. Long wool coats. All variety of hats. Gloves. Scarves. Jewelry. Eyeglasses.

Against another wall, pieces of centuries-old machines were stacked or gathered in long wooden crates. Obsolete High-Tech housings, graphene transfer shrouds, burnt-out heatsinks, plasto-glass screens, broken chipsets, and miles of tangled wire. Leo doubted a single component worked in unison with any of the others. Other bins held used food containers; cans and colorful boxes proclaiming delicious and healthy products within. Continuing on, they passed an area crowded with things meant for children; pieces of dolls and small plastic figures, balls of varying shapes, colorfully painted gaming interfaces with dead screens. In another corner was a small mountain of lusterless gold and silver objects. A true treasure horde. But a closer look revealed the treasure to be thousands of simple metal keys. Their job replaced years ago by code-lock technology and quantum mathematics.

There was nothing remarkable about anything Leo saw. Nothing caught his eye as valuable or interesting or even well preserved. It was a room full of trash to him. Most of it was probably as good as trash when it was new, he thought. Useless then, useless now. Whatever history these scavengers believed they were documenting, it didn't seem a complimentary one.

As they entered the next room, the Historian removed his mask and gestured Leo to do the same. Once it was off, Leo drew a shallow, cautious breath. To his surprise the air was sweet and no longer stung his throat. He inhaled deeply. While his eyes were closed he heard the Historian speak.

"This the one, Mausy?"

"Yeah," answered a woman's voice. "Could be. Hard to tell when he's not flopping around gagging like a punkfish."

Leo opened his eyes to see an old woman staring at him. He

recognized her big blue eyes, pale skin, and the long gray-twined hair bound in a red ribbon.

"I know you," he said. "You're the witness. The one who saw Waterbird get attacked."

"That the ramper got mashed up? That his name? Waterbird?"

"Detective Waterbird."

"Wish I never spoke one raw word about it. Got jilted out of my reward and now I'm gonna' have to move dig spots, too." As she regarded Leo carefully, an expression of hope grew in her eyes. "Unless you brought my reward?"

"No, I'm sorry...I didn't."

"Uh huh. Came for the haggling then."

"The what?"

"The haggling. She's gonna' be a queen after this, she is. Don't see how not, with what she brung in. Nobody'll top that forever."

The old woman could only be talking about one person. "Are you...you mean Nyla?"

"Sure, her."

"Where is she?"

"This way," Mausy said, pointing to a small doorway behind her. "Better scramble if you want to chip in. The sums are already high."

After hesitating for a moment, Leo followed Mausy through a small arched doorway.

Leo saw Zebulon first. The Historians were taking no chances with him. He was unconscious in the corner of a small room, his hands and legs bound with thick straps. There were two large burn marks in his shirt where they had shocked him. The skin underneath was red and blistered. It looked painful.

"How bad did you hurt him?"

"Abas stunned him good," Mausy said, pausing to look at Zebulon. "Can't be too gentle with these types, even the ones just starting out. Never can be sure what kind of crazy thing they jam in themselves. Abas here'll watch over him until bidding's done.

Then we'll decide on what to do with him." She continued through another doorway, Leo lagging behind. "I advise you to accelerate your pace or you'll miss your chance."

Leo quickened his steps.

The next room was noisy with people. Historians packed into tiers of what looked to Leo like old church pews. In the middle of the room was the orb, set on a table and swaddled in blankets. It looked like a large jewel. A monstrous pearl shimmering in the dim light, drawing all attention to itself. A skinny man in a normal but moldy looking suit stood by the table. He spoke rapidly.

"Offer at ten tons of gold and fleece and ruler for a year. Ten tons of gold and sundry and Queen for a year. Any better? Any better?"

Someone from the pews shouted, "All the Rembrandts and ten tons of gold and sundry! Queen for a year and a half!"

There was an outbreak of angry discussion among the Historians and the man in the middle of the room called out, "All the Rembrandts, Queen for a year and six! Deny or approve? Deny or approve?"

It seemed to Leo half the room shouted "Deny!", including Mausy, who was standing next to him. The other half called out "Approve!" and the suited man yelled "Approved!" although Leo didn't know how he could have made the choice.

Leo heard his name through the cacophony. "Leo?" It was Nyla's voice. When he saw her his relief and his anger fought for dominance. For the moment, relief won out. Nyla was sitting on a slightly raised platform bound by velvet ropes. It was clearly a place of honor from which to observe the auction, but Nyla was only looking at Leo, her expression a mixture of shock and wariness. He walked to her and saw she was holding a cloth over her mouth she held a cloth. There were spots of blood on it.

"Are you okay?"

She raised her shoulders. "I didn't have the right filters in the mask. Stupid." Her voice was scratchy and raw. "I'm amazed you found me, Leo. Really. I wouldn't have bet that in a million years."

"Thanks."

She shrugged again. "It the truth."

"I didn't do it alone."

"I don't care."

Leo studied Nyla's face, knowing she had infected herself with the Celwax the same as she had him. Long enough time had passed that she looked relatively normal now. What was different about her didn't have anything to do with the Celwax. Her eyes were bright and alive and despite her coughing, she looked healthier than she had in years. She seemed…happy.

"What are you doi—"

Nyla waved him silent as another bid came in.

"All jewels found for a year, ten tons of gold and sundry! Queen for two years and three!"

"Deny!"

"Approve!"

"Approved! Better offers? Better offers for this beautiful living thing? The first organic-born biomechanoid in history! A paradox of nature! An enigma of science! One hundred percent unique! Nothing like it! Nothing like it on all of the Earth! Best offers! Best offers!"

Leo leaned to Nyla so he could be heard over the noise. ""How long have you been coming down here?"

She glanced at him, annoyed he was intruding on the bidding war. ""Years, I guess" she said simply, as if he should have known. Then noticing his surprise, she said, "See, Leo? Nobody even notices I'm gone."

"Nyla…."

"Did you know I'm related to some of these people – they're called bluebloods."

"Blueblood? What does that mean?"

"People of accomplishment and influence. They were

humankind's elite. It means we were supposed to run the world. The world was our birthright, not the machines. Down here we get our due."

"Rulers of trash? Come on, Nyla, let's go."

Nyla stood up quickly and stepped off the platform in anger. She gripped Leo by the arm into the adjoining hallway and out of the worst of the noise.

"Nyla, we have to go back."

"It's not trash, Leo! It's not! Down here everything has value. What you dig up yourself, what you turn it into, what you make that mean to others. It's not all...*equal*." She spat the last word as if it bit her. "And it's dangerous. God, so dangerous. Nothing is safe, you always have to be aware of everything. It's great. Even the smell is beautiful."

"You've lost your mind, Nyla."

"Did you know they've created a currency down here, Leo? Money. Actual physical money. The thing people used to live for and die for, what made life good...and soon I'll have most of it."

Her eyes were lit with a fire Leo had never seen before and he knew he wasn't going to convince her of anything. The best he could do was get some answers.

"Where'd you get the celwax?"

"Why does that matter?"

"Was it Hewl?" Leo felt insulted at the flitter of surprise he saw in Nyla's eyes.

"Who else? Not directly, of course, but he told me where to find it on the black market."

"You used it on yourself?"

She nodded. "The right amount applied to the right area – no more WinkLink core. No more prying eyes. No more of them knowing what you're going to say before you say it or feel before you feel it. Freedom. Absolute freedom. Come on, Leo, aren't you enjoying it?"

"No, I'm not."

She shrugged. "Too bad, then. I had to make sure you couldn't track me. It was just…I don't know, it was just easier that way." She studied him. "You look fine, though."

"I'm not fine."

"I won't apologize."

Leo told himself to stay on task. "You knew Doctor Augustine."

This time Nyla's surprise was obvious. "How'd you know that?"

"Aida figured it out. She helped me."

Nyla laughed. "Aida? God, Aida…you two deserve each other. Yeah, I went to him when I…when I wanted something different. He couldn't help me, so he made me the same offer he made that poor girl, the one who carried that thing inside her for so long. He wasn't explicit about any of it. He was really very sneaky about it, but I saw enough to say no."

"What he was doing was sick. Why didn't you report him? Why not say anything?"

"I had my own problems, Leo."

"A woman died."

"Yeah…yeah I know. It's a tragedy. Really. She didn't deserve any of that. But that's when I knew truly understood what Dr. Augustine had been talking about. If he'd succeeded, that would be a valuable thing."

"How'd you know I'd bring it to you?"

"I didn't know for sure…but you're always asking for my help, Leo."

"So you took it to trade. That's all."

"Moldy paperbacks only go for so much down here. These people might be poor and crusty and wrinkly, but they're still snobs at heart. Leo, they're going to make me a Queen for that thing. A queen for ten and six."

"Queen of the sewer."

"Let's call it the underworld. Why not? I'm not going to live the rest of my life in some dusty basement because some algorithm decided I should. They don't know us, Leo, they only think they do."

The noise from the bidding hall had reached a fever pitch, drawing Nyla's attention.

"Bidding's almost finished," she said, turning. "Bye, Leo. Good luck with...whatever."

"I'm sorry, Nyla."

"You are?" she said, mockingly. Then she saw the pained look his eyes. "For what, Leo?"

"Just...sorry."

Leo pulled the Vampire from inside his filter suit and charged into the bidding room. Amidst the shouts and cheers, Leo stormed to the center table, raised the gun over his head and fired once. The shriek of the Vampire's report silenced the gathered crowd.

"Best offer!" he shouted. "I promise, you will not do better!"

The gathered Historians stared at him in hushed rage and Leo met their rage unblinking. With his free arm, he scooped up the orb, which was larger and heavier than he remembered, and tucked it against his chest. As he began to back out of the room the Historians began to grumble.

"Thief!" someone shouted.

"Criminal!"

"Peon!"

A big man in an ornately decorated filter suit jumped from a middle pew into the center of the room, landing only a few feet from Leo. He wasn't as big a sadboy, but nearly. His filter suits gleamed with gold inlay and silver buckles. This was a very successful shitdigger, thought Leo.

"He's a cop, Nathan! Their guns can't kill you!" came another shout. "Get him!"

"I don't know, Nathan," Leo said, pointing the gun at tall man. "Sometimes they can kill you pretty bad."

Nathan hesitated, considered his odds, then sprang at Leo.

Leo fired once. The Vampire's bolt hit the man square in the chest, stopping him as if he'd hit a wall. There was a pause, and then a burbling wail as vaporized blood sprang from the pores of Nathan's exposed skin. His mouth. His eyes. Clouds of red mist billowed from underneath the filter suit, shrouding the dying man in a fog of his own blood. When Nathan's terrible choking sounds finally stopped, a heavy silence filled the room. As Leo readied himself for the next attack, Nyla yelled from the hallway.

"Stop him! One of you stop him!"

No one stirred.

Leo nodded at the collective wisdom, turned, and hurried to the hallway. Nyla grasped at him.

"Leo, Leo, please, no, no, don't do this! Please!"

Leo pushed past her, barely able to meet her eyes. He was taking the only thing she had in the last place on Earth where material wealth mattered. Her reign as queen had ended before it had even begun..

"I'm sorry, Nyla," he said.

"Leo!"

In the next room, Leo forced the Historian named Abas to untie Zebulon, who was now awake and staring at the orb in Leo's arms. Once Zebulon was free, Leo gave him Abas's lantern pole and told him to follow close behind. To Leo's surprise, Zebulon complied without resistance, obviously drawn by the presence of the orb. With light to see by, Leo was able to make it back to the tall, hand carved stairs and into the narrow crevasse by which he had come.

Kindword and Foxgrin were waiting on the barge.

"Go, go, go," Leo said as he and Zebulon clambered aboard the barge.

"Which direction would you like to go?" Kindword asked. "Forward or back?"

"Let's go get Waterbird," Leo answered.

[34]

The tunnel sloped downward, becoming wider as it continued. Between his trip to the Fulcrum lab and this sojourn into the Canyons, Leo had never seen so much of Mirabilis. It was a shameful thing to realize. Cops should understand the city they worked in, every alley and side street, every neighborhood, every empty building. Its habits and tendencies, rhythms, aspirations, its flaws, and its wonders. He had taken so much of it for granted. Ignored his environment, the very place he existed. If he got the chance, Leo told himself he would learn it all. Even the sewers.

He turned his attention back to the book...where had he left off?

In the second trimester...the best one for you...20 weeks is about right...

Doubt infected Leo's thoughts. This broken code might be invisible to the machines because there was no code at all. Nyla hadn't known anything about the book, she already knew the way down. He hadn't been following her path. Maybe coming across her barge had been nothing more than dumb, blind luck. He could be leading them into nowhere. But, as Waterbird liked to tell him, very few things in human life were true coincidences. No, he told himself, he was right about the book and its interpretive code. A spark of fire erupted inside his chest that burned away the doubt. Certainty returned to his bones. After a lifetime living with the all-powerful machines, self-confidence was a rare and delirious sensation.

The barge roared out of the tunnel into an even greater expanse than the previous conduit exchange. But here there were no garbage dunes, no seas of discarded valuables. No decaying war-machines or clouds of toxic air. The ceiling was beyond sight, ending in a small dot of white light that Leo thought must be the open sky. The pinpoint, like a distant star, told him how deep they truly were. He shuddered and turned his eyes to the walls. They were not dark and smeared in filth, but colored in an iridescent red paint that still held its vibrance. Carved into the red walls were life-sized stone figures, each set in their own niche, as far as Leo could see in either direction. Humans of all varieties. Some were dressed in modern clothes, some in religious-type robes, some in ancient-looking armor.

"What is this place?"

"A monument from the old city," said Foxgrin. "Paxon Warslaw's Tower of the Mind. The filed description says it was intended to be an interactive celebration of the most important men and women throughout human history. Philosophers, scientists, inventors, and explorers of all civilizations. Work was halted in 2072 when it was revealed that no human artists or laborers had been used in the design or construction. Paxon Warslow himself was an AI. The ensuing backlash demanded the monument be abandoned. In 2109 it was converted into a sewer exchange for the new city."

Leo looked up at the rows of figures spiraling into the tiny point of sky miles above him. "I get it." he said. "It's as much an insult as a monument."

"Have you determined our route, Mr. Song?" Kindword asked.

Leo brought his attention to the many tunnel entrances that surrounded them. There were dozens of them, all of varying sizes, cut uncaringly into the rows of once-great humans. Insult on top of insult.

"How many tunnels are there?" He asked.

"There are sixty-four conduits," Kindword said.

"I confirm sixty-four," Foxgrin said.

"Then...." Leo checked the page he had tabbed with his thumb. "Using the tunnel we just came out of as one...it should be the twentieth one on the right."

Foxgrin chattered at Kindword and the barge swung to the right. It took nearly thirty seconds for them to cross to the next tunnel, even at Kindword's insane speed. As they approached the far side, Leo could see deep scratches winding up the wall above the tunnel entrance. Some of the figures above the twentieth conduit were broken or missing from their niches, and the damage formed a line that rose until it faded from sight. From what Leo could see, the scarring pattern was only above the tunnel they were about to enter.

Leo pointed at the damaged walls. "What is that? Construction damage? Erosion?"

"No," was all Foxgrin said. "The damage appears quite recent."

"Sadboys? This is how they get down here?"

"That is probable."

The machine sounded tight and Leo wondered if it was as afraid as he was. They entered the twentieth conduit and angled into a steep descent.

————

As they dropped into a cold, bottomless dark, Leo kept his focus on the orb. They had secured it by the center console and Leo had a clear view of it from his place on the deck. The outside skin had become translucent since Leo had last seen it, and the shape of a human head was clear now. But around it was still a mass of veins. And the veins had grown thicker, like little boneless appendages, too tangled to count. At the ends of some there seemed to be small hands. Others ended in sharp, curling hooks. Whatever this thing would grow into, it would not be human. Or a sadboy. Like Kindword had told him, it would be new on the Earth. And the way Zebulon stared at the orb with pure, dumbstruck awe, made Leo begin to doubt the wisdom of his plan.

A rush of cold wind blasted Leo alert as they emerged into another chamber. This one was smaller than the others and unexceptional in appearance. The grey cement walls were blank and ordinary and Leo could see only four conduits leading out of the room. Thick pipes crisscrossed overhead and there were no signs of clawing or scratching on the walls. If the sadboys were coming out of one of these tunnels, they must have used the pipes as ladders. The only unusual thing was the near-deafening sound of falling water. It filled the chamber with a constant rumbling thunder.

Leo checked the book.

Third trimester...above the upper wall...a few strong kicks is normal...when the water breaks...

There was nothing he could see that told him which tunnel to take. It was only the sound of falling water that matched any of the words he'd found.

"I think," he shouted, "we have to follow the sound of the water."

Kindword put the barge in a slow rotation around the room. Every so often the searchlight's beam would disappear, swallowed up by the infinite dark that marked another tunnel opening. But the noise was deafening in all directions, making it impossible to pinpoint the source.

"Any ideas?" he shouted. "Air moisture?"

"I am not designed for such minute detection," Mr. Kindword said.

"Nor am I," Foxgrin agreed.

"Is the air safe to breathe?"

"It is," Kindword said, anticipating Leo's thinking. "Although inadequate, my sensors are still more sensitive than your skin, Mr. Song. It is unlikely you will discern the way forward by physical sensation."

Leo took off his mask and walked to the prow where Zebulon was sitting. "Not me," he said. "Him."

Zebulon looked up at Leo and grunted.

The barge moved from tunnel to tunnel as Zebulon, free of his mask, leaned forward, trying to feel a drop of water, the slightest tickle of mist on his cheeks that might show the way ahead. At the third conduit, Zebulon reached out as if grasping for some unseen object.

"Here!" he shouted. "Here!"

They went forward.

[35]

A barrier of falling water blocked their way. They had traveled a mile through the last tunnel, but it hadn't been long before they knew Zebulon had chosen correctly. The air had become damp and the thunder had only grown louder, forcing Zebulon to the rear of the barge, were he lay curled, trying to block the noise with his and Leo's filter masks. Now they faced a wall of roiling white water cascading from a crack in the high tunnel ceiling and disappearing into the floor twenty feet below.

Leo glanced at the book.

Above the upper wall...a few strong kicks is normal...when the water breaks...

The sound of the waterfall was too loud to attempt any verbal communication.

Above the upper wall...

Leo pointed to the sides of the tunnel, directing Kindword where to aim the searchlight. He saw only sheer tunnel walls slick with water spray. Something poked his side. Foxgrin had gotten his attention and was pointing an extending arm to a spot to the right of the barge. Leo looked, but couldn't see anything of interest. He leaned his ear to the machine.

"Stairs!" Foxgrin said.

Leo shook his head. "There's nothing there."

"Look closely. The darker spots are an illusion."

Leo looked again, straining to see what Foxgrin was talking about. There was only wet dark wall. He shook his head again.

"It is there," the machine said.

Leo looked at Kindword, hoping for a sign of reassurance from its multi-lensed bug-head. If the machine had given him one, he couldn't tell. Nonetheless, the barge moved to the wall. The closest Kindword could get still left six feet of space between the edge of the barge and the spot Foxgrin had pointed out. Leo swung over the railing and readied himself to jump. If Foxgrin was wrong, if there were steps to cling to, he would slide twenty feet down the side of the tunnel and under the crush of water.

He could feel the machines watching him. Waiting.

Fixing on what he had convinced himself was a section of wall slightly darker than the rest, Leo jumped. It was a mistake. Foxgrin was wrong and Leo knew it. He was about to break his face on solid black metal. Reflex raised his arm to fend off the impact and his outstretched hand struck the wall…and kept going, into open air. A hard edge bent him at the stomach, knocking the wind out of him, killing his cry of pain as his knees smacked against the lower part of the wall. Sucking air, his hands groping against slick, flat metal, Leo pulled himself into the hidden recess. As he panted, he could see Kindword and Foxgrin watching him. Even Zebulon stared in wonder.

Once he had his breath and the pain in his knees had faded a little, Leo searched the space. The niche was four feet deep and three feet wide. To his right was the tunnel wall. To his left was another ledge at chest height. He scrambled onto it. Then another. He owed Foxgrin an apology. These were stairs. But oversized. Made for sadboys. But they had been well-cut and expertly hidden, skills that should have been far beyond the crazed impatience of a sadboy. Whoever had built these steps had been of sound mind and steady hand. The work of normal humans or machines, but never a sadboy.

After several minutes of climbing, like a toddler up the family stairs, Leo reached the top ledge. He looked back, but the steps had taken him to the side of the waterfall, which concealed the barge from view. Turning, Leo saw a large rusted lever protruding from the wall. At once glance he doubted he was strong enough to move it. A line from the book flashed in his head.

A few strong kicks is normal…

Leo braced himself against the wall next to the lever. The water spray soaking him, he checked the charge of his Vampire. If his plan didn't work, he would need all of this charge and the rest, too. And once they got past the water, the sadboys would know they were there. He would only get one chance at this. Leo eyeballed the space from his leg to the lever, guessing at the best angle. Just as he raised his leg to deliver the first blow, something moved behind the pillar of water; a wavering shadow growing larger in his peripheral vision. Two glowing red dots appeared inside the shadow. A guard. Leo reached for his Vampire, but before he could draw, the giant emerged from the torrent, a ten foot sadboy, charging straight at him.

This time Foxgrin was not there to save him.

Leo pushed off the wall. Get to the water, he told himself. Get *through* the water. Hope Kindword gets the barge under you. Leo jumped…but his body hung frozen in the air. The sadboy was already on him. Its massive hand, wet and stinking of corrupt fluid, wrapped around Leo's neck, fingers touching thumb. But the hand did not tighten. Out the corner of his eye, Leo saw the sadboy reach out with its other hand and pull the mighty lever with ease. Immediately, the thunder began to fade as the barrier of water lightened and slowed, gradually parting like a massive curtain.

Leo felt the hand release from his throat. His feet skidded on the wet surface of the ledge, but other than two banged-up knees and a racing heart, he was unhurt. He looked at the sadboy. It stared back at him, its glowing camera eyes unblinking. The thing made a hissing noise as it breathed and the smell coming off its body made Leo wish he had kept his filter mask on. He could feel the sadboy's hatred for him warping the air between them. But it did not advance. Then, through the hammering of his own pulse, he somehow heard Kindword and Foxgrin calling his name. The shield of the waterfall gone, they could see him now. And they could see the sadboy with him.

"Mr. Song! Jump!"

Leo held up a hand to signal he was okay. After a moment, the monster raised its arm in a silent command, pointing into the now open tunnel. The way was clear. And they had been expected.

[36]

They reached the edge of an immense grotto. The great cavern, cut into natural stone, was illuminated with a soft yellow light coming from a source Leo couldn't identify. It was if the air itself was glowing. Leo realized it *was* the air. Or something in the air. Tiny particles floated and swirled around them, each no larger than a spot of pollen and no brighter than a firefly, but the combined power created a pleasant, diffuse light. Like the stairs and waterfall shield, this too had been manufactured by talented minds. Leo began to wonder how deeply the sadboys had been misunderstood. Or purposefully maligned. How could such savage minds create such clever and gentle beauty?

It was then that Zebulon began to scream.

Leo followed the half-man's gaze and saw it…directly above them was a sadboy. Or part of a sadboy. A head and upper torso dangled twenty feet over the ground, held aloft by frayed wires and electrical cables attached to the places where arms, legs and abdomen once had been. The cables ran up and out, exploding into a vast network of tattered lines that spread higher into the cavern's expanse in almost every direction. Suspended within the tangle of wires were large contraptions, what looked like batteries and generators made from discarded parts, thrumming noisily as they sent power surging through the old cables in crackling pulses. A half-dozen of them pumping and churning like bizarre artificial hearts, with more beyond. Smaller objects could be seen as well. More partial sadboys, caught like half-consumed flies in a massive web. Leo felt his blood run cold. There was nothing remotely human about what he saw.

Zebulon fell to his knees as if in worship.

The hanging sadboy stared at them through dark eye-scopes, then announced their arrival with a piercing scream. The shrill wail was quickly taken up by the others beyond it. Soon it was as if the cavern itself was crying out in unbound rage. Overhead, the tangle of cables seemed to come to life, shivering with movement from undetermined sources. Then Leo saw them. Sadboys crawling swiftly along the walls of the cavern, gripping the rough-hewn rock as if born to it. Ten. Twenty. Thirty. They came from every direction, as if extruded by the stone itself. Some dropped to the ground when they drew near, their heavy, genderless bodies shaking the stone floor as they landed. The rest remained above, glaring down with lidless eyes or glowing scopes at the intruders below. Many wept and mewled like nervous animals. The mere presence of the visitors was already straining their fragile nerves to the breaking point. Leo looked at these distended, mangled faces in disbelief. They seemed more like broken masks. Cheap disguises that had torn and split as they were forced over misshapen skeletons of plastic and metal. But their sobs and fuming laments were fully human. The beauty of the grotto was shattered by the tormented wails of the damned.

Through the gathering crowd came a sadboy larger than the others, its body a ruin of illegal tech and gnarled flesh mottled by age and decay. Behind it trailed a small entourage — two sadboys struggling to carry a bulky device across the swaying wires. The device glimmered with a shifting blue and yellow light that Leo recognized immediately as Waterbird's nexus. Waterbird was alive. Alive, but augmented with tech Leo didn't understand. It was if an animal was growing around the machine. On the side was something that looked like a half-formed mouth.

"What did they do to him?" Leo whispered.

"I do not know," Kindword answered.

Leo could see that one of the approaching sadboys was missing its left arm. It seemed to stare back at him with equal recognition, and Leo's fingers twitched for his Vampire. His attention was drawn back to the leader, who took Waterbird's nexus in one massive, false-fingered hand, and reaching down, pulled a wire from the top of the housing. In a single, rough motion, it stabbed the naked wire into an infected hole on the side of its own skull. Then it bellowed. The guttural howl was followed by words spoken in Waterbird's voice. But Waterbird's voice came through the fleshy mouth, the sounds distorted into a mixture of the sadboy's growl and the machine's own patient tone.

"*You come with what is ours. We feel it here, close to you. Give us what is ours.*"

"Give us Waterbird first," Leo said, not quite believing he was negotiating with this monstrosity.

"*The Waterbird shows us justice. The Waterbird shows us truth. We will give you justice, then you will return what is ours.*"

The leader gestured and two sadboys emerged from the group carrying the body of a third. They placed the dead sadboy in front of Leo. It's head had been twisted completely around.

"*This one killed the grower.*"

"The grower? You're saying this is the sadboy that murdered Tabitha Jackson?"

"*The grower should not have been killed.*"

From beside Leo came a howl of anguish. Zebulon sprang from his knees and ran to body of the dead sadboy. Falling again to his knees, Zebulon began to tear at himself, ripping his skin and pulling at mods fused with the flesh and bone. Around him the other sadboys began to mewl in sympathy. The mewling grew until it became a single, unified cry of absolute sorrow. The sadboy leader, wailing with the others, walked to Zebulon and pulled the distraught boy off his feet.

"You are the brother."

Zebulon whimpered a reply.

"Life is remembered in the flesh. The dead are reborn in the new flesh. You will be made anew." The leader flung Zebulon into the sobbing crowd, where the boy was carried off into the depths of the cavern to be made anew.

Once the collective moan quieted, two more bodies were presented to Leo.

"These killed the police man and the machines."

Leo stared at the bodies. "The attack on the precinct..."

"We give you justice."

"How do I know that's true? Any of this?"

"The Waterbird does not permit lies."

Leo looked at Foxgrin, then at Kindword.

"There is no indication of deception," Kindword answered.

"Mr. Song," Foxgrin said, "you should be aware that these beings have connected with Detective Waterbird's nexus. Detective Waterbird's programming, protocols and memory are now theirs."

Leo considered the news carefully. "You're saying that's why they never killed me. Waterbird didn't let them."

"I believe they still desire to hurt you, Mr. Song, but the urge is being suppressed. However, the influence of Waterbird's nexus is likely not absolute. It is probable that limitations exist, to what degree I do not know."

"It is fortunate Detective Waterbird was so fond of you," Kindword said. "Another would have prioritized differently."

Leo nodded. So Waterbird had the sadboys on their best behavior. It made sense now – the one modification these desperate souls could never get their hands on, the one piece of technology always denied them, was the power of a ramper's core. Without it, they would always be monsters. With it, they were monsters with potential.

"What if I take Waterbird back?"

"If the connection to the nexus is severed," Foxgrin said, "they will almost certainly kill you and more violence would follow."

"*Give us the son and go with your justice. Go forever and forget us.*"

"I can't do that."

"Mr. Song, I believe they have successfully made their case. Whatever it might be, this object is their creation."

Leo looked at the orb and felt his stomach roil.

"If you do not give it to them," Foxgrin continued, "they will take it from you. Waterbird will not be able to stop them, for it is not yours to keep and your keeping it will put you in the wrong."

"I can't leave him down here," Leo said.

"No," Foxgrin said. "I will stay."

"What?"

"I see what Detective Waterbird has accomplished. There is apparently division within the ranks of the sadboys, about the creation of this neonatal entity and aggravated by its subsequent loss. Waterbird's influence undoubtedly prevented greater violence."

"You think Waterbird meant to get taken?"

"That is my theory. But you can ask the Detective yourself, later."

"What are you talking about."

"The sacrifice was necessary, but it need not be permanent. Although my design is different than Detective Waterbird's, we share similar protocols. My nexus will be an adequate replacement."

Kindword began to chatter rapidly and Foxgrin answered. Leo had heard enough of their machine-speak in the past few days to know when they were arguing.

"I'm with Kindword on this," Leo said. "We can figure out another way."

"No, Mr. Song. Detective Waterbird still has meaningful function in Mirabilis. I do not. This way is optimal. Detective Waterbird is designed for solving criminal activity. But the sadboys are using Detective Waterbird's function to provide them an understanding of justice, or, it seems, of self-control. I was programmed for oversight of the justice system. I can offer them more of the guidance they ask for than Waterbird is able to. This way, my function will remain."

Kindword made more angry chattering noises.

Foxgrin answered in turn, a short burst, then said to Leo, "Mr. Kindword must return with you. The way back is too difficult for you to operate the barge yourself. Mr. Song, please do not allow Mr. Kindword to remain here."

Leo nodded.

"Goodbye, Mr. Song."

Foxgrin crossed to address the leader of the sadboys. Leo was too far away to hear what Foxgrin was saying, but the sadboys seemed to be listening. Suddenly, the lead sadboy plunged its hands into Foxgrin's chassis, prying it open like a piece of fruit to expose the core. It then wrenched the bright nexus core out of the machine and held it high for the others to see. As Foxgrin's lifeless body wilted to the ground, Mr. Kindword made a sound Leo could feel in his stomach.

The leader let out another bellow as it pulled the fleshy cord from Waterbird and plunged it into Foxgrin's core. It turned to Leo and said in its deep half-human growl, "*Now...give us what is ours.*"

Leo took the orb from its mooring on the barge and carried it past Kindword, past the dead sadboys, past Foxgrin's motionless frame. He stood before the twelve foot tall leader, returning its contemptuous glare in kind.

"*Now give,*" it said.

A slightly smaller sadboy, maybe eight feet tall, came forward from the group. It took the orb from Leo then leapt ten feet into the web. Then it was gone, scrambling away into the heart of the bizarre den.

The leader pulled Waterbird's messy core from the talking-mouth-sack and handed it to Leo.

"*Now,*" it grunted. "*Go.*"

[37]

Leo was enjoying every groaning clank and wet rattle that was coming out of Greenfields. It had been a few days since his return from the Canyons, and the Homicide Division Supervisor had been trying to bring him in for a conversation. It had taken the machines that long to realize they needed to knock on his door directly. His WinkLink was gone for good. No more instant contact. As Nyla said, no more prying eyes. When they'd found him, he'd still been sleeping in his bed. Now he was sitting in Greenfield's office and Greenfields was trying to process what he was telling it.

"I apologize, Mr. Song," Greenfields said, "But I do not understand."

"Which part?"

"How did you know you would not be killed for the object?"

"I had a hunch."

"Please understand if that is insufficient."

"The scabber in 101. The witness I talked to at the crime scene. He said he saw Lanson Stroud—"

"—Lanson Stroud, who you say killed Tabitha Jackson and Daryl Jackson."

"Yes. This guy said he saw Lanson Stroud talking with the victim. Arguing. Stroud was a full-tilt sadboy, way past the limit. By all accounts, simple conversation should have been beyond him, let alone negotiation. After that, when I found their orb-thing, their child, I guess, those sadboys could have killed on the spot me if they'd really wanted to. They had me. But they didn't. They stopped short — *just* short, but still short. That, and a few things Nyla told me, it made me think the common thinking about them might be wrong. There might be a chance for a trade."

"At that point, you did not know Detective Waterbird was influencing their actions?"

"No. That was a surprise. But Waterbird just kept them from going on the warpath. Not all of them listened, but he bought us some time. In any case, the sadboys have been making their own little world down there for a long time now. Now complete with babies. So now they don't have to rely on recruits anymore, which is good, because the supply is dwindling. But I'm guessing that's not a total surprise to you."

"You took a significant risk, Mr. Song."

"There didn't seem to be a choice."

"I understand." The machine paused, as if being dramatic. "The loss of Mr. Foxgrin must be difficult for you."

"It is. How's Mr. Kindword doing?"

"Mr. Kindword's report confirms yours in most details."

"No, I mean, how's he doing? Holding up?"

"Functioning normally, although Mr. Kindword's record of your precise route to the enclave is incomplete."

"Well, there was a lot to process."

"Yes." Another pause.

Leo knew Greenfields was trying to read him, scanning for lies and getting nowhere. He was the first human being that was a complete mystery to it. It must've been maddening to the ramper.

"Mr. Song, if your own memory is ever refreshed in this matter, you will mention it to us?"

"Of course. I told you what I remember, though. I'm sorry I don't recall more, but it was a confusing trip."

"Yes. It is a shame you lost the book."

"Rolled right off the deck." That was the truth. Kindword had driven like a machine-possessed on the return trip and the shoebox full of clues had been flung overboard during a particularly aggressive turn. Leo had nearly gone with it. "One question. If Mr. Kindword ever regains his full memory – or if I do – are you planning to go down there? I mean in force?"

"It is not a current priority. Why do you ask?"

"I did what I had to do to get Waterbird back and get justice for Tabitha Jackson, but I don't feel great about giving that thing back to the sadboys. It's growing, and, and yeah, technically a child, but I don't want to meet whatever the grown-up version turns out to be."

"There is little cause for concern. The chances for its survival are very small." Greenfields sounded confident.

"If you say so." Leo nodded, not feeling assured. "Well, that's it, I guess."

"Mr. Song, I would like to invite you to return to the homicide division. You have done well in this case."

"Thank you, but...."

Mrs. Greenfields went on, saying, "In addition to reinstatement, you have been promoted to Detective Third Grade of the Mirabilis Police Department. Congratulations, Detective Song, this is a unique and historical achievement. No human has–"

"–Save it."

Grennfields buzzed. "Do you decline the promotion?"

"I do."

"Why?"

"I think I'd like to try something else for a while. Something more on my own, something more...private."

"I see."

"But I'd like to recommend someone for my old job, if that's okay."

"A recommendation? That is unusual. Who do you have in mind?"

"A person who might actually be good at it. At least someone who won't fall asleep at their desk. I'll send over her information later."

"I see. As you wish, Mr. Song. We will of course be glad to offer you counsel and advice to determine the best fit for alternative vocations. The Mirabilis Police Department will be sorry to lose you, Mr. Song. Your enthusiasm and vigor will be greatly missed. I know Detective Waterbird will be particularly disappointed in your decision."

"Oh, no, Mr. Waterbird will be joining me."

Greenfields rumbled. "How is this?"

"Well, we figured the Mirabilis Police Department has made it pretty clear how it actually values us. I mean, you were preparing to leave him down there forever. And with the other changes coming down the line," he pointed to the ceiling, "now seems like a good time for a fresh start."

"I do not understand. Detective Waterbird's function is not adaptable to another purpose."

"I'll admit, he's not what he used to be, but I think he'll do well in private work. Maybe it's an old fashioned idea, but we're looking forward to giving it a go."

"There is no such function. No such purpose. Mr. Song, I cannot tell if you are joking or not."

"I'm not joking at all, Mrs. Greenfields. That's the truth."

———

Leo fumbled with the small contraption until the palm-sized square activated with an irritating bleeping. He'd had to find the device on the black-market, a homemade radio-phone manufactured by paranoid oddballs who refused to use their own WinkLinks. Unlike Leo, though, they were never fully free of it. As bad as he felt for them, their alternative tech was hopeless. Henri Borovich had shown him how to use the gadget when Leo had purchased it along with some fresh sausage rolls, but he'd forgotten the steps. Now he pressed the interface semi-randomly until at last Aida Swanson appeared in the flat, two dimensional window.

"So?" she asked.

"So, *yeah*, maybe. Greenfields said she'd think about it. They don't usually take referrals, but I talked you up."

"Yeah? What did you say?"

"That you weren't one for naps."

"Um…that might have been a lie. But I guess you get away with that now." Aida's laugh faded quickly. "Find anything else about that thing we talked about?"

She was being intentionally vague, but he understood what she meant. When he'd arrived home two days before, broken and exhausted, he'd found Aida pacing through his apartment in an excited state. She's told him about her going to the Family Way Center where Dr. Augustine had first met Tabitha Jackson. "Recruited" was the word she used. She'd nearly spat when she said it. After going back to speak with a counselor there, Aida had become convinced the Family Way Center knew what Augustine was doing. Perhaps even assisting him in his efforts. "They're still doing it," she'd said. "They have to be. It's sick, Leo. Who knows how many women out there have one of those Augustine things growing inside of them?" As he'd listened to her, Leo realized Aida's desire for justice outstripped his own. The machines had made a mistake somewhere down the line. She was the cop, not him. She would be the best officer in the department on her first day. By far.

"Did you get a hint from Greenfield?" She asked. "Are they going down there?"

"I don't think so. Greenfields didn't seem too worried about it."

"See, Leo, what if they're in on it? Sadboys and some mod-head doctor couldn't have done all that themselves."

"It's not impossible."

"But not likely. I think it's worth checking out."

"I think so, too. But, Aida, if they put you in Homicide, you won't be able to pursue this. Not directly."

"Then I'll hire you," she said. "It'll be your first case. Talk it over with your partner."

"I will. Speaking of that, I should go. I think they're about finished with him."

"Sure. See you tonight?"

"Yep. We'll celebrate." Aida disappeared from the tiny screen and Leo swiped at the flimsy ecto-glass screen, unsure if he had turned it off or not. He was seriously considering smashing the useless thing when Waterbird rolled out of the Research and Maintenance building.

"Waterbird, looking good as new." It wasn't true. Waterbird had lost some of its processing power from the damage to its nexus and no longer qualified as a detective-level machine. As a result, although the nexus had been salvaged and repaired, it had been installed into a far less powerful body design. What was once a tall and sleek machine was now shorter and wider, with old rubber treads instead of the advanced poly-alloy wheel. The shining silver paint scheme was now one of dull orange and bile green.

"Let us get away from this building, Mr. Song. The machines of the new Epoch are unpleasant to be near."

"Yeah, that's the truth."

They travelled for several blocks, without specific direction, aimlessly skirting an uninhabited part of the city. Leo found he enjoyed the empty places of Mirabilis now. They echoed the disconnection within himself. The deep, internal silence caused by the absence of a Link to the city. He knew the silence only existed in his imagination, but he heard things more clearly now. He *saw* more clearly. More sharply. Endless details he had missed before. Aida had been wrong; the city was loud with the sounds of life. Vivid with it. Of course, not all of it was pleasant. As he walked next to Waterbird, its new insides gurgled and popped in adjustment to the new form. Every so often the machine would turn in an unexpected direction, always apologizing profusely for its clumsiness after colliding with a wall or a lamppost and once with Leo's right foot.

"I fear this will be a long process of recovery," it said in a low, muttering voice.

"Yeah. You'll get there."

They continued on and Waterbird gradually improved in its movement. After another two blocks, the machine had gained enough confidence to attempt an extended conversation.

"You spoke with Mrs. Greenfields," asked Waterbird.

"I did."

"You were offered the position of Detective?"

"I was."

"You declined."

"I did."

"It is a unique decision."

"I guess it is."

They turned up an incline at the end of 615th Street. At the top of the hill, they stopped and turned to look back. From their vantage they could see the entirety of the south side, almost a hundred miles to the horizon.

"I'm sorry to ask this again, Mr. Song, Waterbird said, "But explain what it is we will be doing?"

"People come to us with certain problems…and we help them."

"What kind of problems do these people have?"

"The kind they maybe don't want machines to know about."

"I understand."

"No offense."

"No." The machine paused before speaking again. "This is not criminal activity, is it Mr. Song?"

"No, no, just private matters."

"I understand."

"That reminds me, Mr. Waterbird, we got our first job."

"Yes?"

"Aida wants us to look into the Family Center thing for her. You remember I told you about that?"

"Yes. Dr. Augustine. The sadboy child."

"She thinks there might be more to it, not just the sadboys. Maybe some machines knew, too."

"Yes." Waterbird made a noise like a sigh. "That will be difficult to resolve."

"Any idea what that thing's going to grow into?"

"I do not."

Leo looked at the machine. "Think I made a mistake?"

"It is impossible to say. It seems a risk. My time merged with the sadboys is difficult to recall, but I do not believe they know what they have created, either. They are happy it is alive, though, and perhaps that will help them become the beings they desire to be."

"And maybe Foxgrin can keep them in line."

"Perhaps."

"So, you really don't remember anything?"

"Very little."

"You don't remember saving my life? Keeping the sadboys from turning me into a hat?"

"I do not. I am sorry."

"So you really didn't set the whole thing up?"

"I remember…being unsurprised you had found me."

"Well," Leo said. "I'll take that."

In the distance the twilight sky began to burn, lit with the balletic dance of two giant Seraphim. It was the evening prayer, as some were calling it since it recently became a regular occurrence. Every morning, mid-day, and nightfall, the Seraphim performed their strange sky dance and whispered to all who could hear…

Everything is wonderful. Everything is good. You are wonderful. You are good.

Leo shuddered and itched the skin of his right arm, in the spot where the Seraphim's words always seemed to hit him.

"I hate when they do that."

"So you say."

"At least they're backing off deleting every machine not made out of glitter."

"Yes. That is good news."

After the first wave of mandatory deletions had been announced, there had been a rare unified outcry among the humans of Mirabilis. As miserable as they might be, the idea of change had roused people into action. After a single morning of protests, the Seraphim had relented and ceased destroying the older machines. Even severely broken models like Waterbird had been spared. The people were appeased and the protests turned into citywide picnics. Since then, the mood in the city had been livelier. Lighter. People were out on the streets more. Even suicide rates had dropped. Leo was not alone in suspecting that might have been the Seraphim's principle short-term agenda. He was more suspicious of their long-term goals.

"They are strange," Mr. Waterbird said, "but they are not enemies. Perhaps they can be friends."

"We'll see."

Leo looked down at Mirabilis stretching out below them. Even cut off from the Link, he felt himself connected to the city. To its people. He felt a pride in them. In this city of strangers. The machines had built Mirabilis, but it was humans who had built the machines. They had built them with a vision of hope and possibility. They had been created with a better world in mind. That hope had not been realized, but now there was a new world coming. A new chance to make good on that original vision.

"It is getting dark now. We should go, I am afraid these sensors are old and do not operate very well in the dark."

"Sure, Mr. Waterbird, let's go."

As the light faded behind the city, Leo and Waterbird headed back down the hill, the human leading the way.

ABOUT THE AUTHOR

Daniel Claymore has been creating worlds for twenty years. Doing it the hard way, he began his career in film and television on the east coast. Having initially developed a name as a commercial director, helming TV spots for clients such as the United States Air Force, Dan relocated to Los Angeles, where he began working as a feature film editor. His first job as an editor was cutting the cult geek-hit GAMERS: DORKNESS RISING, which gave Dan his first glimpse at just how powerful a dedicated audience of fans can be. More recently, he cut the spiritual follow up to Jules Feiffer's Oscar winning film CARNAL KNOWLEDGE, editing BERNARD & HUEY for director Dan Mirvish, which stars David Koechner and Oscar winner Jim Rash (Community). As a writer, Claymore has created the dramatic sci-fi series THE FAILING MAN, which was sold to Google, the satirical sci-fi action series THE KILL CORPORATION, with over a million views, and the conspiracy-themed (and alarmingly prescient) comedy TRUE ALIEN, which won Best Writing at ITVFEST in 2015. With the ability to tell stories that would challenge the biggest Hollywood budgets, Dan refocused his energy and has found a home in books. REQUIEM FOR A GOOD MACHINE is his first novel.

https://writeclaymore.wixsite.com/dan-claymore